# A Christmas to Remember

# A Christmas to Remember

*A Cape Light Novel*

## THOMAS KINKADE
### & KATHERINE SPENCER

JOVE BOOKS, NEW YORK
A Parachute Press Book

**THE BERKLEY PUBLISHING GROUP**
**Published by the Penguin Group**
**Penguin Group (USA) Inc.**
**375 Hudson Street, New York, New York 10014, USA**
Penguin Group (Canada), 90 Eglinton Avenue East, Suite 700, Toronto, Ontario M4P 2Y3, Canada
(a division of Pearson Penguin Canada Inc.)
Penguin Books Ltd., 80 Strand, London WC2R 0RL, England
Penguin Group Ireland, 25 St. Stephen's Green, Dublin 2, Ireland (a division of Penguin Books Ltd.)
Penguin Group (Australia), 250 Camberwell Road, Camberwell, Victoria 3124, Australia
(a division of Pearson Australia Group Pty. Ltd.)
Penguin Books India Pvt. Ltd., 11 Community Centre, Panchsheel Park, New Delhi—110 017, India
Penguin Group (NZ), 67 Apollo Drive, Rosedale, North Shore 0632, New Zealand
(a division of Pearson New Zealand Ltd.)
Penguin Books (South Africa) (Pty.) Ltd., 24 Sturdee Avenue, Rosebank, Johannesburg 2196,
South Africa

Penguin Books Ltd., Registered Offices: 80 Strand, London WC2R 0RL, England

A CHRISTMAS TO REMEMBER

A Jove Book / published by arrangement with Parachute Publishing, L.L.C.

PRINTING HISTORY
Berkley hardcover edition / October 2006
Berkley trade paperback edition / October 2007
Jove mass-market edition / October 2008

Copyright © 2006 by The Thomas Kinkade Company and Parachute Publishing, L.L.C.
Cover image: *Skater's Pond* copyright © 1993 by Thomas Kinkade.
Cover design by Lesley Worrell.

ISBN: 978-0-515-14537-3

JOVE®
Jove Books are published by The Berkley Publishing Group,
a division of Penguin Group (USA) Inc.,
375 Hudson Street, New York, New York 10014.
JOVE® is a registered trademark of Penguin Group (USA) Inc.
The "J" design is a trademark belonging to Penguin Group (USA) Inc.

PRINTED IN THE UNITED STATES OF AMERICA

10  9  8  7  6  5  4  3  2  1

# A LETTER FROM THOMAS KINKADE

Dear Friends,

Every year as we get ready for Christmas, I find myself reminiscing about Christmases past, each one so special in its own way. When I was a child, I would reflect back, trying to recall the presents I was given from year to year. Only now, as an adult, I realize that the most important gifts are the memories that are made—a gift you can truly keep forever.

My family and I like to look back fondly on past Christmas celebrations to trace the path that has brought us here today as we think ahead to the future and all the wonderful things that are yet to happen.

So, come with me now to Cape Light, a town filled with people just like you and me who have learned much from the past and know that there are always many new memories waiting to be created.

Let's visit with Lucy Bates, who is finally making her dream of becoming a nurse come true, though not without many challenges along the way.

Let us look in on Luke McAllister and Sara Franklin, who are both ready to make this Christmas their most special one ever.

And finally, let's spend some time with Lillian Warwick, who will have her own Christmas memories come to life in ways she never imagined possible.

Here the families of Cape Light are gathering to create beautiful new Christmas memories as you and your family create your own special memories to cherish for a lifetime.

Merry Christmas!
Thomas Kinkade

# CHAPTER ONE

*Newburyport Yacht Club, August 1955*

"JUST THIS ONE DANCE, LILY. I'LL BE RIGHT BACK."
Charlotte hesitated.

*Feeling guilty,* Lillian suspected.

"You don't mind, do you?" Charlotte whispered.

"Don't be silly. Go ahead. He's waiting for you." Lillian
Merchant wrapped the silk shawl around her bare shoulders then watched as her cousin practically skipped across
the room.

*For goodness sake, you don't have to run him down like
a bird dog, Charlotte. Have some dignity.*

Charlotte couldn't help herself, Lillian knew. Her cousin
couldn't feign disinterest if her life depended on it. She
wasn't very discriminating either. She seemed to think any
man who donned a dinner jacket was magically transformed into Cary Grant.

Charlotte had promised that if Lillian came to the party,
they would stick together. She wouldn't run off to visit
with friends, or disappear with some man.

*So much for promises. Here I am, high and dry, just as I expected.*

Lillian had been to the Newburyport Yacht Club many times during summer trips with her family, but she didn't know a soul here. And even though she enjoyed dancing—under the right circumstances—she hated to stand around without an escort while complete strangers looked her over like a choice cut of beef in the butcher's case.

She sipped her drink and glanced at the dance floor. Charlotte's expression was animated, her blue eyes bright. Her blond wavy hair bounced around her face and bare shoulders as she talked and laughed with her partner. Who was passably good-looking but undistinguished, Lillian decided.

Charlotte missed a step but her partner caught her, his arm hooking tight around her waist. Charlotte didn't seem the least bit embarrassed while Lillian cringed.

Well, it wasn't her fault. The band was dreadful, though no one else seemed to notice. About fifteen pieces altogether; all the musicians in tuxedos, as if quantity and fancy dress could make up for quality. They were playing an old song, popular during the war, slow and syrupy. The band leader crooned into the microphone from time to time in a vague imitation of Bing Crosby or Frank Sinatra, neither of whom Lillian had ever cared for.

At least the music was fairly dignified and none of that "rock 'n' roll" people were so excited about lately. Undoubtedly, they would get to that later as the evening progressed. With any luck she would be gone by then.

Lillian's gaze sought her cousin again. Her companion was doing all the talking now. Lillian had no idea what the man was going on about but Charlotte looked positively starry-eyed.

Lillian envied Charlotte sometimes. She was bubbly and buxom and easily impressed. She never seemed to see the flaws in people, especially in men. Only the good points, real or imagined.

That's what men liked, Lillian knew. They rarely appreciated someone like herself, a serious girl who asked questions, who had her own ideas and opinions. Who had a brain in her head, for goodness sake. Who rarely fell into a starry-eyed stupor. Lillian was not easily impressed and men seemed to sense this, as if she gave out some sort of low-pitched hum warning them to keep their distance.

Another song began and Charlotte and her beau glided away in a fox trot. Lillian knew her cousin had forgotten all about her. It was hopeless now to even try to catch Charlotte's eye.

Lillian felt conspicuous, sticking out like a sore thumb in her solitude. She tried to blend in, edging closer to a cluster of women who stood nearby. One of them turned. Her eyes swept over Lillian from head to toe, then the woman turned back to her friends, and Lillian heard them whispering about her.

Probably about her dress, a simple off-the-shoulder sheath, icy blue silk with a stole of matching fabric, lined with cream-colored satin. Lillian had found the dress in New York at a boutique that sold only haute couture. She had the figure for Paris fashion. That's what the seamstress who had pinned the alterations said. Lillian knew what that really meant was that she was tall and bean-pole thin, with long legs, long arms and no curves to speak of.

Her ensemble was the latest style but, of course, this Newburyport crowd didn't realize that. The other women were dressed in puffy-skirted chiffon concoctions. They wouldn't see anything close to this dress around here until next fall.

Meanwhile, their stares made her feel horribly self-conscious. The doors to the deck stood open, inviting her to escape. White paper lanterns were strung across the dark sky, and lights twinkled in the dark harbor.

Lillian held back, waiting. If Charlotte didn't return after this song, she would call a cab and go.

A group of men at the end of the bar burst out laughing, and Lillian looked over at them. The man who stood in the center was telling a story. The others sat on bar stools while he stood, imitating various voices, gesturing with his hands. He was tall, with thick dark hair parted on the side and combed back smoothly from his forehead. His dinner jacket draped over his broad shoulders and trim build with a hand-tailored fit.

She had noticed him earlier on the dance floor. Never the same partner twice. He was a good dancer, excellent form and graceful, unlike most of the others.

She didn't realize she had been staring until one of his buddies nudged him. He turned and stared back at her. Then he winked and flashed a brilliant smile.

Lillian felt her expression freeze as blood rushed to her cheeks. She turned her head sharply and stared straight ahead, pretending not to have seen him.

Another wave of male laughter made her cringe. They were all laughing at her now. The evening had progressed from discomfort to utter mortification. Thanks to that preening oaf who had winked at her.

Drawing on every ounce of self-control she possessed, she lifted her chin and swept through the open glass doors to the outside. She crossed the deck and stood at the rough wooden rail, looking at the harbor and star-studded sky. The air was fresh and felt cool against her skin. She could hardly hear the music or the party guests. It was suddenly so quiet; she heard only the water below the deck, lapping at the pilings.

*I should have come out here sooner,* she realized. *What was I doing standing around in that smoke and noise?*

The dark harbor was filled with boats, mostly sailboats tethered to moorings, bobbing in the waves. Lights shone within a few of the sleek vessels where she saw people moving about in the cabins or sitting on the decks.

Lillian felt a sharp longing to join them, to be out on one of those boats, sitting in the quiet night with a few close friends who knew and understood her.

She would wait out here for a few minutes—until those

ill-mannered clods had moved on—then she would slip inside and call a taxi from the lobby.

*Charlotte won't even notice I'm gone.*

Coming to this party had been a mistake. Maybe this entire vacation was going to be one, Lillian worried. She and Charlotte adored each other, always had. They were as close as sisters. But they weren't little girls anymore. They had grown up very differently and had different interests, different priorities.

Lillian had been engaged. She knew what that was all about. Her fiancé, George Tilles, had broken it off a month before their wedding. Her parents had tried in their way, but they really hadn't been very sympathetic. They never said it outright, but the way they looked at her sometimes made Lillian feel they understood George's reservations. As if the broken engagement had been all her fault.

Her father had been annoyed about losing his money on the wedding preparations. If she ever got engaged again, she and her betrothed would have to foot the bill, he told her. As if he would actually miss the money. Her family was quite wealthy, though Albert Merchant, a dyed-in-the-wool banker, fretted over every penny that passed through his fingers.

Romance. You could have it. It never measured up to the storm-swept passion in the movies. While Lillian no longer felt hurt by George's rejection, she did feel disillusioned. And that might be a good thing, she decided. The last thing she needed was more illusions.

That's why an event like this dance seemed so silly and pointless, a thinly veiled pretext for girls like Charlotte to continue their desperate hunt.

"Excuse me, miss." A soft deep voice broke into Lillian's thoughts.

She turned to find the dark-haired man who had winked at her. She took a small step back and stared at him.

He looked amused. His smile was polite but wide enough to show off deep dimples and straight white teeth.

"You dropped this." He held out her shawl, folded in a

neat, silky blue bundle. It looked out of place and awfully feminine in his large hand.

Lillian took the shawl, barely meeting his eyes. "Thank you. I didn't realize."

"You wouldn't want to lose it and ruin that beautiful outfit."

Lillian wondered for a moment if he was being sarcastic, subtly making fun of her dress. She decided not. He watched as she arranged the shawl around her shoulders, his look of admiration seeming perfectly sincere.

He was even better-looking close up, she decided.

"Do you know much about fashion, Mr. . . . ?"

"Warwick. Oliver Warwick." He said his name quickly, as if everyone knew him. Or should know him. "And though I know little about it, I would guess that gown came from New York, or maybe Paris."

Lillian was surprised. Even a bit impressed. "New York," she answered. "I was there in the spring. On business."

His dark brows jumped a notch. "You have a job, do you?" He nodded, considering the idea. "I think that's fine. I think women should be out in the world making their way, if they want to be."

She struggled to keep from laughing out loud. "Thanks so much for your approval, Mr. Warwick. I can carry on now without concern."

He smiled and tilted his head. "I'm sorry. That did sound rather stupid, didn't it? You caught me by surprise. I mean, you don't look the type. . . . Unless you're going to tell me now that you're a fashion model?"

She shook her head. His frank reply—and not so subtle compliment—made her smile. "I work in the Museum of Fine Arts, in Boston."

"Really? What do you do there?"

"I'm an assistant curator." She tried not to sound defensive, but she was almost positive he assumed she had some fluffy job, a fund-raiser or tour guide.

"I should have guessed something like that." He pulled

a silver cigarette case from his breast pocket and offered her one. Lillian shook her head. "So what do you curate?"

He was only asking to be polite. She didn't think her answer would matter one way or the other to him. She had a feeling he knew little about art or museums.

"I'm a specialist in the Egyptian period. Egyptian pottery mainly."

He lit his cigarette with a silver lighter then exhaled a long plume of smoke that floated in the air between them.

"Brains and beauty, too. What a package." His low tone and the way he was suddenly looking at her alarmed Lillian. She hugged the shawl around her slim body and turned away from him to look out at the harbor again.

"You didn't think I was a model. You only said that to flatter me."

There, she would be as blunt as she liked. Her mother said it was rude to be so straightforward, especially to men. But Lillian knew it was the fastest way to cool them down.

Oliver Warwick didn't seem the least put off. "Why would I want to flatter you? I don't even know your name."

Lillian didn't answer.

He waited a moment, watching her. "All right, let me guess."

"I doubt you will. It's very uncommon."

"I expected that. I can already see you're an uncommon girl."

Somehow the way he said it made the words sound like the highest kind of compliment. She watched as he took one more puff on the cigarette then stubbed it out on the railing.

"How about Diana? Goddess of the hunt. Career girl. Brains and beauty."

Lillian had to smile again, surprised to find Oliver Warwick up on his mythology. "Yes, I know the story."

Diana didn't have a very high opinion of men, either, Lillian recalled. "But no, it's not Diana."

He smiled, showing off those disconcerting dimples again.

"All right, let's see . . . What about . . . Chastity? There's an uncommon name for you."

Lillian felt herself blush and was thankful for the darkness. "Wrong again. Give up?"

Before she could protest, he had closed his eyes and touched his forehead, like a magician in a dinner show.

"One more try . . . Silence, please. I need a moment to focus."

Lillian sighed, smiling in spite of herself. Oliver Warwick was really too much. At least he was some distraction in an otherwise dull evening.

He opened his eyes and beamed down at her.

"Your name isn't by any chance . . . Lillian, is it?"

Lillian's mouth made a perfect circle, then she snapped it closed. "You knew that all along."

He feigned an innocent stare that nearly persuaded her. Except for the teasing light in his eyes.

"I know your cousin, Charlotte. But that was fun."

"Fun for you, maybe."

"That should teach you the first thing about me, Lillian. You shouldn't take me seriously. Unless I tell you to, of course," he added with another teasing look.

"Okay, I'll remember that."

As if they'd ever see each other again. Not very likely. He was hardly her type. Just the opposite.

He smiled at her warmly, seeming not to notice her sarcastic tone. "Now that we've got that settled, would you like to dance?"

"No, thank you."

"We can dance right here. It's very picturesque."

What he really meant was romantic. It was a romantic notion to dance with a handsome stranger on a deck that overlooked the harbor.

But Lillian was not swayed. The whole idea . . . annoyed her.

"Thank you, but I was just about to go."

"Go? You can't go yet. I've been waiting all night to talk to you."

This last line was really too much. The man had no shame.

Lillian practically laughed at him. "No, you haven't. You've been well occupied entertaining your friends at the bar . . . and dancing with any number of women."

He beamed, as if she had just confessed her undying passion.

"So you had your eye on me, too? I thought so, but you're so classy and well-bred, Lillian. It was hard to tell for sure."

Lillian felt her face flush with color. She straightened her shoulders and took a sudden step back. "That's not what I meant at all. I didn't even notice you were in the room. . . . I took no *special* notice, if that's what you're implying."

He looked down at her, smiling gently. He reached out and softly ran his fingertips down her bare arm. Lillian knew she should say something. She should step away and not allow him to take such liberties.

But somehow, she felt frozen to the spot and did nothing.

"How many women did I dance with, do you think? I bet you know."

She did know. That was what was so galling about the question.

"This conversation is getting tiresome. I'm going in now. Good night."

She started to walk away, but Oliver Warwick caught her hand. "I was wishing all the time I was dancing with you. I should have had the nerve to ask you, but I didn't dare. I thought you would turn me down."

"You're right. I would have." She tried to sound convincing, but she knew she hadn't quite pulled it off.

She stood facing him, not quite knowing what to do next.

He still held her hand, now in both of his own. She had never been in such a situation with a man before.

"May I have my hand back, please?" she asked quietly. "I don't want to make a scene."

He laughed but didn't release her. "Not yet." He gazed down at her, the smile gone. His gaze wandered over her face, studying her features. Did he like what he saw? Then she was angry at herself for caring. "You're very beautiful," he said quietly.

"No, I'm not. You're just saying that."

"You like to argue, don't you?"

She looked up at him, about to counter that observation, too, when he bent his head and kissed her. Right on the lips. Not too hard but not too soft either. It wasn't the sort of hesitant, testing peck she remembered from college boys.

He wasn't a college boy. He kissed her as if he had a perfect right, his lips lingering for a moment, tasting her mouth. Then just in time to escape her complete wrath, he pulled away.

He watched, waiting for her reaction.

She drew back her hand and slapped him squarely across the jaw.

He took a breath and rubbed his cheek. Then he smiled. "You're stronger than you look."

"You have some nerve, Mr. Warwick."

"Oliver, please. I think we're on a first name basis now, don't you?"

"I don't think . . . anything about you," she sputtered. She took a deep breath and looked out at the water. It was just a kiss. She had been kissed before. Kissed plenty. Why had it rattled her down to her bones?

Oliver's voice broke into her flustered thoughts. "May I call you tomorrow? You're staying with your cousin, right?"

Did he think she was going to go on a date with him? Of all the outrageous assumptions . . .

"Lily? There you are. I've been looking all over for you." Charlotte stepped out onto the deck. Lillian could tell she was surprised to find her with a man. "Hello, Oliver. I see you've met my cousin."

"Yes, I have. We've been having an interesting conversation, getting to know each other. Right, Lillian?"

Why did he have to put it that way? As if there was something going on out here. Lillian knew Charlotte's suspicions were already piqued, just by having found them out here together.

And if mere suspicions weren't enough, Oliver had lipstick all over his mouth, she noticed. She hoped Charlotte wouldn't notice. But of course, her cousin would pick up on something like that right away.

Oliver Warwick leaned back on the railing, his gaze fixed on Lillian. "I just invited Lillian to go out tomorrow, but she hasn't given me her answer yet."

Lillian saw Charlotte's eyes widen. She looked about to bubble over with a fit of girlish giggling. Lillian pinned her with a cold, hard stare.

"I would be happy to take both of you to Plum Island and out to lunch," Oliver offered.

"Oh, we would love to go," Charlotte answered quickly.

"But we can't," Lillian cut in. "We promised to go to the horse show in Hamilton with your mother."

"The horse show? She doesn't . . ."

"Of course she does! She has tickets. We can't disappoint her." Lillian drew closer to her cousin with every word, signaling a silent message with her eyes.

Finally, Charlotte took the hint. "Oh, yes. I forgot. We do have plans. Maybe another time, Oliver."

Lillian wouldn't second that suggestion. She was only visiting for a week. She didn't plan on spending any of her precious vacation with Oliver Warwick.

The man was such a bore. Well . . . not boring exactly. But so pushy. Lillian didn't like men like that.

"Good night, Lillian." Oliver sketched a small bow. "I look forward to continuing our conversation."

"Good-bye, Oliver."

Lillian ushered Charlotte off the deck and led her through the party and out the front door of the club, where a valet brought their car.

She was eager to put a great distance between herself and Oliver Warwick.


*Cape Light, Late November, Present-day*

EVERY WINDOW IN HER GRANDMOTHER'S HOUSE WAS dark when Sara Franklin pulled into the driveway. That wasn't unusual. Lillian hardly kept any lights on. The huge Victorian looked spooky in the wintry late afternoon light. It wasn't quite five, but it was already nearly dark outside. A few loose shutters shivered and creaked in the wind, and the bare branches of trees scratched against the clapboard.

Sara strode up the walk to the front door, a plastic bag of groceries dangling from each arm. Her boots crunched on a thin layer of ice and snow that had fallen only a few days ago, on Thanksgiving morning. *Like clockwork,* Sara thought. Every year since she had come up from Maryland to live in New England, snow had begun falling by Thanksgiving.

Sara rang the bell for the second time and peered in the window. No sign of life. But that wasn't unusual either. It often took Lillian a very long time to answer the door. She might be reading or watching TV and didn't hear the bell or the knocking. She claimed to have perfect hearing, but Sara was doubtful. If Lillian was napping upstairs in her room, she wouldn't hear the bell no matter how many times you rang it.

She also had an aversion to visitors, even those she expected. Lillian never hurried herself to let anyone in.

Sara set the bags of food down near the door and knocked harder. She waited a few more moments then walked around to the far side of the porch where she found the emergency key hidden in a decorative wooden birdhouse that hung from the rafters.

Lillian hated it when anyone let themselves in, even her daughters. The house was her private and sovereign domain, and "to have people traipsing in and out, as they pleased" unnerved her.

*But this is practically an emergency,* Sara reasoned. She had promised to bring her grandmother some groceries and visit with her awhile. She had to meet Luke, her fiancé, later and didn't have all that much time to spend here.

Sara turned the key in the lock, hefted her bags, and pushed the big door open with her shoulder. She stepped into the large foyer and set the bags on the antique mail table. Then she looked around and turned on a low lamp.

"Lillian, are you upstairs?" she called. "It's Sara. I've been standing outside for a while. I let myself in. . . ."

Usually by now, Sara would hear some cackling response from the deeper recesses of the rambling old house. But she heard only silence. The ticking of the big clock in the foyer and the sound of water trickling suddenly through the pipes. She felt a chill and started up the stairs. Slowly at first, then faster.

"Lillian? Are you all right? . . . Please answer me. . . ."

The hallway upstairs was dark, except for a thin shaft of light that streamed down from the attic door. The door was open, blocking her view of the rest of the long hallway.

Sara knew something was wrong. Her grandmother was very particular about watching her expenses. She would never leave the attic door open in the winter. Sara hurried toward the open door.

Then she saw her. Sprawled out at the bottom of the steps, curled on her side, her one leg twisted underneath her at a painful-looking angle.

"Lillian!" Sara gasped and swallowed back a bitter taste at the back of her throat. *Dear God, please let her be alive.*

She dropped down and felt her grandmother's neck. A pulse beat faintly but steadily, thank God.

She gripped Lillian's hand, and her grandmother moaned softly then opened her eyes. She struggled to raise her head.

"No, don't move," Sara said quickly. She didn't know much about first aid, but she knew you weren't supposed to move someone who'd had a bad fall. It could make the injury worse. Especially someone as old and fragile as Lillian. "I'll call for help. They'll be here right away."

Sara pulled her cell phone out of her jacket pocket and dialed 911. An operator came on the line right away. "It's my grandmother. She's had a bad fall. She needs an ambulance right away. . . ."

Sara gave the address and the rest of the information and then checked her watch. How long would it take for them to get here? Lillian might be bleeding internally. She could be very badly hurt, though she was still conscious.

That was a good sign, wasn't it?

Her grandmother's cheek was pressed against the floor. She looked up at Sara. "You . . . you've finally come . . . I was waiting . . ."

"Yes, I'm here. It's going to be okay," Sara promised, hoping that was true. "I've called nine-one-one. The ambulance is on its way."

"I hate ambulances. . . . I hate hospitals."

Could her grandmother actually argue about going to the hospital in her state? Sara was flabbergasted. Then again, her grandmother could argue about anything and often did.

Sara patted Lillian's hand while dialing the cell phone with the other. "Are you in much pain?"

"What do you think? It hurts all over!" Lillian's usually sharp voice was a strained whisper. "Who are you calling now?"

"Emily," Sara replied, naming her birth mother.

"Yes, of course, Emily. Tell her what's happened. Jessica, too . . ." She murmured the name of her other daughter.

Sara hoped Emily was home and would pick up the

phone. She listened impatiently as the phone rang one, two . . . eight times. It was really no surprise. Emily was always so busy—either with Sara's little stepsister, Jane, or her job as mayor—that she rarely picked up the phone at home.

But as Sara began to talk to the answering machine, Emily picked up. "Sara? Is that you?"

"Yes, I'm at Lillian's. I just got here, and she's had an accident. She fell down the attic steps. I just called for an ambulance. You'd better come right away," Sara said quickly.

"An ambulance? What kind of accident? Is she breathing? Is she conscious?" Emily's voice rose, sounding more anxious with each question.

"She's awake and can talk. But she's in pain. She must have broken something."

"I'm not dead yet," Lillian managed to squawk from the floor. "Tell her that for me, will you?"

"I'll be right there. Don't leave without me. . . . I mean, yes. Leave if the ambulance gets there. I'll catch up at the hospital. I have her insurance cards and information. You don't have to worry about finding all that. . . ."

"Okay, that's good to know."

"Try to keep her awake if you can."

"Yes, I will." Sara had heard that was important, too.

The connection with Emily broke off, and Sara turned back to her grandmother again. She softly stroked her wispy white hair. Lillian's usual upswept hairdo had come undone, and Sara realized that her hair was quite long, longer than her own.

"What can I do for you, Grandma? Is there anything I can do?"

"Oh dear . . . you must think I'm done for. . . . You never called me Grandma before."

Sara didn't know whether to laugh or cry.

"You've probably broken something. But I'm sure you're going to be all right." Sara did her best to sound convincing. She really wasn't sure of anything.

As for the other question, Sara didn't think this was the time or the place to get into it.

There was a reason Sara had never called Lillian "Grandma." Lillian had always sidestepped acknowledging their connection. Sara's birth mother, Emily, had eloped at age eighteen, eager to wriggle out from beneath Lillian's thumb. She married a local fisherman Lillian had never approved of, moved to the Maryland shore with him, and lost all contact with her family. Until her young husband died in a car accident, leaving Emily eight months pregnant and injured. Lillian had come down to Maryland to take care of her, which included persuading Emily—strong-arming her really—into giving up her baby for adoption. This way, Lillian had argued, Emily could return home to Cape Light, start college and pick up her life as if the unfortunate marriage—and baby—had never happened.

Sara had been the baby that Emily gave up. Although she was adopted and raised by loving parents, she always wondered about her birth mother. She had found Emily a few years ago, soon after she graduated from college. It had taken Sara a long time to confess her real relationship and to forgive Emily. Now she couldn't imagine her life without her birth mother—or her birth grandmother, as she had come to think of Lillian.

She heard Lillian's soft groan and took her hand. Her eyes were closed again. *Keep her awake*. That's what Emily had said.

"What were you doing up in the attic? You know you shouldn't climb stairs with your cane."

Lillian didn't answer, and Sara wondered if she had lost consciousness. "I needed something," she mumbled finally.

"You knew I was coming. I would have gotten it for you."

"I couldn't remember. . . . It was driving me crazy. . . ." She let out a harsh breath, and Sara could tell it was a great effort for her to say even a few words.

It was suddenly very quiet. Sara heard the ticking of the grandfather clock at the end of the hallway. Then she heard a siren in the distance. She stood up. It was getting closer.

"They're here. I'll be right back." She squeezed Lillian's hand then flew down the stairs.

She swung open the door to find the emergency responders hurrying up the walkway with a gurney.

"She's upstairs. This way," Sara called. With the EMS crew behind her, she ran back up the steps two at a time.

She stepped back as they reached her grandmother and knelt at her side. Sara watched as they pulled out medical instruments and checked Lillian's heartbeat and blood pressure. They looked into her eyes with a tiny flashlight. One of the EMTs leaned over and talked to her quietly. After a moment, he looked up at Sara.

"We're going to put a collar on her and a full-body support. She's broken some bones. She might have some pain."

Sara swallowed hard and nodded.

The emergency crew put the supports on Lillian quickly, then turned her limp body to one side and then swung it over onto the stretcher. Lillian moaned with pain, a heart-wrenching sound, and Sara felt tears well up in her eyes. She stepped closer and touched her grandmother's hand as they strapped her on the gurney.

"Lillian, I'm right here."

"No . . ." Lillian tried to shake her head, but the support held it rigid. "Say the other . . . the other thing you called me . . ."

Sara paused. "Grandma, I'm right here."

Lillian stared at Sara and blinked. Then she closed her eyes.

"She's okay. Her vital signs are steady," one of the EMS workers told Sara. "She's very strong."

"Can I ride with you to the hospital?"

"No problem. Can you turn on a light or something? It's like a museum in here."

*It's true,* Sara thought as she found the hall light and

turned it on. The old house with its heavy antique furniture and knickknacks in every corner did look like a museum.

The EMS crew wheeled her grandmother toward the top of the staircase, then began the careful process of carrying the gurney down the long flight of stairs.

As Sara stood back and watched, she noticed a square of paper on the floor where she had found Lillian.

She bent down and picked it up. It was an old photo. In the dimly lit hallway Sara could hardly make out the image. Then she realized that there were old photographs scattered all over the attic steps and near the doorway.

"You coming, miss?" one of the EMTs called up.

"Be right there." She stuck the photo she'd picked up in her pocket and hurried to catch up with her grandmother, now being taken out of the house.

*Please, God, don't let her be in much pain. Don't let anything really bad be wrong with her.* Sending up a silent prayer, Sara readied herself for the long ride to the hospital.

# CHAPTER TWO

*Southport Hospital, Late November,*
*Present-day*

"YOU'RE VERY LUCKY, LILLIAN. A MILD CONCUSSION and two broken bones. A small price to pay at your age." Doctor Bartow looked up from his notes and smiled.

"Compared to breaking my neck completely, you mean?" Lillian murmured.

"Mother, let the doctor finish. Please?" Emily Warwick stood at one side of Lillian's bed. Jessica, Emily's younger sister, and Sara stood on the other side. The doctor had left out the bruised ribs, Emily noticed, and the swollen spot around her mother's eye, now covered with an ice pack, which would probably darken into a bona fide shiner. For the last few hours, Lillian had been rolled around the hospital undergoing tests. Then casts were put on her left arm and right ankle, which were both broken in her fall.

"Excuse me, Doctor. Are you sure you prescribed a painkiller and not a placebo?" Lillian managed a momentary scowl then closed her eyes. A nurse had given her a painkiller some time ago, but Lillian insisted it wasn't helping at all.

Unsurprisingly, she wasn't a very good patient, complaining at every opportunity and quizzing each medical professional who came near her on their experience and credentials.

"If you want to kill yourself, check into a hospital," she often raved. And had, several times during her tests.

Of course, if she hadn't been complaining, Emily, Jessica, and Sara would have really been worried about her.

Doctor Bartow looked down at the notes in his folder. "She'll need to stay overnight. We want to watch the concussion and her blood pressure. But she should be ready to go home tomorrow or the day after."

"That's good news, isn't it, Mother?" Emily's voice was bright, the tone she used when trying to override Lillian's expected objections.

"Good for the insurance company. No wonder they have that big revolving door downstairs. Pretty soon it will be a drive-through window," Lillian muttered. "Or perhaps the beds will pop the patient up and out like a toaster."

The doctor grinned. "Lillian, I have no worries about you. You're sharper with a concussion than most of my patients are without one."

His expression grew serious again. "I understand she lives alone. She'll need help around the clock for the next two months, at least. I suggest that you check her into a nursing home or a rehabilitation facility so that she can have proper care."

Lillian's eyes flew open. "Why are you speaking about me as if I wasn't here? She *this* and she *that*?" She struggled to sit upright. "I won't hear of a nursing home. I simply won't hear of it!"

The doctor seemed puzzled by her reaction. "Only until the casts come off and you're mobile again. You'll need some physical therapy and—"

"I won't go. You can't make me. I know my rights." Lillian glared at him.

Emily and Jessica exchanged concerned looks. Sara sat quietly, holding back a smile. She had no doubt that her grandmother would win this debate.

"Another alternative would be for you to go home with one of your daughters," the doctor said. "But even then you'll need a home health aide around the clock."

"My sister and I would both be happy to have her," Emily said.

Lillian smoothed the edge of her blanket across her chest with her good hand. "You know that I prefer to be in my own home. Besides, both of you are out working all hours. I'll be stuck in a tiny room, listening to noisy children and baby-sitters all day. And those vile cartoons on the television—"

"I get the picture," Dr. Bartow cut in.

"We went through all this when she had her stroke, five years ago," Emily explained. "She can be very stubborn—"

"I'm comfortable in my own home. As most people are, or should be. There's no crime in it," Lillian insisted. "If I can be dumped in one of their houses with some medical attendant hanging over me all day, then why can't I do the same in my own house, Doctor?"

Dr. Bartow looked resigned. "It wouldn't be my first choice, but if you won't agree to any other alternative, I guess it will have to do. You'll both be looking in on her, I assume?"

"Every day," Emily promised.

"We both will. And Sara," Jessica added, glancing over at her niece.

Lillian sighed and closed her eyes. "Oh goody. I can hardly wait for all these visitors, traipsing in and out."

"Oh, Lillian, you know you love the attention," Sara said with a laugh.

"Yes, I've gone to great lengths to get some, haven't I? I must crave attention desperately."

"What's next, doctor?" Emily asked.

"I'll give you the information for the local agencies.

She'll need someone with her twenty-four hours at first, even with all of you visiting."

"Not at night," Lillian piped up. "I'll just be sleeping. Why does someone have to be there at night?"

"In case you need to get out of bed or have some unexpected emergency," Emily explained patiently.

"Someone must be there at night, or I can't approve this plan," Dr. Bartow said firmly.

"I don't want a stranger in my house at night—wandering around, peering in at me, going through my things. . . . I won't sleep a wink. They're liable to give me a heart attack."

Emily touched her mother's hand, hoping to calm her down. "We'll figure it out, Mother. Jessica and I can come stay with you until we find someone you feel comfortable with. How's that?"

Lillian peered at her. "How can you manage that? And don't tell me you're going to bring your babies along with you. That would be even worse."

"We do have husbands, Mother," Jessica reminded her. "Husbands can take care of babies when necessary. They'll all be just fine."

"That remains to be seen," Lillian huffed.

Sara stood up and walked over to the bed. "Lillian's right. It will be hard for either of you to stay over. I can do it. At least until we find someone she likes."

"What about your fiancé?" Lillian asked. "I don't think he'll like the idea much."

Lillian did not approve of Luke McAllister, Sara's fiancé, and had never pretended otherwise.

"Luke will understand. He'll want to come visit you, too," Sara said.

"That's just what I was worried about."

"Mother, really," Emily said. "There's no pleasing you. If it's not one thing, it's—"

"Luke McAllister. All right, I give up. One can't expect perfection in this world. I already know that."

Lillian closed her eyes again and rested back on her pillow. Everyone else in the room exhaled sighs of relief.

"Do you think we should have her sign something?" Jessica whispered in a teasing tone.

"I heard that," Lillian said, her eyes still closed.

The doctor struggled not to laugh. "All right. We have a plan. If you three can step out into the hallway a minute, we can go over a few more details and Lillian can get some rest."

"Excellent suggestion. I wish you would all go now and leave me alone."

Emily and Jessica kissed their mother good-bye then followed the doctor out to the hallway. Sara stood at the side of the bed a moment, then kissed Lillian lightly on her forehead, thinking she had already drifted off.

Lillian surprised her, gripping her hand. She opened her eyes a tiny slit. "Thank you," she mouthed the words.

"You're welcome. I'll see you tomorrow," Sara whispered back.

Twenty minutes later, Sara found her way to the elevators and punched the button to go down. She reached into her jacket for her car keys and found instead the old photo she had picked up off the floor by the attic door.

Two young women stood together, one with fluffy blond hair and a round face, who looked directly at the camera with light blue eyes and a guileless smile.

The other was tall and thin, with chestnut-brown hair in a smooth, sophisticated upsweep that looked a bit severe. But the young woman was beautiful enough to carry it off. She had high cheekbones and a wide sensuous mouth. Large blue eyes were enhanced by the color of her ice-blue dress, a silk sheath with a matching stole. She wore long white gloves and a wide gold bracelet.

Her gaze seemed to challenge the photographer, as if she dared him to take her picture. Sara had no idea who the blonde was, but she had a strong suspicion about the brunette. She would know that look anywhere.

She flipped the photo over and checked the inscription on the back. *Charlotte and Lillian. Newburyport Yacht Club. August 1955.*

Grandma had been a stunner. No doubt about it.

## Cape Light, August 1955

LILLIAN LED THE WAY DOWN THE SHORELINE TO AN empty stretch of beach with a determined, long-legged stride. She carried an umbrella, a beach bag, and a cooler, which didn't seem to slow her in the least. The others trudged behind, rolling their eyes at one another.

"I feel like I'm marching across the Sahara," Bess, one of Charlotte's friends, complained.

"Did you ever see that movie with Frank Sinatra, when he signs up for the Foreign Legion? He's dreamy," another named Penny replied. "I'd follow him across a desert anytime."

"That was Gary Cooper, you goose," Charlotte corrected her.

"I don't care who it was," Bess cut in sharply. "How far are we supposed to go? I haven't been hiking like this since summer camp."

Lillian sensed a mutiny on her hands, but she wouldn't be swayed. Crane's Beach was the best in the area for swimming and one of the prettiest. But also, the most crowded. She rarely spent time at the shore anymore, and she wasn't about to sit in the middle of Grand Central Station, blankets edge to edge, noisy children kicking sand at you. She wanted to see the water without peering around a forest of umbrellas and beach chairs.

"Lily, I can't walk another step." Charlotte let out a long breath. Her face was glowing, the same color as her flamingo-pink sundress. "I have to sit."

Charlotte dropped her chair and did just that, plunking down on the sand without waiting to open it.

"Me, too. For goodness sake. I've had it, girls." Bess did the same. She wore a white turban over her hair with large dark glasses and pedal pushers over her halter-top bathing suit. Lillian suspected Bess thought she looked very glamorous, but Lillian didn't think she had any taste at all.

Bess quickly pulled a compact out of her straw bag and checked her lipstick. It was perfectly applied, her lips taking on an exaggerated bow shape, but she swiped an extra coat on anyway.

Lillian hardly used cosmetics; her mother insisted it made a girl look "cheap." She certainly didn't wear any to the beach; it didn't make sense to her at all. But Charlotte and her friends seemed to think they were naked without their artfully applied layers and were always asking each other if their lipstick was still fresh.

Lillian jabbed the bottom half of the umbrella pole into the sand, anchoring it firmly, then fit the top half in, and opened the umbrella. The others spread out blankets, undressed down to their bathing suits, and stretched out to sun themselves while they paged through the latest issue of *Screen Magazine*.

They barely spoke to Lillian and she could tell she was only tolerated for Charlotte's sake. She didn't care. She felt the same about them. They had no serious interests or stimulating conversation. Lillian took out the book she was reading, a current bestseller, Herman Wouk's *Marjorie Morningstar*. She doubted any of Charlotte's friends had cracked open a real book since college. She wasn't even sure Bess had gone to college. Maybe some no-name, two-year school. She was just a second-rate debutante, waiting for a rich, young man to marry her. At least Charlotte had become a teacher; that Lillian could respect.

"How was the party at the yacht club last night? Did I miss anything?" Bess spoke without looking up from her magazine.

"I didn't go either." Penny had taken out a manicure set

and was industriously working on her nails. "Charlotte went—with Lillian, right?"

Bess seemed amused. "Did you have fun, Lily?"

Lillian didn't know what to say. "It was interesting."

"Oliver Warwick cornered her out on the deck. He wouldn't leave her alone," Charlotte added. "He asked her to go out with him today, but she kept saying no. He's called three times this morning."

Lillian stared at her cousin. Charlotte was probably trying to defend her, but she had asked Charlotte not to mention Oliver again. Charlotte had given her an earful of gossip about the town's leading bachelor last night, and Lillian was sure she didn't want anything more to do with him.

"Oliver Warwick? Really?" Bess put down her magazine, looking as if she didn't believe it.

Lillian felt stung. *As if an attractive man wouldn't look twice at me.* "I don't know why everyone around here thinks he's such a catch," she said. "I found him quite full of himself . . . and annoying."

"He could annoy me anytime," Penny cut in with a giggle.

"To each her own, I guess," Bess said languidly.

"He is wild." Charlotte glanced at Lillian. "My parents would never let me date a man who's been divorced."

"My parents wouldn't mind, not with all his money," Bess said. "There are two sides to every story, girls. I heard his wife walked out on him. What else could he do?"

"I heard she walked out after she caught him running around," Penny countered.

Charlotte had mentioned Oliver's divorce last night, though she hadn't given Lillian any details. It sounded as if no one knew the facts, and Lillian didn't want to ask more questions and reveal her curiosity. Not to these girls.

She kept her gaze fixed on her book, though she wasn't reading a word, her ears tuned to every word.

"Well, he got that girl from Ipswich in trouble. Louise . . . what's her name. She worked at the bank, remember?" Penny shrugged a bare shoulder. "I heard Oliver's father paid off the family, and she went to stay with relatives down south."

"Really? I thought she went up to Maine," Charlotte said.

"I don't know where she went, but I heard she was trying to trap him. And she wasn't even pregnant either." Bess closed her magazine and stretched out on her blanket. "She's just a gold digger."

Once again, none of them seemed to know the facts of these shocking stories. Lillian found herself annoyed at them for the careless gossip, then she felt even more annoyed at herself for caring.

Lillian forced her attention back to her book for a few minutes but was too restless to concentrate. "I think I'll take a walk. Would anyone like to join me?"

The other three looked at each other and practically groaned. "I've had enough exercise for one day, thank you." Penny stretched out on her blanket. "I'm ready for a nap."

"Me, too," Bess said, laying her magazine aside.

Charlotte already had her eyes closed, so Lillian set out alone. She preferred her solitude anyway. She had just invited them to be polite.

The stretch of shoreline ahead of her was just about deserted. The sky was clear and the sun strong, but a stiff wind whipped the waves to high, rough peaks. Lillian watched a few boats out on the water, dipping and bobbing. She walked at a purposeful pace, her steps tracing through the foam on the smooth wet sand.

A walk on the beach was an excellent way to clear your mind, Lillian had always found. And she was in need of a clear mind. As hard as she tried and no matter what she told the others, she couldn't stop thinking about Oliver Warwick. The way he had looked at her. The sound of his voice. The way he touched her arm, held her hand.

The way he kissed her.

She certainly didn't want to see him again. She didn't even like him. So why couldn't she stop thinking about him?

Lillian didn't understand her feelings. She didn't like it. She didn't like it at all.

## Cape Light, Present-day

THE CLAM BOX WAS PRACTICALLY EMPTY, EXCEPT FOR A man eating at the counter and a couple sitting in the booth at the back. Sara took her usual table near the front window and settled in, waiting for Luke.

Charlie Bates, the diner's owner, was busy at the grill and hadn't noticed her come in. Which was fine with Sara. Though she and Charlie didn't get along, she came here anyway. It was convenient and the food was pretty good.

Lucy Bates swept out from the kitchen and served the man at the counter. She smiled when she noticed Sara and raced over to her table. "How did you sneak in? I didn't even hear the bell."

She leaned over and gave Sara a hug.

"I know all the secrets. I used to work here, remember?"

"How could I forget? When you worked here I used to look forward to coming in," Lucy said ruefully. "So what are you doing hanging around alone on a Saturday night? Where's Luke?"

"He's meeting me here. We had plans to eat out in Newburyport, but my grandmother had an accident. I just got back from the hospital."

"Oh, dear. Is she all right?" Lillian did not have many fans in town, but Lucy's big heart accepted everyone.

"She'll be okay. She had a bad fall down the attic stairs. She broke her arm and her ankle and is pretty shaken up. It could have been a lot worse, though."

"Yes, I guess she's lucky she didn't break a hip. Or get so upset it sent her into a stroke. She'll probably need physical therapy after the casts come off."

Sara sat back. "I'm impressed. You sound just like the

doctor, Lucy. Are you sure you aren't going to medical school instead of nursing school?"

"Don't be silly. Anybody knows that stuff." Lucy smiled, color rising to her cheeks. "But we are getting into the heavy-duty phase now. I start hospital work tomorrow. Can you believe it? Real live patients. No more dummies in the nursing lab."

"Wow. That is serious."

Lucy nodded, looking like she hardly believed it herself.

"I really don't know how you do it, Lucy. Working at the diner, your school work, and now the hospital, too. Plus the kids and Charlie. I can't even imagine juggling my job at the paper and being married to Luke," Sara admitted.

Lucy laughed. "Don't worry. Luke's the enlightened type. He'll be doing the laundry and the dishes and walking around with the baby strapped to his chest in one of those Daddy pouches."

Sara's eyes widened. "Who said anything about a baby?"

"Lucy?" Charlie leaned over the edge of the counter and rang the little order bell until it sounded like it was going crazy.

Lucy slowly glanced at him over her shoulder. "Yes?"

"When you're done entertaining the customers, there's an order up for you."

"Be right there." She turned back to Sara. "It's just a sandwich. The man's still eating his soup."

Sara was glad to see Lucy didn't jump when Charlie barked at her. She used to just about jump out of her skin if he so much as gave her a dark look.

"I bet you can't wait until your nursing degree is done and you won't have to work at the diner anymore."

"You got that right." Lucy sighed. "Sometimes I think I might miss it. . . ." She leaned over so that only Sara could hear her. "Then I say to myself, *Are you out of your mind?*"

Sara grinned. "I can't believe you're almost done."

"Me, either. I never thought I would get this far. I just took one step at a time and kept going." She looked down at Sara and met her gaze with a serious look. "I never could have done it without you, Sara."

Sara felt embarrassed by her friend's gratitude. "Of course you would. I didn't do anything."

"Yes, you did. You helped me fill out all those college applications. You kept telling me I could do it."

"Well, maybe I encouraged you but you did the rest yourself. You have a lot to be proud of."

Lucy smiled quietly. "Thanks. It ain't over till it's over, though. I still have all this training to get through."

"You'll do fine," Sara told her. "I'm sure of it."

Charlie had walked to the end of the counter and now leaned over, speaking in a low growl. "Sorry to interrupt, ladies. But maybe Lucy could take a short break from socializing to wait on the tables? You know, that thing you do when you carry the food to people?"

"Okay, Charlie. Cool your jets. I'm getting to it." Lucy winked at Sara. "Catch you later," she said, heading toward the order window.

Charlie stood glaring at Sara a moment. Sara glared back.

She knew Charlie saw her as the source of his troubles—the high-minded college girl who had put the idea of going back to school into Lucy's head. Not to mention his perennial feud with Emily, who he believed did not deserve to be mayor of Cape Light nearly as much as he did.

He hated the idea of Lucy going back to school and had done all he could to discourage her. Lucy had even left him for a short time a few years back. She had taken the boys and moved in with her mother. The separation hadn't lasted long, just long enough to show Charlie that even Lucy had her limits.

"Did she even take your order?" Charlie growled.

"I'm waiting for Luke," Sara said.

Charlie's mouth curled in a disdainful smile. He didn't

like Luke much either. "Right, I should have guessed. . . . When are you two getting married?"

"We haven't set a date yet."

"Well, don't rush into anything. Marriage is a tough row to hoe, I'll promise you that."

*Married to you, it would be,* Sara wanted to say. She was more like her grandmother sometimes than she liked to think.

The bell over the door jangled and Luke walked in. His gaze swept the diner, quickly settling on Sara.

"Well, here he is now. Don't get too comfortable. We're closing at ten tonight."

"Don't worry, Charlie. We'll eat fast and get out." Luke gave Sara a quick kiss, then sat down in the seat across from her. "And thanks for the hospitality."

"You shouldn't provoke him, Luke," Sara said, trying to look serious.

"I know but it's hard to resist." Luke took her hands and held them in his own. "How's Lillian doing?"

"She was pretty good when we left. She felt well enough to argue with her doctor. But she's in her late seventies with two broken bones and a concussion."

"Your grandmother's head is as hard as a rock. I wouldn't worry about that part of it."

"Fine Italian marble, maybe," Sara conceded. "She wouldn't like hearing her cranium described as any old kind of rock, you know."

"How long will she be in the hospital?"

"Why? Are you planning on sending her flowers?" Sara teased.

"I'd send her a roomful if I thought it would make her like me any better."

"Oh, she likes you. She just enjoys taking a contrary position."

"Sara, the woman despises me. I know she tells you to dump me every chance she gets. She had a fit when she found out we were engaged. At least admit it."

Sara stared down at the table. It was true. For some reason, Lillian had never liked Luke. She told Sara time and again that he wasn't good enough for her and she could do much better.

Luke was the finest man Sara had ever known. He had endured so many challenges in his life that had only made him stronger.

"I know Lillian has her blind spots about you. But in time, she'll get to know you better, and she'll—"

"She'll find something new to complain about," Luke finished for her. "Maybe when we get married, she'll finally get it."

*Finally* was the key word, Sara knew.

She cleared her throat, hoping to sidestep the when-are-we-getting-married conversation tonight. "There's something I need to tell you about Lillian," she began. "When she comes home from the hospital, she's going to need help around the clock. But she doesn't want a stranger staying overnight. She gets very upset by the idea. Emily and Jessica said they would stay, but you know how hard it would be for them. . . ."

"Uh-oh. I don't like where this is heading at all." Luke rested his chin on one hand, already looking glum. "Go on."

"I said I would stay over at night and keep her company. Is that so awful? She's my only grandmother, you know."

"Sure, I know. But will she ever admit it?"

"She admits it," Sara answered quietly.

She thought about telling Luke how Lillian had asked her to call her Grandma while they waited for the ambulance. But somehow the moment seemed too private, almost secret.

"I need to help her out. I need to help Emily and Jessica. They'll be visiting during the day and doing their share."

Luke didn't look very happy about the situation. "All I know is, now I'll see you even less. And don't tell me to come and visit you there. Your grandmother practically calls the police if she spots me walking down her block."

"She'll be bedridden. She won't even know if you come by to see me."

"Come on. I'm not going to sneak in and out like a teenager. I'm too old for that stuff."

"Yes, I'm marrying an old man, aren't I? I almost forgot," Sara teased him.

Luke was older than her by almost ten years. Sara didn't think about it much, though she knew he did.

"That's right. I'm getting older every day. You better marry me before I need a walker to come down the aisle."

Lucy came over with her order pad in hand. "Hi, Luke. Are you guys ready?"

Luke and Sara ordered sandwiches and coffee, and Lucy returned to the kitchen.

"I guess we can go across the street to the Beanery and have dessert," Sara said, gazing out the window. "They stay open until midnight on Saturdays."

"We should have had dinner there, too," Luke added.

Sara didn't answer. She knew he really didn't care where they ate, that he was annoyed at her. Frustrated about their wedding plans, or lack thereof.

"So?" He stared at her.

"Yes?"

"When are we getting married, Sara? People keep asking me. It's getting embarrassing. We've been engaged a year."

"Not quite . . . well, at Christmas I guess it will be." She sighed. "It's not unusual for couples to be engaged for a year. Or even longer. I don't know what you're embarrassed about."

"Because those people are *planning* weddings. Big, fancy weddings that take casts of thousands. We haven't even set a date yet. We haven't done a thing. . . . Do you even want to marry me? I'm starting to worry."

"Don't be ridiculous. Of course I do. . . . I've done stuff. Lots of stuff." Sara knew she sounded defensive but couldn't help it. "It's just so hard to figure out. It's like a full-time job, except I have a full-time job. So who has time to do this, too? Besides, why should it be up to me to plan everything? Men can read a bridal planner. The print doesn't turn into invisible ink."

"Very funny. Give me the planner. I'll fill it in."

"Fine. But a football game on wide-screen TV, accompanied by beer and pizza do not qualify as Entertainment, Beverages, and Dinner."

Lucy appeared, carrying their orders. She glanced at Sara and then back at Luke. "Whoops, sorry to interrupt. Just remember, don't argue at mealtime. Impairs the digestion. Too much stomach acid."

Luke smiled at her despite his foul mood. "Thanks for the health tip, Lucy."

Lucy set their food down. "Enjoy your meal . . . and don't worry too much about the wedding. These things have a way of working themselves out."

"I hope so," Luke said.

Luke started eating his sandwich, but Sara felt too nervous to touch hers. "Listen," she began, "the thing is, every time I start thinking about the wedding, I get all confused. My family in Maryland wants us to have the wedding down there. My mother keeps telling me about all these nice places she's been looking at. I know my parents will be very hurt if we decide to get married here."

Luke shrugged. "So let's get married in Maryland. My family can get there from Boston. They don't care where it is. I think they're all still in shock that a girl like you would marry me."

"Luke, I'm trying to be serious here. It's not your family I'm worried about. It's Emily. I know she wouldn't make a big deal about it, but I think she has her heart set on us getting married in Cape Light. I don't want to hurt her feelings either."

Sara picked up her sandwich and put it down again. "And even if we do decide where to have it, then we have to decide what kind of wedding we want. Whenever I read those bridal magazines . . . I don't know . . . the Bridezilla mind-set just scares me. So many choices. How do people figure it out? Gowns, veils, flower arrangements, Hummer limos, DJs, heart-shaped chocolate fountains . . ."

"Okay, I get your point." Luke looked up from his plate. "At least we're getting to the bottom of it. We don't have to have a big fancy wedding. It's not a law, you know."

"Not yet." Sara sighed. "Emily said she would help me. She has a restaurant for us to see. She wants us to meet her there for dinner one night next week."

"That sounds promising."

"Not to my parents in Maryland. For them it promises to be a disaster."

"You know," Luke said, "I'm starting to think I have to kidnap you and drag you off, caveman style. Just you, me, and a justice of the peace."

"Oh, Luke. Not that again."

He smiled and nodded. "Time to go to Plan B, Sara. I don't know why you keep resisting. It would make life so simple."

Every time they had this conversation, Luke came up with the same solution. Sara knew she should have expected it. Plan B: run off and elope. At first she had dismissed the idea, but as their engagement dragged on, it was starting to sound better and better. She was tired of fretting about where to have the wedding and stressing over whom she might upset with her decision, Emily or her adoptive parents. She loved them all so much, it seemed impossible to choose.

Besides, she just wanted to be married to Luke. Period. A big party for their wedding didn't seem at all important to her.

"Just give me a little warning. So I can have my hair trimmed or something? And I'd rather not get married in jeans and a ratty old sweater." She looked down at herself, surveying her usual outfit.

"No warning. I'll be wearing the same. We want to make

a statement. Maybe you could write a column about it for the paper. An anti-wedding-industry-that-exploits-young-couples-in-love kind of thing."

"I think you're trying to weasel out of wearing a tuxedo."

Luke shrugged. "Okay, that, too." He grinned and leaned across the table to kiss her. "Now finish up before Charlie shuts the lights off and makes you take that sandwich home in a doggy bag."

Sara poked at her sandwich. She was starting to agree with him. She wished they could skip a real wedding and just run off to get married on their own. It would make life so simple.

But of course, Luke had only been teasing her. And she had been teasing him back . . . hadn't she?

### Crane's Beach, Cape Light, August 1955

LILLIAN HAD WALKED ALL THE WAY TO THE STONE JETTY, rested there for a few minutes, then started back toward Charlotte and her friends. As she grew closer to their striped umbrella she noticed a man sitting there in the midst of the three women, looking like a satyr among the nymphs.

Oliver Warwick. Who else would it be? She stopped in her tracks then realized they had all turned to look at her. Charlotte waved. Lillian realized she was too close to turn around and walk down the beach again. She took a breath, fixed her face in a neutral expression, and headed up the sandy slope to meet them.

"That was quite a walk, Lily. You've been gone an hour." Charlotte rose and walked a few steps to meet her. "We were worried about you."

"I guess I lost track of time. The beach is beautiful at that end, so empty and quiet."

"Lily loves the quiet," Bess said to Oliver. "She made us hike out here to no-man's-land. I'm surprised you found us."

"It wasn't easy," Oliver admitted. He looked up at Lillian and smiled. She didn't smile back. She poured herself a cup of iced tea from Charlotte's cooler and drank it down quickly.

Oliver looked completely different today from the way he had the night before. Though unfortunately, no less attractive.

He wore khaki Bermuda shorts, boat shoes, and a short-sleeved cotton sports shirt, dark blue with vertical grey stripes. His shirt hung open, revealing his bare chest; he was more muscular than she would have expected. The wind tossed his dark hair in all directions, and sunglasses hid his eyes. She could still feel him watching her every move, like the heat of the sun on her bare skin.

"Why don't you sit down, Lily? You must be exhausted." Charlotte jumped up from her chair. "Here, sit in the shade a while and cool off."

The chair in the shade did look inviting. But Oliver sat on the blanket right beside it, his arms folded loosely around his long legs. She was angry at the idea of him following her and afraid of what she might say.

She had plenty to talk to him about. But not in front of Charlotte and her friends.

"I do need to cool off. I think I'll take a swim." Lillian grabbed a towel and headed for the water.

Charlotte wasn't much of a swimmer, and Lillian knew she wouldn't follow. Neither would any of the others. Penny and Bess were too busy flirting with Oliver, and he wasn't even dressed for swimming.

"The water's rough today, Lily. Be careful," Charlotte called after her.

Lillian nodded. "Don't worry. I'll be fine."

The surf was rough. The wind was strong and the waves were coming in close together, peaking high and breaking with lots of spray and foam. There were no lifeguards on this stretch of shoreline, but Lillian wasn't concerned. She had been swimming in the waters of Cape Light and

Newburyport all her life. She was a strong swimmer who knew how to handle herself in the surf.

She waded in a bit until the water swirled around her hips, then dove in, slipping under the breakers. She popped up on the other side and floated. Even at this relatively calm point, the waves rose and fell quickly, lifting and dropping her into deep ocean troughs.

The rough, cold water quickly cleared her head and cooled her temper. She felt ready to return to the group on the blanket. After a few moments, she turned on her stomach and did a breast stroke, swimming back toward the beach.

But while it had been easy to get into the water, it was another matter to get out. She bobbed up and down in the big waves, waiting for the chance to ride one to shore. But the waves were coming in so close together and from several different angles. She could bob around here until midnight, Lillian realized. There would never be a really good time to make her move.

She waited for the next big wave and started swimming madly, feeling it sweep her into the shore, just as she had planned. She noticed the group on the blanket watching her and as she reached the shallow water she tried to get up and exit the water as gracefully as she could, despite the load of sand—and maybe even a few small crustaceans—that had been swept down the cleavage of her suit.

Lillian rose on wobbly legs and shook out her hair. Foamy whirlpools swirled around her legs. She started to walk out of the water, while the sand beneath her feet was sucked from under her by the outgoing wave.

The last thing she saw was her cousin, leaping out of her chair, her expression terrified. Charlotte yelled something to her. Lillian couldn't hear anything over the roar of the ocean, but Charlotte was pointing madly and Lillian glanced behind her to see what Charlotte was pointing at.

A wave had crept up behind her, and the swell of water was now towering over her head. Lillian turned and tried to dive into it but she wasn't fast enough. The wave smashed down on her, knocking her off her feet. She fell face-first into the water and immediately tried to push herself up. But it was impossible. Tons of water crashed down over her, pushing her down. She gasped and flailed her arms and legs, her lungs about to burst. She felt her body sucked under, swirling in the blue-green water. Finally, she felt herself making some progress. *Up,* she thought. *Swim up!*

Then she felt the sand in her hands. She had been swimming in the wrong direction, to the bottom. She turned, feeling her lungs about to burst. She tried to head up toward the light, but the undertow gripped her, twisting her as if she were a bit of seaweed.

*I'm going to drown,* Lillian realized. *This is it. I can't breathe. I'm being suffocated. I can't get up. I'm not strong enough. . . .*

WHEN SHE OPENED HER EYES AGAIN, OLIVER WAS STARing down at her. His face was very close. He looked so serious. She hadn't imagined he could ever look that serious.

She felt his hand under her head, lifting it off the sand.

"Thank God," he said quietly. "Say something," he prompted her.

She swallowed and made a face. She had sand in her mouth and tried to spit it out. "I feel sick. . . ."

Unable to stop herself, she rolled away from him and spit up in the sand.

She felt his hand rub her back in soothing circles. "You must have swallowed half the ocean out there."

"Here's a towel," she heard Charlotte say. "I put some fresh water on it."

Lillian quickly wiped her face and took a long, shaky breath. She felt as if she were going to cry and fought to hold it back.

"Go ahead and cry if you want to," he said quietly so

that only she could hear. "I might feel better after a good cry myself."

Lillian glanced up at Oliver, his dark lashes spiked with water, his hair slicked back wet. She realized he must have jumped in and pulled her out. He had saved her life. Just narrowly.

"I'm sorry," she said awkwardly. Apologies had never come easily to her. "That's never happened to me before. I'm a very strong swimmer. . . ."

"Of course you are." He patted her shoulder, his hand lingering there. "You were knocked down. That could happen to anyone."

"You weren't breathing, Lillian. You didn't move. I thought . . . the worst." Charlotte's face was pale as paper, and Lillian realized she had scared her cousin half to death.

Had Oliver given her mouth-to-mouth resuscitation?

Lillian was too embarrassed by the idea to even ask.

"I'm all right now, Charlotte. Don't worry." She forced herself to sound much stronger than she felt and started to get up. She wasn't about to lie there like a hospital patient.

Charlotte moved toward her. "Here, let me help you."

"I'm fine," Lillian insisted.

Oliver didn't ask permission and didn't believe her either. As she tried to stand he hooked his arm around her waist, lifting her up off the sand as if she weighed nothing at all.

"Come on, lean on me. Don't be so stubborn, or I'll toss you back in the ocean again."

Her legs did feel weak. Having no choice, she leaned on him for support. He kept his arm around her as she walked back to the blanket.

Lillian managed to lower herself to the blanket, only to have Charlotte and her friends begin to fuss. They insisted she sit in the shade. They brought her a cold drink. They covered her shoulders with a towel. Lillian wished they would just leave her be, so she could get her bearings and pretend the whole thing had never happened.

She felt so embarrassed. So foolish. Oliver sat on the blanket in the sun, sipping a bottle of cola. He hadn't put his shirt back on, and she saw now his physique was impressive, with heavy muscles in his shoulders and arms. Across one side of his back near his rib cage, jagged white scars crisscrossed his skin.

After a few minutes, Bess, Penny, and Charlotte decided that the excitement had made them hungry. They were going to the snack bar for lunch.

"I'll just stay here," Lillian said. "I'm not very hungry."

"Care to join us, Oliver?" Bess glanced at him over the top of her big sunglasses.

"No thanks. I'll stay here and keep Lillian company," he said politely.

Bess answered with a knowing smile, then glanced at Penny in a way that made Lillian feel self-conscious. Finally, the three young women left, and Lillian and Oliver were alone.

"You must think I'm an idiot," Lillian said finally.

He shook his head. "Not at all. I nearly drowned myself one summer, just that same way. Luckily my older brother was watching and pulled me out."

She nodded, wondering if he was only saying that to make her feel better.

"Well . . . thank you. You saved my life."

It was difficult to say the words. She wasn't sure why. She didn't like appearing weak in front of him—or feeling indebted to him.

"I guess I did, didn't I?" He looked as if he wanted to smile but was trying hard not to. "I think we should celebrate. Will you have dinner with me?"

He never gave up, did he? She had to give him an A-plus for persistence.

"Dinner? Oh . . . thank you. But I don't think that's necessary."

"Of course it's necessary. You have to eat dinner, don't you? I'd like to take you out tonight, if you're free."

"I really need to have dinner with Charlotte's family to-night. I'm not here for very long," she hedged. Then, see-ing the disappointed look on his face, she felt herself give in. "How about lunch? Would you settle for that?"

His expression brightened. "Okay, lunch is a start." He picked up his shirt and pulled it on. "There's a new restau-rant that's just opened on Main Street, the Clam Box. I've been meaning to try it."

"Right now?" She hadn't meant she wanted to go out with him right that minute.

"Why not?"

She couldn't think of a good reason. Why not go with him now and get it over with? She certainly had had enough of the beach for one day. And Charlotte's friends. "All right. Let's go. I'll just leave a note for Charlotte."

He stood up and picked up his shoes and towel. "She'll understand."

She would understand, Lillian knew. She was probably expecting it.

Lillian pinned her wet hair in a loose knot atop her head. She pulled on her shorts and cotton blouse then quickly packed her canvas bag.

She was soon walking off the beach with Oliver. He took her bag and then took her hand, as if it were the most natural thing in the world. She thought about resisting but for some reason she just didn't.

# CHAPTER THREE

～

*Southport Hospital, Present-day*

"You there . . . Lindy?" Margaret Sherman, Lucy's supervising nurse waved Lucy over to the main desk.

"Lucy Bates." Lucy corrected her in a respectful tone.

"Lucy, right. I need a blood pressure reading in Room 203; patient's name is Helen Carter."

"No problem." Lucy took the chart and the blood pressure cuff and set off for Room 203, glad for the assignment.

She had been at the hospital since the early morning but hadn't gotten to do any hands-on nursing yet. Most of the time had been taken up with a group orientation and a tour of the building. Then she had been assigned to the second floor, east wing, where the patients were either in for tests and diagnosis or recuperating from surgery.

"Most of the patients in this wing are in relatively stable condition," Margaret had told them. "Which is not to say that caring for your patients will be any easier or less exacting than more acute cases. One small, seemingly unimportant error could put a life at risk."

The warning had made Lucy nervous. She had done well with her coursework but it never came easy. Making a mistake here would be a lot worse than getting a bad test grade, especially with Margaret Sherman as her supervisor. Magaret was tough and intimidating, and Lucy suspected she enjoyed making the student nurses jump.

Lucy reached Room 203, knocked on the half-open door, and went in. Though it was the middle of the day, the shades had been drawn, and the room was so dark Lucy could hardly see where she was going.

Lucy made out a figure huddled under the covers in the room's single bed. "Excuse me . . . Ms. Carter?"

No answer. She walked closer to the bed, and Helen Carter slowly turned her head in Lucy's direction.

Lucy smiled. "I need to take your blood pressure."

"What's the difference?" the woman asked bitterly. "It's all so pointless."

Lucy was a bit unnerved by the reaction but tried not to let it show. She unwrapped the rubber cuff. "If you could just lean a little closer and hold out your arm, please."

Helen shook her head and turned away from Lucy. "Get that thing away from me. I don't want to be jabbed or poked or stuck with anything."

Lucy took a step back. Her first day as a nurse, and she had to deal with a genuine, fire-breathing dragon. She stood beside the bed a minute, not knowing what to do.

"I'd like to be alone, please," Helen Carter said. "Can you just go now?"

Lucy winced inwardly. It was going to be hard to explain to Margaret Sherman that she had been chased away by the patient on her very first assignment.

But the woman did seem upset.

Lucy rolled up her equipment. "Is there anything I can get you, Ms. Carter? Would you like me to raise the shades?"

Again, a swift shake of her head. "Leave the blinds. I want it like that. . . . Some fresh water would be good. I've been asking for it for hours."

"Water? No problem." Lucy took the plastic pitcher from the bedside cart, brought it to the ice machine in the hallway, and filled it with ice and then fresh water.

Maybe after she had a drink, Helen Carter would be in a better mood and let her take the pressure reading. Lucy hoped so.

"Here you are." Lucy entered the room again and set the water pitcher on the cart. "I'll pour you a cup."

As Helen Carter watched silently, Lucy pulled a disposable cup from the stack on the bedside cart and started to fill the cup with ice water. For some reason, her hand was shaking. This woman unnerved her.

*Get a grip. You're not doing brain surgery here, Lucy.*

"So, how are you doing today?" Lucy asked, trying to make pleasant bedside conversation.

"How am I doing? *I'm dying.* That's how I'm doing. Do you find many healthy people in these beds?"

Startled by the outburst, Lucy stepped back and knocked into the cart. The pitcher tumbled and flooded the bed.

"Aaaaah!" Helen Carter screamed. "You idiot! What are you trying to do, kill me?"

She jumped out of the bed, the bottom of her nightgown and robe soaking wet. She held it away from her body, doing a little dance.

"Oh, my gosh. I'm so sorry!" Lucy ran over to help her, trying to keep her head. It was only ice water. Yes, she was a clumsy clod to have spilled it, and she was sure it wasn't comfortable, but the woman was absolutely hysterical.

"No, get away from me! You've done enough. Get out!"

"Please, let me help you. Just . . . sit in this chair. I'll get some help and change the bed. . . ."

But help already seemed to be on the way. Lucy heard buzzers sounding and footsteps running toward the room. Lucy wasn't sure how, but she and Helen Carter had set off alarms at the front desk.

A flock of nurses and doctors raced into the room. Lucy stood at the foot of the bed. She had just pulled the blanket and sheets off. The plastic mattress cover had done its job, and a puddle the size of Lake Michigan filled the middle of the bed.

Lucy couldn't bear to look at all the faces that were now staring at her—a few nursing students along with doctors and nurses from the floor, several of them whispering together, fighting not to laugh out loud, she thought.

A doctor walked up to the irate patient and spoke quietly. Lucy couldn't hear what he was saying but his tone sounded soothing.

Helen answered him loud and clear. "I will not calm down! That woman should be fired! Get her out of here, right now." Helen sat up and pointed at Lucy. "That one!"

Lucy felt her face turn flaming red.

"Student nurse," she heard Margaret Sherman murmur to the doctor. Then Margaret walked up to Lucy and touched her arm. "All right, Lindy, you can go now. We'll take care of this."

Lucy didn't have the heart to correct her name again. She let the wet bedding drop and walked from the room, Helen Carter's voice ringing out clearly behind her, "I could sue this hospital. I could have slipped, jumping out of bed like that . . ."

Lucy hurried down the hallway, fighting back the urge to cry. She would have felt worlds better if she had been allowed to help clean up and make the bed again.

Could she possibly be cut from training on the first day?

She went back to the nurses' station, where another nurse asked her to sort out some patient consent forms.

Twenty minutes later, Lucy looked up to see a grim-faced Margaret Sherman standing over her.

Lucy summoned up her courage. "I'm very sorry about spilling the water. The patient started yelling at me, and I was just taken by surprise. I usually work as a waitress and I've rarely even done that in a restaurant."

Margaret stared down at her, sizing her up, Lucy thought. "A waitress, huh?" she asked finally.

Lucy nodded. "My husband and I own a diner."

"Don't quit your day job," Margaret said dryly.

"What would you like me to do now?" Lucy asked, forcing out the words. All she really felt like doing was crawling into a hole and disappearing.

Margaret glanced at her watch. "Why don't you take a break? Sign out on the sheet over there. I think you've done enough around here for one afternoon."

Lucy headed for the elevators, feeling exiled. Two other student nurses passed her in the corridor, nodded hello, but didn't stop to talk. Lucy could tell from the way they smiled back that they had heard the news: Lucy Bates nearly drowned a patient in her own bed.

The hospital cafeteria was almost empty. Lucy bought herself a cup of tea and a packet of cookies and sat at a table near a window overlooking a courtyard. The day was dreary and gray. Lucy turned away from the bleak view. Someone had a left a newspaper behind and she paged through it, too upset to concentrate.

Charlie was right. She wasn't smart enough to be a nurse. Whatever made her think she could actually pull this off?

Maybe this was a sign, a sign that she should quit before she really hurts somebody. Today it was just ice water. The next time, it could be fatal.

She felt tears well up again and pressed a tissue to her eyes. When she took the tissue away, a man was standing at her table, gazing down at her. She guessed from his green scrubs and stethoscope slung around his neck that he was a doctor. He carried a tray of food and looked down at her with concern.

"Are you okay?" His voice was quiet, calming. Lucy recognized it immediately. He was the doctor who tried to calm down Helen Carter.

She nodded quickly. "Sure, I'm fine. The newsprint—" She pointed down to the paper. "It gets my nose going."

"Interesting. You're either allergic to the ink . . . or all the bad news."

She laughed. "Maybe both."

"Would you mind if I sit here?"

Lucy gazed around at all the other tables, which were completely empty. "Sure, have a seat. I can see that it's hard to find a spot."

He grinned and set down his tray. She eyed his large paper cup filled with ice and water and pointed to it as he sat down. "Better keep that away from me."

He set the cup on the far side of the table. "Better?"

Lucy nodded and smiled. "Thanks. It hasn't been my day."

"Is this your first day at the hospital?"

"Yes. I just hope it's not my last."

"Hey, you'll have to do a lot worse than that to get kicked out of training. It was just a little water."

"My supervisor seemed pretty mad. She told me not to quit my day job."

He laughed and took a bite of his sandwich. "She was just trying to scare you."

"It worked," Lucy admitted.

"Listen . . . what's your name?"

"Lucy Bates."

"Listen, Lucy, when you start your training it's nerve wracking. You want to do everything right, but nobody's perfect. You're bound to make mistakes. Dumping water on a patient may be the least of it."

"That's encouraging . . . I think?" Lucy gave him a doubtful look. "I'm going to screw up even more before this is all over, is that what you're saying?"

He nodded, his thick brown hair falling down across his eyes. "There's a reason they call it training."

"That's supposed to make me feel better?"

He smiled and wiped his mouth on a napkin. "That patient who blew up at you? She had just gotten some upsetting news about her condition."

"Oh." *I should have guessed something like that was*

*going on when I saw her sitting in that dark room,* Lucy thought. "What's wrong with her, or can't you tell me?"

He looked away a moment. "I guess it's easy enough for you to read her chart. She has cancer. She had a tumor removed about five years ago, but it's come back, spread to her kidney. It's not operable and she's refusing other courses of treatment."

"That's awful. She looks so young." *About my age,* Lucy thought.

"She could live a long time with the right treatment—if she's lucky."

"I guess it's hard for her to see it that way," Lucy said, trying to imagine how Helen Carter must feel. "It's hard to know the right thing to say in a situation like that."

"It is," he agreed. "That's why most doctors don't say anything."

"That seems wrong, too, though, don't you think?" Lucy looked up at him. "Are you her doctor?"

"Just an attending on the floor. I'm a resident here." He held out a hand to her. "My name is Jack Zabriskie."

Lucy shook his hand. "Nice to meet you, and thanks for the words of wisdom."

He laughed. "I'm only a few rungs up the food chain from you, so I guess I can identify. I am a bit older than most of the residents, though. So they do call me Yoda from time to time."

"Yoda's not so bad. The other student nurses call me . . . Mom," she admitted. "Not to my face, of course."

"They do not."

She shrugged. "Maybe I just imagine that."

"You should be proud of yourself. Lots of people think about a career change or going back to school when they're older, but few have the guts to really do it."

"It wasn't easy," she admitted. "It still isn't. But I always wanted to be a nurse. Until today, that is."

"I always wanted to be a doctor but ended up driving an

ambulance instead. I couldn't get into med school right after college. Then I gave up for a while. But one day I just decided to go for it. I couldn't go on doing the EMS work anymore. It was worthwhile, but it wasn't what I really wanted."

Lucy understood that. She had felt the same way about running the diner with Charlie.

"I know what you mean. Even if nursing doesn't work out for me, I can't see myself going back to the diner."

"Don't worry, your training will work out," he assured her. "What was it that you used to do at a diner?"

"I love hearing that past tense," Lucy admitted. "Actually, I still work there. My husband and I run the Clam Box in Cape Light. I'm a waitress there . . . when I can't avoid it."

"You're married?" He glanced at her left hand, and Lucy realized she had taken off her rings to wash up and had forgotten to put them on again.

It made her feel odd to think Jack Zabriskie had even noticed. For one thing, he was light years younger.

"Charlie and I have been married . . . oh, almost twenty years now. We have two boys. Are you married?" she asked quickly.

"My wife and I are separated. We'll probably get a divorce."

Lucy wished she hadn't asked. "That's too bad."

"These things happen." He shrugged and glanced at his watch. "I'd better go."

"Me, too." Lucy stood up and gathered up her trash. She had lost track of time talking with Jack. She didn't want to return late from her break and give Margaret Sherman another reason to be annoyed with her.

Jack had to stop at the radiology department before returning to the floor, so Lucy went back on her own. She felt anxious heading back to the scene of her disgrace, but Jack's words had helped. He was right. She wasn't going to be Super Nurse in one day. She had to expect a few mishaps.

Nursing was what she had always wanted to do, and she wouldn't let a silly accident discourage her.

"LUCY, IS THAT YOU? WHAT TOOK YOU SO LONG? YOU said you would be home by six-thirty."

Lucy heard Charlie call out to her from the kitchen before she was even halfway through the door. She dumped her book bag near the front door and shrugged out of her jacket as she walked to the back of the house.

The boys sat at the kitchen table frowning over their homework. Charlie stood at the stove. At least he could fix a meal. But since he worked over a hot stove all day, he claimed it wasn't his place to cook at home, too. She could tell he was annoyed now by the rigid set of his shoulders.

"Hi, boys." Lucy kissed each of her sons on the cheek.

C.J., the oldest, didn't even look up from the thick textbook he was reading. He wore headphones hooked to a CD player, listening to music while he studied. Or supposedly studied.

Lucy pulled one of the earpieces out. "No music while you're doing homework. You know the rules."

He made a face but took the headphones off and put them aside. "Bummer."

Lucy knew that was all she would get out of him for now. At thirteen, C.J. was at a stage where he only replied in one-word answers.

Jamie was two years younger. He, at least, was still at a communicative stage and clearly missed her while she was out of the house.

"I got a ninety-five on my math test, Mom. Look." He held up the sheet proudly.

"Wow, that's great, honey. I'm so proud of you." Lucy squeezed his shoulder. "Charlie, did you see Jamie's test?"

"Yeah, I saw it. Pretty good." Charlie glanced over from the stove. "C.J. has a report due tomorrow. American History.

As usual, he's barely started. You'll probably have to write it for him."

C.J. wasn't the best student but he tried hard. Charlie never gave him any credit, though. Criticism didn't help. It only made C.J. feel worse and do worse. But Charlie didn't seem to understand that.

Lucy caught her older son's eye. He looked as if he expected her to be angry at him, too.

"Don't worry, we'll write it together. How long does it have to be?"

"Three pages, typed."

Lucy forced a smile. She had a pile of her own schoolwork to do tonight. This extra assignment was definitely going to set her back. But her family came first. Her son needed her. She wasn't going to let him down.

"That's not much. We'll start right after dinner."

She quickly washed her hands and pulled an apron over her nursing outfit. "Can I help you, Charlie?"

"Just set the table, everything's ready here. I've got to get back to the diner. Jimmy came in at three to cover for me, and he doesn't want to close up, too."

"At three? What happened to my mother?"

"Your mother got stuck late at her job. So I had to pick up the boys at school. Again."

"Something must have come up."

"Yeah. That's what she always says."

Lucy knew it wasn't her mother's fault. She had a daycare job watching small children. The woman who employed her was a teacher, but she wasn't always able to come home right after the school day ended. Lucy knew her mother wanted to help with the boys, but she couldn't just walk out on her own job.

The boys cleared their books off the table, Lucy set out the dishes and utensils, and Charlie served some chili he had brought home from the diner, his usual fallback. Lucy was getting sick of it, but she didn't dare complain. Fortunately, the boys would eat anything.

"Did you get any calls about the job today?" she asked as they began to eat. Charlie had been running an ad in the *Cape Light Messenger* for waitressing help, to fill in for Lucy's absence. The sooner he had more help in the diner, the better his mood would be.

"I got a few. Nobody with the right experience."

"Maybe you could train someone. Start them off when it's slow. I could help."

"When are you going to help? You're hardly there as it is. I'm darned if I do hire someone and darned if I don't. I'm not looking forward to shelling out that extra paycheck every week. We're skating on thin ice as it is, Lucy."

According to Charlie, they were always on the brink of financial disaster. Lucy had begun to doubt these dire reports, though. Her husband seemed to find resources when he needed them to buy a new piece of kitchen equipment, or even a new truck last year. Of course, she was never privy to the financial side of the business. Charlie laughed off her inquiries, claiming she wouldn't understand.

"It's just temporary," she reminded him. "As soon as I finish the training and get my degree, it will be much easier for us."

"If we make it till then," he mumbled.

"Of course we'll make it. Don't be so negative." Lucy took another bite of chili. The boys were quiet tonight, she noticed. She didn't like to talk about the family finances in front of them. Kids didn't need those worries.

"I hope you're right, Lucy. This whole family has made an awful lot of sacrifices. I hope it's worth it."

Charlie didn't say more about it, and Lucy was thankful he let the matter drop.

She had wanted to tell them all about her first day at the hospital, but no one asked her about it. Then again, if she ever admitted today's mishap to Charlie, he would pounce on it as another sign that she wasn't cut out for nursing and should just give it up.

She didn't need that. She wasn't going to tell him about

having coffee with Jack Zabriskie either. Charlie would just get the wrong idea.

"Well, I should get going." Charlie pushed back from the table and got up. "I'll be home at the usual time."

"I'll be here." Lucy watched him grab his jacket off one of the pegs near the back door and head out into the night.

Lucy carried the dishes to the sink. The kitchen looked like a cyclone, even though Charlie hadn't really cooked. The dishes from breakfast were still piled in the sink, and the dishwasher needed emptying.

"I don't have any clothes to wear for tomorrow, Mom," Jamie said. "Can you wash my basketball uniform, too?"

"Just bring it all down. I'll get to it."

"Me, too. I need some clean jeans and underwear." C.J. set a stack of books for his report on the table. Quite a big pile of books, Lucy noticed with dismay.

She filled the sink with soapy water and started washing the pots. "What's your topic, C.J.?"

"The Louisiana Purchase. You have to write out a speech, like, if you were in the Congress and trying to talk for it, or against it."

"That's interesting." Lucy dug into the burned bottom of the chili pot with a soap pad.

"Right, Mom. It's so interesting, I'm going to fall asleep."

Lucy laughed at him. "Let's save some of those wise remarks for the essay. You crack those books and take notes, the way I showed you the last time. I'll help you get organized and do a first draft."

"First draft?" he groaned. "Can't we just write the stupid thing?"

"Just take the notes. I'm not going to write it for you, you know."

C.J. made a face but started working.

Jamie came into the kitchen with a notice for her to sign about a field trip. The fifth grade was going to a science museum in Boston. Jamie had been talking about it all year.

"Just put it on the table, honey. I'll sign it when my hands are dry."

"Can you be a chaperone? Mrs. Effron says they need a lot of parents, and you didn't come on any school trips this year, Mom."

Lucy could tell he really wanted her to go with his class on their trip, but she couldn't see how she would manage it. "Let me check the date. I'll try to come if I can, honey."

He gave her a look, and she knew that she had disappointed him once again. His expression brightened a few moments later, though. "Hey, Mom, I think I know what I want for Christmas."

"Really? What is it?"

Christmas! Was Christmas coming already? Lucy felt an unhappy jolt. She wasn't ready for Christmas, financially or emotionally. She felt so overburdened right now, Christmas would push her right over the edge.

"Rollies. They're these really cool shoes. They have wheels on the bottom and you sort of roll around. A kid in school has them, and—"

"A kid wore those to school? The principal allows that?"

"Well, he wasn't supposed to. He had to take them off and put on his regular shoes. I wouldn't wear them to school. I just want them, though."

"Rollies. Okay, write it down on a list or something for me," Lucy said. "Now go inside and let your brother study. Don't forget to take a shower. You need to be in bed by nine."

"I know." Jamie headed for the TV. He was a good kid. Never gave her any trouble. A good student, too. He would get his Rollies. Lucy just hoped they didn't cost a fortune.

She felt bad about not going on the field trip and vowed that she would try to make it up to him somehow.

She could only spread herself so thin, and tonight it looked like she needed to be on top of C.J. He had been staring at the same page for the last half hour.

She sat down next to her older son and pulled his textbook over so that they were sharing it. "Let's see what we have here," she said.

It was going to be a long night.

# CHAPTER FOUR

❧

*Cape Light, August 1955*

$\mathcal{J}$UST AS SHE WOULD HAVE PREDICTED, OLIVER DROVE
a shiny red convertible, a sports car made in Britain. He
drove fast, too, which Lillian would have also predicted.

They weren't able to talk much on the ride to town
along the winding beach road. Oliver would glance over at
her and try to point out some landmark he thought interesting, shouting at her through the wind. By the time Lillian
understood what he was talking about, they had flown by it
and were miles down the road.

She was blown to bits, her hasty hairdo dispersed in all
directions. She imagined she looked a perfect wreck, but
she told herself she didn't care.

*The worse I look, the better. Maybe he'll decide he
doesn't like me as much as he thought.*

Oliver parked in front of a diner. The sign out front read
THE CLAM BOX and there was a "Grand Opening" banner
slung across the doorway.

Lillian was surprised at the choice. She had expected

him to take her to a fancier place—lunch at the yacht club, perhaps, or a real restaurant.

He turned to her with a grin, and she wondered if her reaction was obvious.

"I know it doesn't look like much, and frankly, it isn't. A buddy of mine—Otto Bates—just opened the place. I thought we could give him some business. Do you mind?"

"Of course not. This will be fine." Lunch at a diner would be faster than at a restaurant with more elaborate service. Their date would be over in no time. That's what she wanted, wasn't it?

They walked up to the entrance and Oliver held the door open for her, dipping his head to avoid hitting the banner. It was thoughtful of him to give his friend some business. Maybe he wasn't as self-centered as she suspected.

A man behind the counter called out to him cheerfully. "Well, look what the cat dragged in."

"Hello, Otto. How's business?"

"Booming. Business is booming. Did you come by to try some of my world-famous clam rolls?"

Oliver grinned. "Are they world-famous already? You only opened last week."

Otto Bates laughed and Lillian did, too.

"Take any table you like. I'll be right out with menus."

Oliver led Lillian to a table by the window, where they had a clear view of Cape Light's Main Street. "So, what do you think of my hometown? It must seem very provincial to a girl like you."

Lillian gazed out the window. "I guess it is a small town, but I don't mind it. My parents brought our family up here every summer when I was growing up. I've always liked Cape Light."

"Really? I would take you more for summers on the Vineyard or Nantucket."

"My father liked to visit with his brother in Newburyport. That's Charlotte's father, my uncle Joshua," Lillian explained. "He also found it very . . . economical."

Oliver understood her implication; she could tell by the twinkle in his eye. "Well, economical or not, it's a pleasant place in the summertime, an undiscovered place. I'll take it over the Vineyard or Nantucket anytime."

"But you live here year round, don't you? Charlotte said your family owns a factory or something?"

Lillian could have bit her tongue. Now he knew she had been asking about him. Not that Charlotte had needed any coaxing. Her cousin had given her an earful last night after the dance, eager to tell Lillian more than she ever wanted to know about the town's most infamous native son.

"My father owns a cannery, the largest in the area. And there are some other interests as well. We stopped canning for a while during the war and did some manufacturing for the defense department—bullet casings."

"That sounds both patriotic and profitable."

"It was profitable." Oliver shrugged. "Some people resent the fact that my family profited from the war. Did Charlotte tell you that?"

Lillian was surprised at his honesty but found it refreshing. "As a matter of fact, she did."

"I thought she might. What else did she tell you about my family?"

Lillian hesitated. He was daring her. She didn't know if she should go much further, but what did she have to lose? So what if she insulted him? She didn't care if he liked her or not, so what did it matter?

"She said your grandfather ran gin boats down from Canada during Prohibition. She told me that was how your family made all their money."

"Most of our money, not all of it," Oliver said. "But there you have it—the complete Warwick family history in a nutshell. I'm the grandson of a bona fide bootlegger. Are you shocked?"

"I'm not sure yet what to think," she said slowly. "I will say your background's more colorful than most people I meet. Was your grandfather ever caught?"

"Never. He was a clever man, very daring. I'm sure if anyone ever tried to arrest him, he talked his way out of it. He could charm a dog off a meat wagon."

*Just like you,* Lillian nearly said aloud.

Oliver stared at the entrance, and she turned quickly to see a man entering the diner. He called a greeting to Oliver and walked toward their table. "I thought that it was you, Warwick. I waved from the window but you didn't see me."

"Of course, I didn't see you. Who would notice your ugly mug when I have a beautiful young woman sitting right in front of me?" Oliver glanced at Lillian. "You'll have to excuse me for talking like that to this fellow, Lillian. We grew up together."

"One of us grew up," Oliver's friend added. "The other will remain Cape Light's own Peter Pan . . . with a trust fund."

"Very funny. He's a great wit," Oliver said, looking annoyed at the comment.

Lillian couldn't help smiling at the joke.

"I don't know how you get all the gorgeous ones, Oliver." He bent his head toward Lillian. "How do you do? I'm Ezra Elliot." He extended his hand politely and Lillian shook it. "Doctor Elliot, actually."

"Doctor Elliot?" Oliver stared at his friend. "So you're a real doctor now? How did that happen?"

"The usual way, only longer. But I made it." He glanced at Lillian. "I had just started med school when I was drafted, sent to Korea. But I made it back in one piece and started all over again."

"That's very admirable," Lillian said sincerely. She admired all the young men and women who had served their country. So many had lost their lives or come home wounded beyond repair.

"So what's the plan, Ezra? Coming back home to set up a practice?"

"No plans for that right now. I'm at Children's Hospital in Boston," Ezra explained. "I like practicing in the city. I might come back here someday when I'm old and gray and ready to settle down."

"Lillian lives in Boston. She works at the Museum of Fine Arts." Oliver sounded as if he were bragging about her, Lillian thought, though he hardly had the right.

"That's an interesting place to work. What do you do there?" Ezra asked, leaning toward her.

"I'm an assistant curator in the Egyptian department."

"Did you study art history or archaeology?"

"A little of both," she answered, impressed that he knew it took a knowledge of many fields to master that era.

"Lillian's a very unusual woman," Oliver cut in. "And I saw her first. Remember that." Oliver's warning was delivered in a jesting tone, but Lillian noticed his expression was serious.

"In this case I might be likely to forget," Ezra retorted. He smiled at Lillian in a way that made her blush. "You would be better off with me, Lillian. Oliver has a scandalous reputation."

"Oh, don't believe him. He's just joking." Oliver's tone was airy and casual, but a muscle in his jaw tightened and Lillian knew Ezra had hit a nerve.

"Yes, of course," Ezra said agreeably. "Oliver and I like to joke around with each other. A pleasure meeting you. Enjoy your lunch."

Ezra smiled again at Lillian then slapped Oliver on the shoulder, and the two men made vague promises to meet soon.

Lillian and Oliver both watched from the window as Ezra left the diner and headed on his way down Main Street. He wasn't nearly as tall as Oliver or as handsome, Lillian noticed. But he was clever and intellectual, more the type of man she was used to socializing with.

"You really shouldn't believe what Ezra said about me," Oliver told her. "He's just jealous. He would love to meet a girl like you, beautiful and accomplished and intelligent."

Lillian snapped open her menu and glanced at the list of

dishes. "Everyone in town is warning me about you," she pointed out. "Are they all jealous?"

Oliver laughed and picked up his own menu. "People like to talk about me and my family. You'll have to get used to that once we're married. You seem very level-headed. I think you'll do fine."

Lillian dropped her menu and stared at him an instant then looked away, trying to hide her reaction.

*Married, indeed.* They hadn't even ordered lunch yet.

These outrageous pronouncements seemed to be part of Oliver's flirting technique. He didn't mean anything by it, she was sure. The man didn't have a serious bone in his body.

Otto approached the table, order pad in hand. "Sorry for the wait, folks."

"Now here's a man who'll stand up for my character." Oliver turned to Otto. "Will you kindly tell this young woman that she can trust me?"

Otto looked surprised. "Trust him? I trust him with my life." He leaned closer to Lillian, making her feel suddenly uncomfortable. "Didn't you know this man won the Purple Heart?" He nodded, his expression serious. "That's right. He saved my life and the lives of about a half dozen other soldiers in our unit."

"I didn't even know he served," Lillian said. Somehow the girls on the beach hadn't mentioned that chapter of Oliver's life, nor had Charlotte.

"He served all right. We were on patrol and—"

Oliver rested a hand on his friend's beefy forearm. "Otto, please. Lillian doesn't want to hear boring old war stories."

"No, go on, Otto," Lillian insisted. "You were on patrol, you said?"

Otto nodded. "That's right. Night patrol, south of France. Me and Oliver had just come over. We were boys, only eighteen . . ."

Oliver stared down at the table, impatient for his army

buddy to finish—or lost in painful thoughts of the past? Lillian couldn't be sure.

"We were ambushed and a few men fell. Oliver crawled on his belly, got to the gunner up on a hill and somehow knocked him out. He took over the gun and covered us, so we could get to safety. Then he went down and helped the wounded men back to camp. I was one of them."

Otto rested a hand on Oliver's shoulder. "He doesn't like to talk about it, but you couldn't find a better man than this one, right here, miss. That's my opinion, anyways."

Lillian nodded, moved by the story and by Otto's heart-felt testimony. Oliver didn't seem the heroic type. He was too glib and irreverent, for one thing. Then again, you never know who will rise to the moment in a crisis. And he had saved her life today; she couldn't discount that.

"You never mentioned that you were in the army," Lillian said.

Oliver shrugged. "I don't like to talk about the war. I would rather pretend it never happened." He glanced at his menu. "Are you ready to order?"

"I suppose so," Lillian said, surprised by the swift change of topic. She ordered a cup of chowder and a clam roll, Oliver ordered the same, and Otto took the menus and headed for the kitchen.

Lillian wanted to ask more about Oliver's time in the service, but it was clear he didn't want to pursue that topic. She had met other men who felt the same way. Usually, they were the ones who had seen the most bloodshed and destruction.

The food came out quickly. Oliver carried the conversation, asking her opinion on popular books and movies. Lillian could tell he wasn't a great reader but was trying hard to make the right impression on her.

He was surprised—and pleased—to learn she was a baseball fan. "Lillian, you just get better and better," he told her with a charming smile. "I'll come to Boston and we'll see the Red Sox."

Lillian didn't answer. She didn't want to encourage him. She had no intention of seeing him after this lunch date that she had only agreed to because he saved her from drowning.

When they finished lunch and stepped outside, Oliver suggested a walk down to the harbor. It seemed like a good idea to her. She needed to stretch her legs after their filling lunch, and she wasn't in any rush to take another windy ride in the little red convertible.

They walked down Main Street, headed for the village green. It wasn't nearly as hot as it had been earlier on the beach. A light breeze blew off the harbor, ruffling the leafy treetops and the sails of boats tethered to the town dock.

"What did you think of the Clam Box, Lillian? Do you think he'll stay in business?"

"I thought the chowder pasty and the clams too chewy, and I don't think that place will last very long . . . though he's certainly a very nice man."

Oliver slung his arm around her shoulder. "You don't mince words, do you?"

"Don't ask me a question if you don't want an honest answer."

"I'll remember that," Oliver promised with a grin. "But for Otto's sake, let's hope the rest of the world isn't as particular as you are."

Lillian felt as if he was teasing her but in a good-natured way. Her mouth twisted as she fought off a smile, but finally she couldn't help herself.

Oliver led them out onto the wide dock. The harbor was filled with boats, all shapes and sizes, many tied up to the dock for the day, and more anchored out in the harbor. Seagulls swooped and swirled overhead, occasionally coming to perch on one of the wooden pilings jutting from the water.

The far end of the dock was reserved for working fishermen and their sturdy, homely vessels. Lillian saw piles of nets and box-shaped lobster traps. A few men in black rubber boots worked together, loading buckets of fish onto a truck.

A fisherman sat by a shed on a wooden crate, smoking a pipe while he worked on a trap with a pair of pliers. He wore a stained work shirt, tattered dungarees, and big rubber boots.

As they drew close, Lillian could see he wasn't much older than Oliver, though his long shaggy beard initially gave the impression of a man much older. He looked like the Ancient Mariner, she thought, or what you would think the Ancient Mariner might look like.

Two big dogs lay at his feet, one a black Labrador, the other a shaggy brown hound of undistinguishable origin. They both had thick, wet fur and smelled badly. A little girl sat beside him, too, dangling her bare feet over the edge of the dock. She wore a yellow cotton sundress and had dark brown braids hanging down her back. Her skinny arms stuck out as she held a fishing pole over the water.

"Hello, Digger. Are you going after lobster now?" Oliver greeted the fisherman.

Digger shook his head. "Just working on this trap for a buddy. Nothing better to do until the tide goes out."

"This is my friend Lillian. Lillian, this is Digger Hegman."

Digger nodded. "How do you do, miss?"

"Digger is the best clammer in town. Maybe even in all of New England."

Digger shook his head, looking embarrassed by the praise. "Not so loud, Ollie. The clams are always listening." He glanced around, as if the bivalves were eavesdropping that very minute. "Haven't seen you on the flats much this summer. You lose your rake?"

"I haven't had much time for clamming lately, Digger. But I'll meet up with you soon," Oliver promised.

Lillian found it hard to picture urbane Oliver Warwick and this crusty fisherman digging up clams together, but Oliver did have an unexpected side.

"Don't forget now. You rich boys need your exercise." Digger patted Oliver's flat stomach and laughed. Then he tapped his daughter on the shoulder. "Say hello to Mr. Warwick, Gracie. Show him your manners."

The adorable little girl tipped her head back and smiled up at Oliver and Lillian. "Hello, Mr. Warwick."

Oliver crouched down to talk to her. "Catch anything?"

"Not yet."

"Fishing is hot work," he said sympathetically. "You look like you could use an ice cream cone. Strawberry maybe?"

Grace considered the suggestion very carefully. Lillian could see she was a very serious child.

"I think I could," she said finally.

Oliver laughed, reached into his pocket, and gave Grace a folded bill. The ice cream would only cost a nickel. The rest could buy a few bags of groceries for her family. *Very generous*, Lillian thought. But the girl and her father looked like they could use a little charity.

"You go ahead. I'll hold the pole for you."

Grace looked at her father, who nodded his consent. Oliver took the pole, and Grace jumped up and ran down the dock. The dogs lifted their heads, then the black one rose and slowly padded after her.

Lillian smiled. "I guess she likes strawberry ice cream."

Digger nodded. "Females favor pink food. That's what I've found."

"Not me," Lillian said.

"Then you must be the exception, miss." Digger turned to Oliver. "Here, give me that."

Digger took the fishing pole from Oliver, stuck it on the dock, then held it in place with his boot, while he kept working.

"I told Grace she wouldn't catch anything out here this time of day. But she's an awfully stubborn little girl."

"Women can be that way in general, I've found." Oliver glanced at Lillian, a teasing light in his eye.

They said good-bye to Digger and headed for the village green. The shady path under the tall trees felt like an oasis. They found an empty bench, and Oliver wiped it off with his pocket handkerchief, offering Lillian a seat.

The bench faced the harbor and they soon saw Grace return with her ice cream, skipping down the dock toward her father. The black dog followed, licking the trail that dripped from the cone.

"I enjoyed talking with your friend Digger, but clams can't actually hear," she said finally. "I doubt they have any senses at all."

"Don't tell Digger that. He's sure they can even smell him coming." Oliver looked so serious, Lillian had to smile.

His arm was slung over the back of the bench, not touching her but close enough. He leaned even closer when he spoke, his face so near all she could think about suddenly was the way he had kissed her on the deck the night before.

"I'm not sure what to make of you, Oliver. Everyone has a different story. It's hard to sort it all out."

Oliver looked pleased. "At least you're trying. I think you just have to spend more time with me and decide for yourself."

Lillian looked out at the water. "I'm only in town for a few more days. It doesn't make any sense to start dating. It can't lead anywhere."

"Boston isn't so far away. I go into the city fairly often. I can come and see you anytime you like."

Lillian glanced at him. He wasn't going to be put off. Not like most men who would politely accept her excuses.

Even if half of the gossip Charlotte had related was true, Oliver Warwick was not the type of young man her family would approve of. For one thing, he was divorced. For another, despite all the Warwick money, her parents wouldn't be eager to tie their good name to a bootlegger's fortune.

Lillian knew there was something more—the strong

attraction she felt was mixed with a feeling of . . . unease. She had always been able to hold her own with men and often took the upper hand, even with her former fiancé, George.

Oliver was another type altogether. He was older than she was, about six or seven years, she guessed. He was much more experienced with women. Impulsive and unpredictable, exciting to be around, she never knew what he was going to do next. Which she didn't like at all.

"Do you want to know what I think?" Lillian asked, turning to him again.

He gave a comical wince. "I have a feeling you're about to be painfully honest with me. Go ahead. I can take it."

"I think you're bored and something about me amuses you. Maybe I'm different from other women you meet." She shrugged. "I don't know. But I'm really not your type. I think you know that. We had a nice day together. So why not just . . . let it go?"

He stared at her a long moment. "You are different, I agree with you there. But I'm as serious as I've ever been. I mean to keep seeing you, Lillian. You're not going to get away from me that easily."

He cupped her face with his hand. Then he leaned over and kissed her. Lillian resisted for a moment, trying to pull away. But it was no use. She felt herself melting toward him, as if she had no will of her own.

### Southport Hospital, Present-day

EMILY SAT BY HER MOTHER'S BED, WATCHING LILLIAN sleep. Dr. Bartow had decided to keep Lillian a day longer than he initially expected. He had some concerns about her blood pressure, which fluctuated on Monday but had stabilized today. If all remained stable, she would be sent home tomorrow morning, he said.

The extra day had given Emily and Jessica time to get their mother's house ready. Not much time, but somehow they had managed, bringing in a hospital bed and making a bedroom for her on the first floor in one of the many spare rooms. Like so much of the house, the room was drab and needed painting, but there hadn't been any time for redecorating.

Emily was sure her mother would insist that she needed to be in her real bedroom. But there was no way they would be able to get her up the stairs. And even if they did, how would she get back down?

They had also hired a day nurse. Luckily, Sara was still planning on staying there at night. Emily knew that it was going to be a sacrifice for her daughter and thought it was very good of her to offer. She hoped Lillian wouldn't be too difficult with the day nurse or Sara. But that was probably hoping too much.

Lillian opened her eyes and turned to stare at Emily. "What time is it?"

"Nearly six. I have to go in a few minutes. Jessica will be by later and you're going home in the morning."

"Yes, I know." Lillian closed her eyes again.

Emily worried that her mother had been sleeping too much the past few days, drifting in and out. But Dr. Bartow said it was normal, the result of the pain medication she was still taking and the trauma of the fall.

"Ezra called. He wanted to come visit you here, but I told him you would be home tomorrow. He'll probably call back later."

"Ezra . . . he fought in the war. Korea. Went to medical school on the GI Bill . . . Did you know that?" Lillian spoke with her eyes closed, as if she were reporting from a dream.

"No, I didn't," Emily replied. She stood up and touched her mother's arm. "Your dinner is here. Do you want some help before I go?"

Lillian shook her head, her eyes still shut. "The chowder is pasty and the clams are very chewy," she complained. "I doubt that it will last."

Emily smiled. Her mother was having a dream. And complaining about her food in it, obviously.

"It's baked chicken, Mother, with carrots and rice."

Lillian's eyes opened. "Oh, never mind. I'm not hungry," she grumbled, turning to her side. "Just let me sleep, will you?"

A knock on the door made Lillian turn around again. Emily turned, too, to see Reverend Ben Lewis step into the room, his coat draped over one arm. "I hope this isn't an inconvenient time. I was visiting Vera Plante and thought I would drop by to see you, Lillian."

Lillian frowned. "What's wrong with Vera? Did she fall down a flight of stairs, too?"

Reverend Ben came closer to the bed. "Not at all. She had a dizzy spell and needed a test. It's probably her blood pressure medication. Her doctor wanted her to stay overnight for observation."

"I hope it's nothing serious," Emily said.

"I don't think so. But she does have that big house to take care of, and there are two people boarding there now. She's doing too much for a woman her age. I've told her to drop out of the Christmas Fair committee this year. We don't want her spending the holidays in here."

"Vera works so hard on the fair. We'll miss her." Emily pulled an empty chair closer to her mother's bed and offered it to the reverend.

"Everyone works hard. It's a big job," Ben said as he sat down.

Lillian shifted against her pillows. "Maybe the church should skip that silly fair altogether. Maybe it's a sign from on high, Reverend. It's much ado about nothing, if you ask me."

Ben glanced at Emily. *Lillian is in fine form,* his look seemed to say. *Despite her broken bones.*

"The community seems to enjoy our fair, and it's a big fund-raiser for the church. It would be hard to meet our budget next year without it," he admitted.

"Money, of course. The root of all evil," Lillian reminded him tartly. She sat back and smoothed the sheet over her lap. "Perhaps I have a solution. I've been thinking of giving the church a gift, a special gift for Christmas. A sizable offering."

He sat back in his chair, looking puzzled. "Oh. Well . . . that would be very much appreciated, Lillian. We would be very grateful."

Emily knew why Ben was surprised. Her mother was a fixture at Sunday service, but she rarely participated in the church beyond that. She never joined any committees or became involved with the events. She claimed she didn't have the patience for the meetings, but Emily knew her mother considered herself above such efforts. That was for the worker bees, not Lillian Warwick.

"When I get home, I'll take care of it," Lillian promised. "Then maybe you won't have to worry so much about hawking those chintzy-looking crafts and tins of broken cookies. It's just not dignified."

Ben gave her a long, thoughtful look. "I don't think we can call off the fair. But your gift, in any amount, will be greatly appreciated."

Emily glanced at her watch. "Oh, dear. I've got to run." She grabbed her coat and purse, and gave her mother a quick kiss on the forehead. "Good night, Mother. I'll see you tomorrow. I think Jessica will be by later. If you need anything, just ring the nurse."

"I could press that button till my finger falls off. Do you think they ever come?"

The nurses had already gotten wise to her, Emily knew.

"Don't worry, I'll look after her. You go along, Emily," Reverend Ben said.

He turned back to Lillian as Emily left the room. "Have you been thinking about this a long time, Lillian? This gift to the church, I mean."

She didn't answer immediately, her mouth set in a thin tight line. "I'm not sure. That tumble down the attic stairs may have brought it to the surface, like shaking a snow globe."

The image made Reverend Ben laugh. There was nothing wrong with Lillian Warwick's wit. Even falling down a staircase couldn't blunt it.

Ben had the urge to ask her more questions but instead waited for her to speak. He had long ago learned that listening was more important than speaking during these bedside visits.

"I've been thinking about the past. It's seems more real to me lately than the present," she admitted. "Sometimes I feel as if . . . as if I might get lost back there and never return."

"Does that concern you, Lillian? It's not uncommon at your age to reminisce."

She sighed and fingered the edge of the blankets. "So I've heard. I don't fancy turning into one of those mumbling seniors who think they're living back in 1957." Then, seeing his expression, she suddenly sat up straighter. "Don't look so alarmed, Reverend. I'm not saying I think I'm going senile. It's nothing like that. Maybe it's just feeling my own mortality approaching, the way you sense someone sneaking up behind you. It's getting closer, you know. It's not a good feeling."

"I imagine that it's not," he said quietly.

Ben had rarely seen Lillian let down her defenses this way. That part was almost as surprising as her frank admission.

"Were you frightened by your fall?"

She nodded, her chin trembling a bit. "Of course I was. *Well, that's it*, I said to myself. *They'll find me down here, my head cracked open like a coconut. Quick. Efficient. Practically painless. Better than a long drawn-out drama in some nursing home.*"

"You really were very lucky, Lillian. It could have been far worse," he said.

" 'And to die is different from what any one supposed,

*and luckier.*' " She looked straight at him. "A line of poetry, Reverend. Walt Whitman."

Lillian looked away. "It makes you take stock, a fall like that, a near miss. They say we'll all be judged, a full accounting, your good deeds and your bad. As if God is some big, cosmic bean counter. Do you believe that's true?"

Ben wasn't quite sure how to answer. "I don't know, Lillian. I surely can't say exactly what happens when we die. I believe that we have a soul that survives our physical body and goes on to join our Creator in some better place. I also believe that God wants us to follow the teachings of the Gospel and to do good in this world. He wants us to love one another. That's what he asks first and foremost."

Lillian took a deep breath and rested her head back on her pillows, shutting her eyes. Ben couldn't tell if she was satisfied with that answer or had quickly dismissed it.

"No one would describe me as a loving person," she said finally. "No one. Not even my children. I may have been better at it when I was younger, but life changes you, hardens you. My life has."

Ben felt both compassion and shock at the quiet confession. He sat back, glad she had her eyes closed and couldn't see his reaction.

"Does that mean my soul will be condemned to hell, do you think?" Her tone was light, conversational.

"I'm not sure there is such a place," he answered. "But I do believe that God knows your heart, Lillian. He knows that we're all flawed, all imperfect. Maybe all that we can be judged upon is our will to do good, our effort to be kinder and more loving. It looks as if you have time to work on that. If you want to."

She opened her eyes and shook her head. "I don't know, Reverend. I consider these essential questions and yet, I don't believe I can change. Not at my age. This is who I am. If that's what's required, I'm not sure if there's much hope for me."

Ben leaned closer and touched Lillian's hand. "There's always hope, Lillian. Ask for God's help and see what happens."

She didn't answer, only stared down at the blanket again. He wondered if he had overstepped some boundary or if she had simply retreated behind her usual defenses.

"Thank you for the visit, Reverend. I need to rest now."

"Yes, of course." He stood up and took his coat from the chair. "I'd like to visit when you get home."

"Don't trouble yourself, Reverend. I know how busy you are. I will call the church if I need you."

"Good night, Lillian. I'll pray for your speedy recovery . . . and that you find some answers to your questions."

"Thank you, Reverend. It's nice to know at least one person is praying for me. Good-bye now."

That was a dismissal he could not ignore. Ben smiled and left the room.

He wasn't surprised by Lillian's polite refusal to have him visit her at home. She had revealed her fears and doubts to him—her secret weakness—and now felt embarrassed. He could have predicted as much. He wouldn't give up that easily, though, and he suspected she knew that, too.

# CHAPTER FIVE

***

*Newburyport, August 1955*

"𝒴OU TWO ARE GOING TO CHURCH THIS MORNING, aren't you?" Charlotte's mother called from the bottom of the staircase.

Still dressed in her cotton robe, Lillian's cousin ran out into the hallway to answer her. "Yes, Mother. We're getting dressed."

"Well, don't take all day. It's not a fashion show. The service starts at eleven and we have to walk. Your father's gone golfing and taken the car."

"Oh, rats. We'd better hurry." Charlotte ran back into the room. "Have you seen my stockings? I thought I left them on the dresser top. That's my last good pair—"

"They fell on the floor. I'll get them for you." Lillian loved Charlotte, but sharing a bedroom for a week was a challenge.

She picked up the stockings and handed them over. Charlotte smoothed the hose up her legs, fastened her garters, then pulled on a full slip.

Bright sunlight streamed through the voile curtains. An electric fan on the night table slowly turned back and forth, circulating the warm air. Lillian could tell it was already hot outside. It was going to be a long, hot walk to town.

Standing in front of the big mirror that hung over her dresser, Charlotte began working on her makeup. Lillian sat on the bed and fanned herself with a magazine.

"I hate wearing stockings in this heat, but my mother will have a fit if we aren't dressed *properly*." Charlotte mimicked her mother's voice, making Lillian laugh.

Lillian already felt herself melting in her own outfit, but her Aunt Rebecca was right. A proper appearance was important, especially at church. The gray cotton suit was warmer than she would like, but it was all she had brought for Sunday. It had a long straight skirt and a short, fitted jacket with white piping on the lapels. She wore a pale pink silk blouse under the jacket and already had her hat and crocheted white gloves on.

"Maybe my father will take us for a sail later, when he gets back from golf. Or we could go for a drive." Charlotte brushed out a chunk of her golden hair and twisted the ends around her fingertip to make it curl. "Unless you'd like to go to the beach again?"

"I could skip the beach for a day, I think." Lillian forced a smile. She tried not to think about her near-drowning the day before. Or about Oliver Warwick.

"I still can't figure out how Oliver found us out there," Charlotte said, patting on face powder. "He must have looked for you all over town. But it was lucky after all, wasn't it?"

"I guess so." Lillian opened her neat clutch purse and stared inside. She already knew she had what she needed: lipstick, compact, handkerchief, wallet. But she didn't like talking about Oliver. It unnerved her.

They both heard the phone ring. Charlotte looked at Lillian, a gold tube of lipstick dangling from one hand. "It's him," she said breathlessly. "I just know it."

Lillian snapped her purse closed. She wished Charlotte wouldn't be so . . . dramatic. It only made things worse.

"Your mother knows what to say; she'll get rid of him," Lillian said curtly. She stood up and smoothed down her skirt, then checked the seams of her stockings.

"That was Oliver Warwick again," Charlotte's mother called out from the bottom of the stairs. "I told him you were both out, and I didn't know when you'd be back. I hope he gets the hint."

Aunt Rebecca sounded annoyed. Oliver had called several times yesterday and last night. He was nothing if not persistent; Lillian had to grant him that.

Charlotte glanced at Lillian and giggled. "He's got a terrible crush on you, Lily. I bet he sends you flowers today."

"Aren't you girls ready yet?" her mother called again. "I'm starting out without you. I'll see you at the service." Lillian heard the front door close.

Charlotte was at the closet now, pulling out dresses and skirts and tossing them on the bed. "Our church is like a steam bath in the summer. A woman fainted last week, and the deacons had to carry her out like a corpse. I would hate to have that happen to me."

She held a sun dress up to her chest. It had a halter neck and pink polka dots on white fabric. "What do you think?"

"A little revealing for church, Charlotte. Unless you wear a sweater over it?"

"Are you mad?" Charlotte turned back to the closet. "He's after you. It's so exciting. I've heard he's irresistible once he gets going. He's a womanizer though," she said over her shoulder. "They say that's why his wife divorced him."

Lillian felt a jolt. For all his disclosures the day before, Oliver had never mentioned his marriage. Now, though, Lillian wished he had; she was curious about his version of the story. Then again, what did it matter? She wasn't going to see him again, no matter what he said.

"That dark blue dress is nice," Lillian suggested.

"I can't wear that. I'm not going to a funeral." Charlotte sighed and tossed it on the pile. "I don't think we should tell my parents you had lunch with him yesterday. They don't approve of him. Your parents wouldn't either. But isn't it fun to have a man like Oliver Warwick after you? I think it's thrilling."

"Charlotte, he's not after me. He's just very spoiled and used to having his way. It must be a novelty to have someone say no to him. He'll get tired of it soon."

"Oh, I don't think so. He's head over heels for you, Lillian. You can't deny it. I don't see why you won't go out with him—for dinner and dancing and all that. I bet he would take you someplace swell. And he's such a good dancer."

"What's the sense of dating him, even once? I have no interest in encouraging a relationship with him. Not after everything you've told me."

"You do like him, is that what you're saying?"

Lillian shook her head. "Not the way you mean." Charlotte gave her a look. "Oh, well . . . yes, of course, he's good-looking . . . and charming. He has nice manners and can carry on a decent conversation. . . ."

Charlotte laughed. "You're not fooling me, Lily. I know what you're thinking. I bet when he kisses you, your toes curl. That's a sure sign."

*A sure sign of what?* Lillian wasn't prone to blushing, but her cheeks went flaming red. She had told Charlotte about Oliver's advances. Clearly, *that* had been a mistake. But she had to tell somebody.

The truth was, she was attracted to him. Wildly attracted, despite all the reasons she knew she shouldn't be. She didn't find it thrilling or exciting or any of the inane adjectives Charlotte was prone to. She found her attraction mainly . . . frightening. She felt something inside of her that she knew could veer out of control. And she didn't like that, not at all.

Charlotte finally found a dress she wanted to wear, a yellow shirt waist with a flare skirt, cap sleeves, and a neckline trimmed with a white collar and a bow. She stepped into it and turned so that Lillian could pull the zipper up the back.

"Charlotte, I hope you aren't sharing my secrets with all your friends. I told you about Oliver in the strictest confidence."

"I haven't told a soul." Charlotte smoothed her dress. "Why don't you just relax and enjoy it? Oliver can be your summer fling. It will do you good, help you get over George."

"I never think about George," Lillian huffed.

Charlotte laughed. "I'm sure of that. I doubt you thought about George very much when you were planning on marrying him."

Lillian couldn't help smiling. It was true. She had felt more sparks fly with Oliver Warwick in the last three days than she had with her ex-fiancé in three years.

"What I mean is"—Charlotte hesitated—"it's hard for a girl to get dumped like that, right before the wedding. Oliver can help you feel . . . attractive again."

Lillian knew this was true. Even though she hardly believed a word of it, Oliver's outrageous flattery had already boosted her confidence.

But just having a fling . . . that would be using him. Lillian didn't like playing romantic games and knew she was bad at them. Besides, Oliver wasn't the type you toyed with. At least, she wouldn't chance it.

"No, that's not for me, Charlotte. I don't need an ego boost or a fling."

"How do you know, Lily? Don't knock it till you try it."

She winked and scooped her gloves, hat, and purse from the dresser top and stepped into her heels.

"Are you going to walk to church in those shoes? You'll never make it," Lillian predicted.

"Don't worry. I'm calling a taxi. But don't tell my

mother," Charlotte added. "She thinks it's too indulgent, especially for going to church."

The taxi arrived quickly and drove them through the streets of Newburyport, past the fine old homes in Charlotte's neighborhood and into the large village, set on a hill overlooking the harbor. The streets were narrow and many were paved with cobblestone, unchanged from the Colonial era when the town was founded.

The taxi pulled up in front of the church, and the young women paid the driver then hurried through the front doors and took seats in the back of the sanctuary.

The Newburyport church, which stood at the very top of the hill that crowned the town, was an elegant white building with a high slate-covered steeple. The stained-glass windows in the sanctuary diffused the strong sunlight into an amber glow.

Lillian had always enjoyed worshiping here with Charlotte's family when she came to visit. It was just as a church ought to look, she thought, pristine and untouched by time. She settled back, prayer book in hand, and focused on the sermon.

The minister, Dr. Van Houten, had been there as long as she could remember. Charlotte always rolled her eyes when she spoke about him, wishing the church would find a younger minister who didn't ramble on. But Lillian enjoyed his sermons, which dealt with serious and complex topics.

This morning Dr. Van Houten was talking about God's will for our lives. "Life must be lived forward but can only be understood backward," he began. "That's a curious irony and a grievous impediment. We set off for one point and soon find ourselves at some other. And yet, the art of life might be to accept the course that God charts for us, a course that is rarely the most direct route from point to point. But a zigzagging, even circuitous, path where we are confronted with many unexpected trials . . . and unexpected blessings. Where we learn, like the experienced sailor, to use the wind when we are able and to prevail through rough weather without giving up our hope and faith of arriving someday at our destination. But accepting the course God has set for us. Accepting that God may have a better destination in mind than we had ever hoped for . . ."

Lillian considered Dr. Van Houten's premise. She believed in God, she knew that much. But did she believe he had a plan for her, one she would only see clearly in her old age, as she took a backward glance over her days?

Lillian balked at the idea. She believed she had control of her life. She made her own choices. Yet some part of his argument niggled at her. On Saturday, she had nearly drowned. She hadn't had any inkling when she woke up that morning that she might not live to see the end of the day. Had God known what was going to happen to her?

Oliver had saved her. Just in the nick of time. Had that been part of God's plan? What was she to make of it all?

Charlotte nudged her. "Lillian?" She held out her hymnal. Everyone was up and singing while Lillian was lost in her troubling thoughts.

Lillian stood up and leaned toward her cousin, reading the song over her shoulder. "Are you all right?" Charlotte whispered.

"Yes, I'm fine. Just . . . thinking about the sermon," she whispered back.

Charlotte looked surprised. "It got me thinking too . . . about a nap. It was so boring I could hardly keep my eyes open."

Ten minutes later, the service ended. The two cousins were walking out of the church when Charlotte's mother came up to them. "There you are. I didn't see you come in. Aren't you coming to the coffee hour, Charlotte?" Aunt Rebecca leaned closer so that only Lillian and Charlotte could hear. "Muriel Granger's son is visiting for the weekend. He's at Yale Law. I want you to meet him."

Charlotte looked stricken. "Lillian and I are getting a ride to the beach. We have to go right away. Tell Mrs. Granger . . . another time."

"But Charlotte, what will I say? I promised Muriel."

"Say I have heat stroke or something. Sorry, Mother."

Charlotte took Lillian's arm and pulled her through the crowd before her mother could stop them.

"Charlotte, that wasn't very nice. Why don't you want to meet Muriel Granger's son? Is something wrong with him?"

"I'm sure he's a horrible bore, just like all the other nice young men my mother finds for me. I've told her a million times to stay out of my social life. . . . Oh, dear. Look who's here."

They had set off walking quickly down the street, arm in arm, while Charlotte chattered. So quickly that they were steps away from Oliver Warwick before Lillian even noticed him.

He stood leaning against his shiny car, wearing a navy blue blazer and cream-colored trousers with an open-neck white shirt that contrasted with his dark hair and tanned skin.

"He looks like a movie star," Charlotte whispered.

Lillian didn't answer. He did look like a movie star. But she would be the last one to admit it.

Oliver smiled when Lillian met his eyes, his dimples creasing his lean cheeks. "Morning, ladies. How was church?"

"I found the sermon very interesting," Lillian said.

"I couldn't follow a word," Charlotte admitted. "Too much talk."

Oliver laughed. "That's just the trouble with church, I've always found."

Lillian frowned and pulled her gloves on. "Well, nice seeing you, Oliver. Have a pleasant day." She turned to Charlotte, urging her with her eyes to continue on their way.

But Charlotte wouldn't budge, standing her ground like a little toy poodle in a stubborn snit. Lillian glared at her. Charlotte ignored her.

"I would offer to drive you both home, but my car only has room for one," Oliver apologized.

"Take Lily. Please. She was complaining about the heat. I don't think she should be out in this hot sun."

"I wasn't complaining about anything," Lillian said.

"She's so stoic," Charlotte explained. "I have to go back to church anyway. I promised my mother I would stay with her for the coffee hour." Charlotte turned to Lillian. "You go on with Oliver, Lily. Don't be so stubborn."

"Come on, Lillian." Oliver opened the passenger door and made a sweeping gesture. "Let me be your chauffeur today. I'll take you wherever you want to go."

Half-resentful, half-willing, Lillian stepped toward the car and slipped into the front seat. Oliver closed the door and smiled down at her, pleased to have finally gotten his way. So much for all her efforts to avoid him.

## Southport Hospital, Present-day

LUCY STOOD BESIDE MARGARET SHERMAN AND WATCHED as her supervisor checked the flow of liquid dripping through the IV line then checked the point of insertion on the patient's arm. "Please stop fiddling with that catheter, Mr. Krall. I don't want you to pull it off again."

"It itches," said Mr. Krall, a man in his seventies.

"Bates will bring you some cream. Just don't pull it out again," she warned in an even sterner tone.

He leaned back against his pillows and clicked on his TV set. "I shouldn't even be here. I'm not sick. My wife runs me into the emergency room if I so much as burp."

"Your doctor should be by in a little while. He'll let you know what's going on."

Mr. Krall had arrived on the floor that morning, and Lucy hadn't had a chance to check his chart. "Does he have a stomach problem?" Lucy asked after they left the room.

"Upper GI. I would be surprised if it's not the gall

bladder. He's got all the classic symptoms. Learn to read the chart when you enter a room."

Margaret Sherman was brusque and impersonal. She had been supervising Lucy for almost three days and had done nothing but issue curt instructions. But Lucy knew she could learn a lot from her. The woman could look into a patient's eyes and tell if their medication level was off. Just this morning, she had called a code on a patient who was going into diabetic shock, catching it just in time. Lucy wondered if she would ever be as knowing and capable as Margaret Sherman, if she would ever be as confident.

Since the unfortunate incident with Helen Carter, Margaret had been watching Lucy closely. Lucy knew her supervisor didn't trust her, but in a way, she didn't mind the scrutiny. After her little scare, she didn't entirely trust herself.

Next, Lucy was sent out with a medication cart. Lucy found this fairly easy. Though some patients were stubborn about taking pills and others asked all kinds of questions about what she was giving them, most swallowed whatever was in the cup.

The last two days Lucy had been kept busy with simple tasks: bringing patients their medication, taking temperatures and blood pressure, helping patients get mobile again after surgery.

Luckily, there had been no more mishaps. Most of the patients seemed to like her. She had been afraid at first to be too friendly or chatty, but most patients looked for a kind, reassuring word. That was part of her job, too, a part she was naturally good at.

Lucy was rolling the medication cart down the corridor when she noticed Jack Zabriskie walking toward her with another doctor. This was the first time she had seen him since they talked. She wasn't sure why, but she suddenly felt her heart race; if she had been hooked to a monitor, an alarm would have gone off. She felt her cheeks flush. She was a redhead and blushed easily, for no reason at all. And this was no reason, she reminded herself.

*What in the world is wrong with me? I think the pressure's putting me over the edge. . . .*

She ducked her head, hoping he wouldn't see her.

"Lucy? Hey, how's it going?" he called out.

"Just fine. Uh . . . see you."

She picked up her pace and walked past quickly. The med cart rattled wildly, but she acted as if she didn't hear it, setting her face in a serious, focused expression.

Back at the nurses' station, Margaret gave Lucy her next assignment. "Go down to Room 203. The patient had an invasive test yesterday. We want her sitting in a chair for a while, then walking down the hall if she's able. Think you can handle it?"

Lucy drew in a sharp breath. Didn't Margaret realize that was Helen Carter's room? Something in her gray-blue eyes told Lucy she did. She was doing this on purpose.

"Do you have a question?" Margaret prompted her.

"No, no questions." Lucy turned and headed for the room.

Lucy reached the door to Room 203 and nearly lost her nerve. But she knew she had to at least try. Bracing herself, she knocked on the doorjamb then walked in.

The shades were drawn again, the room dark. Helen Carter sat up against the pillows. Her eyes widened as she recognized Lucy.

"Ms. Carter, I'm here to help you up out of bed. You need to get up and sit in a chair awhile."

"Really? Why?"

Lucy was stumped but only momentarily. "So that you don't get bed sores or pneumonia. And to keep your circulation moving . . ."

"All right. I get your point."

Lucy walked over to the bed, feeling she had won the first round. She got the patient to sit up and swing her legs over the side of the bed. Then Lucy put her slippers on her feet.

"You might feel a little light-headed. Let me know when you're ready and I'll help you to that chair."

"I'm ready now," Helen said. Lucy helped her slip down off the bed and held her arm as she took a few steps across the room to the chair. Then she helped Helen sit down and stuck a pillow behind her back for support.

Helen took a deep breath. "I do feel better getting up."

"Good." Lucy willed herself to keep her naturally chatty tendencies under control. She straightened the bedding and then brought in a fresh pitcher of ice water, feeling very self-conscious.

Helen Carter must have been thinking of the spill, too. "I'm sorry I yelled at you," she said abruptly.

Lucy looked up at her, surprised. "You don't have to apologize. I understand."

"I'm sure you don't." Helen pulled the shade aside and glanced out the window.

Margaret peered in. "Everything okay in here?"

"Just fine," Lucy said.

Margaret took another look around the room then left Lucy on her own again. Lucy was relieved. Her supervisor had been breathing down her neck the last few days. It was a relief to do one thing on her own.

Lucy cleaned off the bedside cart, removing an empty box of tissues. She wiped it off and put back Helen's belongings, a book and a photograph that showed Helen with two teenage girls. There was no question they were her daughters.

"Are those your girls? They're very lovely."

Helen nodded. "Thank you."

"How old are they?" Lucy picked up a pillow and gave it a good shake.

"Nineteen and twenty-one. They're both away at college. Robin is at Amherst and Julie is at MIT."

"You must be very proud."

"They're good students," Helen admitted. Then after a

long moment she added, "They don't know I'm in the hospital. I didn't want to worry them."

"That must be hard for you," Lucy said honestly.

Helen frowned and turned her face away. Lucy wondered if she had spoken out of turn and made Helen angry again. Then she realized Helen was upset; her eyes were glossy and she wiped them quickly with a tissue.

"I don't know how to tell them I'm sick," she said quietly. "Their father and I are divorced, a long time now. He sends his checks, but he doesn't take any real interest in the girls. He has a new family with young children. I'm all they really have. If anything happens to me . . ." Helen covered her face with her hand, and her body shook with silent sobs.

Lucy wasn't sure what to do. She walked over, put her arm around Helen's shoulder and leaned toward her. "I'm very sorry."

Helen cried quietly then took a quick, shuddering breath. She pushed Lucy gently away. "You can go now. Please."

Lucy stepped back. "Would you like to get back in bed?"

"Not just yet."

"All right. Someone will come in a few minutes to help you. Don't try to get back on your own, promise?"

"Yes, I promise. Now, please, just go. I'd like to be alone."

Lucy felt uneasy leaving her but had little choice. She returned to the front desk and told Margaret that Helen wanted to stay out of bed for a while longer.

The older nurse glanced at her watch. "All right. I'll send someone in to check on her. I need you to work on the supply closet. We just got a delivery that needs to be recorded and stored."

Lucy had learned in school that nurses nowadays rarely had to fill the supply closet or do many of the lowly jobs that they used to be responsible for. But once in a while there was an emergency, and the scut work would naturally fall to the lowest one in the pecking order. Namely, her.

"Is there some problem?" Margaret stared at her.

"Not at all."

Lucy headed off to the closet, a narrow space with cupboards lining the walls on either side, now completely jammed with cartons of new supplies.

She had barely gotten started when Margaret appeared, filling the doorway with her large frame.

"Yes? Do you need me for something?" Lucy jumped up, stumbling over a carton of rubber gloves.

"There's a call for you, your husband. Says it's an emergency." Margaret sighed audibly and stalked back down the hallway.

Lucy wasn't allowed to have her cell phone on while she worked, but she checked her messages frequently, especially after three o'clock when the kids got home from school.

She had specifically asked Charlie and the boys not to call her at the hospital unless it was an emergency. She knew Margaret Sherman didn't approve when staff took personal calls at the nursing station. Especially the students.

She rushed down the hall to answer the call, hoping nothing was seriously wrong. She picked up the phone. "Charlie?" she asked breathlessly. "What's wrong?"

"Jamie's sick. The school nurse called. She says he has a fever and somebody needs to pick him up. I got my hands full here, Lucy. You need to get him."

"I can't leave, Charlie. My shift isn't over until tonight."

"Well, just tell somebody your kid's sick and go. What's the big deal?"

Lucy tried to hold onto her patience. "Charlie, be reasonable. It will take me at least an hour to get back to Cape Light, maybe more with the traffic. You're five minutes away."

"Don't you tell me to be reasonable. You be reasonable. I'll have to bring him back here. I can't bring a sick kid into the diner."

Lucy wracked her brain for an alternative. She knew her

mother couldn't help; she might be able to come later, but she couldn't leave her job.

"Maybe Jimmy can come in early and cover for a few hours," Lucy suggested. Jimmy was their extra cook, who often managed the diner at night.

"Jimmy's here already."

Now she was really annoyed. "So? What's the problem?" Lucy didn't want to raise her voice or stay on the line any longer arguing about this. The other nurses at the desk were already glancing at her.

"The problem is, it isn't my place to get stuck at home, with a sick kid. I have work to do. I'm the only one bringing in a dollar these days," he reminded her.

Lucy could have screamed—partly because what he said was true—but she forced her voice into a calm, firm tone. "I'm not leaving, Charlie. You can handle it. You have to. Your son is sick and I'm too far away to help. You know that."

"Lucy, for crying out loud . . ." Charlie's words were garbled in a low, growling sound. Then he didn't say anything. Lucy wasn't even sure if he was still there. Had he hung up on her?

What if he brought Jamie back to the diner? The child would be miserable hanging around all afternoon. Would Charlie dare do that to his own boy just to show her?

"Charlie? Are you still there?"

She was on the brink of giving in when he finally answered.

"Okay, you win. This time. But I don't know how much longer I can put up with this baloney."

"You're going to pick up Jamie and bring him home?"

"Yes, I'm going right now."

"I'll call my mother and see if she can stay with him later. Then you can go back to the diner."

"That's some help, I guess."

Charlie hung up without saying good-bye. Lucy knew he was mad at her and this wouldn't be the last of it.

It did seem ironic that she was stuck here, taking care of

strangers and storage closets while her own child was sick and needed her. Lucy didn't feel entirely right about that. But like so many of her problems lately, this one had no real solution.

The rest of the day dragged, and Lucy felt relieved when her shift finally ended. Though she was eager to get home to Jamie, she peeked in as she passed Helen Carter's room. Helen had the lights on and sat in bed, reading a book.

"Hi, how's it going?" Lucy braced herself, not knowing what to expect.

Helen looked up and marked her page. She wore reading glasses with stylish red frames that complemented her dark hair.

"You never came back this afternoon to help me out of my chair."

"Somebody did though . . . I hope?" Lucy asked nervously.

"Oh, yes. I wasn't left stranded there," Helen said with a smile that made her look much younger.

Lucy, glancing at the dinner tray, noticed Helen hadn't eaten much. "Would you like something different?" she asked. "I could get you a sandwich or a salad from the kitchen before I go."

Helen held up her hand. "No more hospital food, please. All I really want is a big, gooey slice of pizza. I don't think they serve much of that around here, do they?"

Lucy laughed. "No, pizza's not high on the dietician's list of healthy entrées."

"Good night, then," Helen said as Lucy started out of the room. "And thanks for asking."

At the nursing station, Lucy glanced at Helen's chart. She wasn't on any dietary restrictions, not even low salt. But Lucy decided to check with Margaret Sherman just to be sure it was okay.

"The patient in Room 203 didn't eat her dinner. She wants a slice of pizza. Can I bring her one from the cafeteria?"

Margaret frowned at her. "Did she ask you to go get her a slice of pizza?"

"No, not at all. I just know she wants one. And she didn't eat her dinner," Lucy repeated.

The older nurse studied the chart and let out a long noisy breath. "I guess that would be all right." Then she looked up at Lucy. "You're not a waitress anymore. You're a nurse, Bates. Or about to be."

Lucy grinned. "I remember. But it's sure nice to hear you say that."

Lucy bought a slice of pizza in the hospital cafeteria, covered it with an extra plate, and brought it back up the second floor. The door of Room 203 stood open, so she knocked on the door frame and walked in. The pizza was still hot, and the smell made Lucy's mouth water.

Helen looked surprised to see her again. "Yes?"

Lucy set the pizza down in front of her. "It might not be the best you've ever tasted, but it's hot."

Helen sat up straight and wide-eyed. "Is this a mirage?" She looked up at Lucy with a small smile.

"It's real. And if you don't eat it, I will."

Helen laughed. She picked up the slice and took a bite. "Mmm . . . that's just want I wanted." She swallowed a bite. "I thought nurses were too busy these days to be so nice."

"I'm not a real nurse. Not yet anyway. Just a student do-ing hospital training."

"Oh . . . I didn't realize."

Lucy could tell what she was thinking. "I know, I look too old to be a student. I got a late start."

"Better late than never. I always wanted to be a teacher, but I quit college to get married, then had my girls. It never seemed like a good time to go back."

"Once you have a family it never is, is it?"

"Once I got divorced, the idea seemed impossible. Now that my kids are out of the house, I wonder if I made the right choice." She glanced at Lucy curiously. "Do you have children?"

"Two boys. One is in middle school, the other's still in elementary. I didn't think I could do it, but I couldn't seem to live with myself if I didn't try. A friend encouraged me, helped me apply and all that. My husband didn't want me to do it, though. We nearly broke up over it, but I can be just as stubborn as he is when I have to be."

"It's good to be stubborn about some things," Helen agreed. "That's what I tried to teach my girls. Calling it motivation or commitment is, of course, a better-sounding personality trait to own up to," she added with a small smile.

"Well, if I can do it, anybody can," Lucy assured her. "I have this friend, Sara. She's a reporter, really smart. She read me this quote once that really stuck in my mind. It's from a writer named George Eliot. She said, 'It is never too late to be what you might have been.' "

Lucy saw the sudden change in Helen's expression and felt a sinking feeling of dismay.

"It's too late for me," Helen said in a flat voice. "My doctor won't admit it but he isn't very hopeful."

Lucy felt terrible. She was such an idiot sometimes. Charlie was right, she did talk too much. Why couldn't she ever quit when she was ahead?

"I'm sorry," she said.

"No, it's okay. I know you didn't mean anything by it. I am tired, though. Thanks again for the pizza."

Lucy nodded and took away the empty plate. "Good night. Have a good rest."

"Thank you, Lucy. Good night."

Lucy grabbed her belongings and headed for home. She felt sad and empty, as if her clumsy remark had undone her good deed. And she felt terrible for Helen Carter. She might die. Modern medicine with all its high-tech equipment and miraculous treatments couldn't save everyone. It was still up to God.

*And would always be,* Lucy reflected. Of course, she knew she would encounter some very sick people once she started nursing. She would see people dying and know there was nothing she could do, nothing anybody could do. But being in the midst of it was different than she had ever imagined. She didn't think she could ever get used to it.

She sat in her dark, cold car, not turning the motor on. She closed her eyes and whispered in the darkness.

*"Dear God, please help Helen Carter. If you can't save her life, please make the rest of her days filled with the love of those she loves most and bring her . . . peace."*

# CHAPTER SIX

*Newburyport, Present-day*

"WHAT DO YOU THINK?" EMILY ASKED, AS SOON AS the maitre d' had seated everyone. "Nice, right?"

Sara and Luke nodded but neither got a chance to answer.

Jane started fussing in her high chair, and both Emily and Dan turned to her. Ever since Jane had begun walking a few weeks ago, it was hard for her to sit still. Emily waved a stuffed dog with a music box inside it, Jane's favorite toy of the moment. It looked as though they were going to hear a lot of "You Are My Sunshine" tonight. Sara didn't mind. She thought her little step-sister was totally adorable. Sara had never thought much about having children of her own. That always seemed a long way off. But Jane coming into the family had given her some ideas in that direction lately.

While Emily waved the music box dog, Dan dug through a big tote bag. He pulled out a plastic container of crackers. "Look what Daddy has for you. Snack box, Janie."

Sara and Luke shared a secret smile. The baby distractions were not only expected but welcome tonight. They gave her a few minutes to compose herself. Luke didn't seem nervous, she noticed. He took her hand and gave it a squeeze.

"It's a very pretty place, Emily," Luke said. "I can see why you think it would be nice for a wedding."

"Yes, lovely," Sara agreed.

The restaurant had once been an old house and retained a warm, welcoming atmosphere while also being quite elegant, with crisp white linens, flickering candlelight, gilt-edged mirrors, and overflowing flower arrangements everywhere you turned. It was decorated for Christmas, with pine wreaths strung around archways and across the big hearth. Tiny white lights sparkled in the dark branches.

Emily waved Jane's toy with one hand, while turning to face Sara and Luke. "In the warm weather they open those back doors. Perfect for a cocktail hour, right?"

"Perfect." Sara glanced at Luke. He slid his chair closer and put his arm around her shoulder.

"But it's just a little too late, Emily. Sorry." Luke smiled, not looking sorry in the least.

Dan and Emily stared across the table, looking confused.

"You've already found a place you like?" Dan asked.

Sara shook her head. "No, but—"

"We don't have to worry about all that anymore," Luke offered cheerfully. "We finally figured it out."

"We're married," Sara announced. She paused and let the news sink in. "We were married on Saturday, up in Maine."

"Married?" Emily stared at Sara in total shock. "You can't be married."

"Yes, we can," Luke corrected her. "We are."

Emily dropped the stuffed dog and didn't even notice. Sara could tell she was speechless, a highly unusual state for Emily.

Dan sat back and chuckled, shaking his head. "You guys

eloped. I should have guessed." He looked at Luke and laughed even louder. "I knew something was up."

"Well, I didn't. I had no idea." Emily looked hurt and Sara felt a sudden pang.

"I'm sorry, Emily. I know you really wanted us to have a big wedding—"

"Not a big wedding. That's not the point. I wanted to be there. I wanted to see you get married, Sara." Sara could tell her mother was trying hard not to cry. Sara felt even worse.

"Oh, come on now, Emily. They're just kids. They didn't want all the fuss and bother, right?" Dan turned to Luke, his expression coaxing him to pick up the ball.

"That was it. That was exactly what happened. This whole wedding scene just started to make us crazy. We couldn't handle it. We just wanted to get to the married part. Right, Sara?"

"It seemed so hard to decide what to do, and where to even have the wedding," Sara confessed. "My folks down in Maryland expected us to have it down there, and everyone here wanted us to get married in Cape Light. I didn't know what do."

Emily's expression softened. She had tried hard to avoid conflict with Sara's adoptive parents and to avoid making Sara choose between them. "Have you told your folks in Maryland yet?"

"Yes, I did." Sara met Emily's glance, hoping this wouldn't upset her again. "We spoke to them Sunday night."

"If it's any consolation, they were pretty blown away by it, too," Luke added.

"My mother also had some nice restaurants picked out for the reception," Sara explained. "Luke and I might go down there soon for a family party."

Dan nodded, and Sara could tell he understood. "That sounds like an excellent idea."

"Yes, my parents are looking forward to it."

Her parents never said so outright, but she knew they felt Sara's ties in Cape Light had taken her away from them. At first, they were patient, accepting Sara's need to meet and get to know her birth mother. But they always expected she would "get it out of her system" and return to Maryland. Now that she had married Luke, her parents could see that would never happen. So for them, her elopement had been a double blow.

Still, they were the only parents she had ever known. They had raised her in a caring, loving home and Sara loved them dearly. Most of the time she thought of finding Emily and the Warwicks as an amazing blessing. How many people are part of two wonderful families? Other times, though, it felt like an emotional minefield she needed to navigate. She was starting to learn that, try as she might, she could rarely please everyone.

Emily finally smiled. "All moms think alike, I guess. But I understand. Really, I do."

Emily had eloped with Sara's father, Sara knew. She certainly did understand these things.

Dan smiled affectionately at his wife and covered her hand with his own. "You have to forgive Emily, Sara. She had her heart set on planning your wedding. She won't admit it, but the bridal books and magazines have finally outnumbered all the baby-care literature around our house, and that's saying something."

"Dan!" Emily gave him an indignant look, then reluctantly smiled. "I suppose it's true."

She leaned over and hugged Sara tight. "Good luck, sweetheart. I know you'll be very, very happy together."

Sara hugged her back—Emily's good wishes meant a lot to her—and both women were misty-eyed when Jane let out a happy shriek and clapped her hands.

Dan beamed. "She's so bright. She understands everything."

Emily rolled her eyes. "At least I have one more chance when she grows up."

Sara laughed. "It's not as if we don't want to celebrate at all. We were thinking of a small party up here, too."

"Really?" Emily's expression brightened. "I think that's a great idea. So many people will want to congratulate you. Of course, your folks in Maryland will be invited and any other close relatives or friends there you think should come."

"The operative word here is *small*, Emily," Dan reminded her. "Nothing in a baseball stadium or on the village green," he added, recalling their own wedding nearly two years earlier.

"The village green was your idea, dear," Emily reminded him.

"Uh . . . no, dear. I'm sure it was yours," he corrected her. "Only you would decide to invite the entire town."

Sara laughed. "I think you both wanted it. And it was perfect for you. But we really do want something much more intimate and simple."

"Low-key," Luke added in a firm tone.

"Whatever you want. It's your party," Emily said. "The last thing I want to be is a meddling mother-in-law."

Dan rolled his eyes. "Though she might have a few suggestions from time to time."

Sara would never call Emily meddling, but she did have a knack for getting people to do things her way. Which was probably why she was such a successful mayor.

"We have time to talk about a party. It will all come together." Sara picked up her menu, hoping to change the topic of conversation. "What's good here?"

"Everything." Emily opened her menu and quickly put it down again. "Where are you going to live? Are you looking for a new place?"

"We're not totally clear on that yet," Sara admitted. "Luke's cabin is too small for all of our stuff together. And my place is bursting at the seams with just my junk in it."

"We're shuffling between the two right now," Luke explained.

"We'll work it out," Sara added. "Besides, we're going to be at Lillian's house for a while."

"Oh, I don't think you should be staying there now," Emily said at once. "That's not fair to either one of you."

"It's okay," Sara said. "I promised I would do it. It will be fine. Luke can stay with me. We are married, after all."

Luke shrugged. "Hey, why go to Hawaii when you can honeymoon right here in town in a spooky, drafty old mansion . . . with a cranky old lady waving her cane at you every five minutes?"

Dan grinned. "You're a good sport, Luke. If you guys can stay married under those circumstances, you're set for life."

Jane was fussing and Emily pulled her up out of the high chair to sit in her lap. Jane was dressed in a really cute outfit tonight, Sara noticed. A hooded white sweater trimmed with fur and a red plaid skirt. With her white tights and shiny little black boots, she looked as if she were headed for a skating party.

"I don't know, Dan," Emily said doubtfully. "I don't think it's a good idea. Starting out their marriage staying with Mother? She can make anyone miserable."

"It's a big place," Luke pointed out. "She might not even know I'm there."

Dan gave him a look. "You don't know her very well if you think that's possible. Lillian's like a bloodhound. She can smell an intruder from a mile off."

Emily laughed but stopped bouncing Jane. "Dan, stop. That's not nice to say."

"Okay, maybe that's a slight exaggeration," Dan admitted. "But only a slight one."

"Don't worry," Sara said. "I'll smooth it over with Lillian. I don't think she'll argue much once she knows we're married. And it won't be for very long—just until you find help for the nights, right?"

Emily nodded. "Yes, that's the plan. It isn't going to be easy taking care of her at home. I'm almost sorry now we let her have her way."

"Your mother was very lucky. It could have been much

worse," Dan said. "How did she ever get up those attic stairs in the first place? That's what I want to know."

"*Why* is more like it. She was looking for a box of old photos. I think I told you, I found photographs scattered all over the stairs, and she was holding on to one when she fell."

"Yes, I found the pictures and some letters on the stairway when I went over there to get the house ready." Emily stroked Jane's downy reddish gold hair. "There were several pictures of my father, some I've never seen before."

"Maybe it was Lillian's secret cache." Luke leaned forward. "She might have had them hidden in a secret spot up there."

"Thank you, Sherlock Holmes." Sara gave him a mock-glare.

"Well, I *was* a detective, you know."

"I think Luke's right," Emily said. "Whatever Mother was searching for must be important to her."

"I'm curious about what's in there myself," Sara admitted. "There must be something interesting in that box if Lillian risked life and limb to find it."

"Just be careful, Sara," Dan warned. "You might end up discovering more than you expected."

Sara laughed at him. "Do you really think Lillian has any dark secrets we don't know about?"

Dan smiled at his stepdaughter. "Sara, I'm surprised at you. Don't you know by now that everybody does?"


*Newburyport, August 1955*

IT WAS CHARLOTTE AND HER ROMANTIC NOTIONS. Lillian knew she would never have been sitting in Oliver's little car this morning otherwise.

*Either Charlotte or God's plan,* a little voice in her head countered. But was Oliver her fate or a test of her willpower? Lillian shook her head, trying to shake loose the ridiculous notion.

"Something the matter?" Oliver asked her.

"No, not at all. I'm fine."

Oliver threw the car into gear, and they pulled away from the church with a roar.

"That hat is very smart," Oliver said as they stopped at a light in the village. "But maybe you should take it off. It might blow away."

"Oh. Yes, that's probably true." Lillian pulled out the large pin holding her hat in place. She lifted it off, taking care with the scrap of netting that draped over her eyes.

Oliver smiled at her. "That's better. Now I can see your eyes. The eyes are the windows of the soul, you know."

"Don't expect to see into my soul so easily, Oliver. That's a privilege not lightly given."

"Which makes the prize even more appealing."

Lillian didn't answer. She turned and looked straight ahead as the light turned green and the car picked up speed again. She noticed people on the street turning to look at them. *Everyone in town must recognize this car and its driver,* she thought. They were about as inconspicuous in the shiny red car as they would be driving around in a fire engine.

"What type of car is this?" she asked over the motor's loud roar.

"A Jaguar. I bought it in England. Would you like to take a turn driving?"

Lillian shook her head. "No, thank you!"

She hadn't done her hair with such a ride in mind. With her hat removed, her upswept hairdo quickly came loose from its pins, and her long brown hair blew in every direction. She gathered it up with her hand and held it to one side.

"You have beautiful hair," Oliver told her. "You ought to wear it loose like that all the time."

"I don't like it loose. It bothers me."

He looked out at the road. "It bothers me, too," he added with a small smile.

Lillian twisted her hair into a bun and held it with her

hand as she stared out the window. They weren't going back to Charlotte's house. This wasn't the route she was familiar with.

"Where are we going?"

"Down to the harbor. I would like to take you out for lunch."

"Oh . . ." Lillian didn't know what to say. She was getting tired of arguing with him. That was saying a lot, she realized, considering how much she had always enjoyed verbal sparring. But Oliver Warwick had worn her down. Or was starting to.

That notion scared her.

Still, she told herself that lunch couldn't hurt. Besides, she was more or less trapped. She had gotten into his car, and now she had to go wherever he wanted.

"Never agree to ride with a strange man in his car," her mother had warned her. Well, there was reason for that. Even though Oliver wasn't really a stranger anymore, he was still a man, dead set on having his way.

Oliver parked his car at the far end of the harbor. He helped Lillian out of the car and then took her hand, leading her out onto the dock.

She didn't see a restaurant or even an open-air snack bar, only a long dock with shorter docks extending every ten feet or so and boats tied up on either side. The docks were crowded today with people working on their boats, hosing them down or doing repairs. A few waved to Oliver as they walked by.

"Where is this restaurant—out here?"

"Who said I was taking you to a restaurant? I said I wanted to take you to lunch."

"So, you tricked me somehow. Is that it?" she asked sharply.

"I don't know, did I?" Oliver glanced at her innocently. "Here we are," he said, "my pride and joy."

They stood beside a long, sleek sailboat. The hull was a light-colored, highly varnished wood, with black and red trim and a pure white deck. It was a large boat with several sails and a tall mast. The sails were partly raised and they rippled and snapped in the breeze. The deck was wide and covered by a white canopy. The shade underneath looked inviting, Lillian thought.

"So, what do you think?" he asked her.

"It's a beautiful boat. . . . Are you taking me for a sail?"

"That was my intention."

Lillian hesitated. They had been isolated enough driving around in the car, but now she would be out on the water alone with him. Anything could happen.

"Do you sail this all by yourself?" she asked.

"It's just me, captain and crew rolled into one."

"Is that safe?"

He laughed. "Usually." Then, seeing her hesitate, he added, "The water is very calm today and we won't go far. Just a short sail across the harbor. It will be much cooler out there, you'll see."

Lillian met his gaze and sighed. He really was so persuasive. He had a way of getting around her, that was for sure. She would have to be very careful.

"All right. Just a short sail, though."

He walked around the boat, loosened the lines, then holding one taut, he jumped aboard the boat and extended his hand to Lillian. "Jump down, I've got you."

Lillian pulled off her heels and tucked them under her arm. She jumped down and Oliver caught her quickly around the waist. He hugged her close for a moment. Longer than was necessary, she thought. She pushed him away and took a seat on a canvas deck chair under the awning.

"Why don't you leave your heels off? You'll be more comfortable and less likely to stumble if we hit any waves."

She didn't answer but didn't put the shoes back on. Her hair was undone, her shoes were off . . . she was in shambles. And they hadn't even left the dock yet.

What would anyone think if they saw her?

Oliver used the boat's motor in order to steer out of the tight dock and crowded harbor. They were soon out on the open water. He shut down the motor and raised the sails.

"Do you know anything about sailing, Lillian?" he shouted back to her.

"Not a thing. I've never liked boats much."

She knew he had gone to some trouble to get her out here, but she didn't see any reason to spare his feelings.

She had been boating many times. It was hard to avoid it when her family spent summer vacations up here. But she had always hated motor boats, with all the noise and the smell of gasoline making her feel seasick. Sailing was somewhat better, but she was no great fan.

"You were right about the breeze," she conceded. "It's much cooler out here . . . and quiet."

Oliver stood at the steering wheel in front of her. "I thought you would appreciate the solitude."

Was he getting to know her likes and dislikes already? Lillian brushed the thought aside. He didn't know the first thing about her.

The sleek craft cut through the blue water, gently rising and falling with the waves. Lillian leaned back and closed her eyes. She finally let go of her hair and it blew behind her like a banner.

It was very quiet, only the sounds of the water flowing past, the creak of the ropes and wood, and the wind in the sails. The canopy above protected her from the harshest light, but the sunshine still felt warm on her skin.

*Sailing can be pleasant,* she thought. *This is very relaxing . . .*

Lillian never even realized she had fallen asleep in her chair. She simply opened her eyes to find Oliver standing over her, holding out a glass of iced tea.

"I'm sorry." She felt flustered. "I didn't mean to fall asleep. It must be the sun."

She straightened up and took the drink he offered, sipping it quickly. How stupid to fall asleep like that. She imagined him watching her while she slept and it made her feel uncomfortable, as if he had been spying on her.

"It's the perfect afternoon for a nap. I'm glad you felt so relaxed." Oliver sat down next to her. She set her glass on a small table and then quickly gathered up her windblown hair. She pulled some pins from her pocket and stuck them into a knot at the back of her head.

Oliver smiled at her, and Lillian gave him a look. "I realize this isn't your preferred hairstyle, but it isn't your hair, either."

He laughed. "I didn't say a word."

"You didn't have to. I know what you were thinking."

He shook his head, looking suddenly serious. "Not at all. You don't have any idea what I'm thinking about you, Lily."

Lillian picked up her glass and took another sip of tea. She looked out at the water then turned to face him again.

"You didn't tell me that you've been married. And divorced."

Oliver looked shocked by her question, but only for a moment. "Does that matter to you?"

"Not at all. I just thought it was odd, since you told me so many other things about yourself yesterday. I wondered why you left that chapter out."

He shrugged. "It was a long time ago. I was very young, only eighteen and about to be shipped out to France. She was my high school sweetheart. So we got married. It seemed like a good idea at the time."

"How long did the marriage last?"

"About three years. Though we actually only spent about three months together. When I got out of the army and came home, she told me she had met someone else. She was young and pretty and she had been lonely." He shrugged. "It happened that way for a lot of guys I knew back then."

"You don't sound very upset about it."

"I was at the time. But as I said, that was a long time

ago, over ten years. I look back now and see that it was all for the best. A man should be at least thirty before he settles down and chooses a wife."

"Perhaps," Lillian agreed.

"I didn't mean to mislead you. I was afraid you wouldn't want to see me because of that. I was right, wasn't I?"

"I didn't want to see you again anyway," Lillian reminded him. "So it really wouldn't have made much difference."

"I think you do want to get to know me better. But something holds you back."

His observation hit a nerve, but Lillian did her best to ignore it. "That's just wishful thinking on your part. I'm not sure why you're so intent on starting a relationship with me, Oliver. Probably because I'm not in awe of you, like all the other young women around here."

"I like a challenge. And you certainly present one—on the surface anyway." He turned to her and smiled, then took her hand. "Besides, we already have a relationship, Lily. You just won't admit it."

Lillian sighed and stood up. She walked over to the railing and looked out at the water and the village of Newburyport now some distance away. "I wish you wouldn't talk like that. If you continue to, I'll have to go."

Oliver laughed at her. "Jump in. It's a great day for a swim, though I hear there are sometimes sharks in this water. Careful they don't have you for lunch."

She turned her head quickly and glared at him. "Speaking of lunch, where is this place you're taking me to? Or was that just a trick to get me out here?"

Oliver walked to the other side of the boat and trimmed a line. Then he stepped over to the steering wheel again. "We're almost there. The dock is coming into view. See, over there."

Oliver pointed ahead to a sharp hillside where thick woods met the shoreline. All Lillian could see through the trees was a very large stone house with several chimneys atop a black slate roof. A few outer buildings were tucked into the green hillside, and a dock extended out at the shore, a small boathouse just beyond it.

"You'd better sit down again. I'm going to drop the sails and motor in."

Lillian returned to her chair. She still had no idea where they were going to end up, but Oliver was too busy for further explanations.

She took a moment to repair her appearance, smoothing out her hair again and adding a dash of lipstick. She put her suit jacket on, fastened the buttons, then put on her hat and shoes.

The boat pulled up alongside the dock, and a man ran down to meet them. Oliver tossed him a line and the man pulled them in closer. While the man secured the boat to the dock, Oliver jumped out and then helped Lillian up.

"Vincent is waiting with the car, sir. Will you be going out again, or shall I close up the boat for you?" The man, who looked old enough to be Oliver's father, spoke with an Irish accent.

"No, we won't be going out again. Thank you, Patrick."

Oliver took Lillian's arm as they walked up the dock. She still didn't know where they were, and she was getting worried.

As they left the dock Lillian could see that a wooden path led over a short sandy stretch of beach to a narrow paved road. The road was flanked by dense, shady woods and seemed to lead up the steep hill. A shiny black sedan was parked at the end of the road, and a man in a chauffeur's uniform stood by the car.

Lillian stopped and looked up at Oliver. "Where are we?"

He paused, as if deciding what to say. "Lilac Hall, our family home. My parents are expecting us for lunch."

"You brought me home . . . to meet your parents?" His audacity was astounding. He might even be a little unstable, maybe some trauma, from the war. "I've only known you for two days, Oliver. Do you take many women home to meet your parents?"

"Only once before. My first wife. But we've already talked about her."

"I *can't* meet your parents. What will they think?"

He laughed. "They'll think I've finally met a polished, sophisticated, intelligent young lady."

"Come on, Oliver. Be serious." Lillian was thoroughly frustrated with him. She had no intention of getting in that car and having lunch with the Warwicks. "I can't meet your family. It wouldn't be right. Take me back to Newburyport. Right away please."

"If that's what you really want." His expression was innocent but unrepentant. "But we are here. And we are hungry. And they are expecting us—"

"Which is none of my doing," Lillian pointed out.

"What should I say? What excuses should I make?"

Lillian hated lies, even tiny, social ones. "Oh, I don't know. Say I'm seasick from the sailing."

"They'll wonder why I didn't bring you inside to rest."

Lillian sighed with exasperation. He wasn't giving up on this, was he?

"I'm sorry, Lillian. But it's rude to cancel at the last minute. They're going to be very disappointed."

Now on top of everything else, he had her feeling guilty and ill-mannered. She stared at him, not knowing whether to scream or laugh. She had never met such an outrageous man in her life.

Lillian took out her gloves and tugged them on. "All right, I'll go. But this is it, Oliver. I mean it."

"Thank you, Lily." He forced a serious face, as if he was trying hard not to laugh at her. "Honestly, you're going to enjoy this more than you think."

# CHAPTER SEVEN

### *Cape Light, Present-day*

"CHARLIE, PLEASE. JUST STAY WITH HIM FOR A FEW hours. I'll be back by lunchtime, I promise."

"You knew he was going to miss school today. Why didn't you find a sitter?"

"I tried. It's hard to find someone to come in the middle of the day."

Not that Lucy even knew that many sitters. The hours at the diner made it hard, if not impossible, for her and Charlie to go out in the evenings much.

"I need to go to the hospital for a meeting. I'll come right back." Lucy kept her voice low. Jamie was in the family room, lying on the couch and watching cartoons. She didn't want him to hear her and Charlie arguing over who was going to stay home with him today.

When Charlie didn't answer, she added, "It's the first week. I can't miss sessions this early in my training."

Charlie shook his head and pushed his plate aside.

"Sorry, Lucy. I have deliveries coming in, a guy coming to fix the freezer, and bills to pay. There's no way I can stay home this morning. I told you that last night."

He had told her. But that was before she called all over town for help and came up empty-handed. She had thought she might persuade him this morning by compromising and only going in for part of the day.

Now she would miss a meeting of the student nurses on her floor with Margaret Sherman. She dreaded the idea of calling to say she would be absent. Sherman didn't like her much as it was. This was going to be one more mark against her and give the impression she wasn't serious and responsible.

Charlie took a last sip of coffee, set the mug down in the sink, and kissed Lucy on the cheek. She stood stiffly and didn't kiss him back. With his head ducked down as he pulled on his jacket, he left the house.

She heard the front door close and felt stuck, abandoned. But there was nothing she could do. She picked up a few of the breakfast dishes and dumped them in the sink, then poured herself more coffee.

Even if she made more calls and did find someone, by the time a sitter got to her house and she got up to the hospital, the meeting would be over. Half of her day would be over. It wouldn't make any sense.

She picked up the phone and dialed the hospital. When an operator came on, she asked for Margaret's line.

"Margaret Sherman." Her greeting was crisp, and nononsense.

"Margaret? It's Lucy Bates." Lucy felt her mouth going dry. She was losing her nerve. She forced her words out in a rush. "I'm sorry but I can't make it to the hospital today. My son is home sick from school, and there's no one to stay with him."

Margaret didn't answer for a long moment. Her silence made Lucy even more nervous.

"Nothing serious, I hope?"

"Just a cold and a sore throat. But he has a temperature and I needed to keep him home."

"Yes, of course. They can't go to school with a fever." Lucy heard some papers rustling. "Let's see . . . you'll miss this morning's meeting. I'll have to see you privately to review that information."

"Yes. Thank you."

"We only permit three absences from training. This is only the first week and you're already using one up."

"Yes, I know. But it couldn't be helped. My husband has a business and he had to go in today. He—"

"When you have a real nursing job, situations like this are going to come up. You're going to need to be better prepared. People will be counting on you. Did you ever hear that Woody Allen saying 'Ninety-five percent of the secret to success is just showing up'?"

Lucy sighed. "No, Margaret, I don't think I ever did."

The way she was talking to her was so unfair, Lucy thought. *As if I'm the irresponsible type, a regular slacker. She has no idea how hard I work and what I can really do.*

"This won't happen again. I'll make sure of it."

"Let's hope not," Margaret said. "I'll expect you on time tomorrow."

Lucy hung up, feeling deflated and depressed. There were a million jobs around the house she had to catch up on. The kitchen looked like a tornado had struck, and the laundry was piled to the ceiling, and she didn't feel like tackling any of it.

Jamie wandered in and walked over to her. She felt his forehead with her hand, pushing back a short fringe of brown hair. "How do you feel, honey?"

He shrugged. "I'm bored. Can you play a game with me?"

"Sure." She nodded then glanced at the clock.

Three minutes past nine. It was going to be a very long day.

"I DON'T UNDERSTAND WHY I CAN'T BE IN MY OWN room. If you can roll me in here like a sack of potatoes—"

"Mother, we can't carry you up the stairs safely. Even if we could, what if you needed to get back down again? What if there was a fire?" Emily struggled for a patient tone, but she felt like a prerecorded announcement. She had already gone through this with her mother a dozen times.

"Who cares if there's a fire? Let the place burn to ashes." Lillian gazed around the newly converted sewing room with a look of profound distaste. "I'm not comfortable down here, though I don't suppose that matters to any of you."

Jessica walked into the room with a vase of flowers. "Look, Mother, these just came for you. I don't know who sent them. There's a card though."

Jessica handed down the card and Lillian opened it. She picked up her reading glasses, which were hanging from a chain around her neck. "Ezra. Who else?" She looked over the bouquet with a critical eye. "At least he told them to leave out the carnations. He knows they remind me of those cheap arrangements in funeral homes."

"Ezra called again this morning and asked if he could visit you," Emily said.

"When I'm up to it. I don't think I want any visitors yet." Lillian shifted in her wheelchair, reaching to place the card on a nearby table. Emily could tell from her expression that she was still in a lot of pain.

She also suspected that her mother didn't want Ezra to see her until the angry bruise around her eye had healed. Which could take some time. It hadn't looked nearly as bad right after the fall, but now that a few days had passed, Lillian looked as if she had been in a fistfight and emerged with a classic shiner. Emily knew how vain her mother was. It probably bothered her to no end, though she would never admit it.

"Where's what's-her-name?"

"Jeanette, Mother. The nurse's name is Jeanette. She's making your lunch."

Lillian frowned. "Do I have to eat in this room?"

"Of course not. I'll wheel you out to the dining room," Jessica offered. She got behind the chair and released the brakes. "You've hardly seen the kids. Sam has the little ones in the living room. Darrell's at school but he made you a card."

"I'll look at it later, thank you." Lillian sighed heavily as Jessica rolled her into the dining room.

Emily pulled aside the heavy armchair at the head of the table, and Jessica steered Lillian into the spot.

Dan walked in, carrying Jane. Sam followed, bent over as he led two-year-old Tyler by the hand.

"Look at these men, toting around babies." Lillian shook her head. "Were you exchanging tips about diaper rash in there?"

"As a matter of fact, we did have a good conversation about teething." Dan turned to Jane and bounced her in his arms.

"I know it's the modern thing, but I find this New Age fatherhood awfully unnatural."

"How are you, Lillian? Holding up all right?" Sam asked, knowing better than to take her bait.

"Not bad for an old lady with half her body covered in plaster. They should have done the other half and made a garden statue out of me."

Sam glanced at Jessica. He couldn't win.

Lillian's new day nurse, Jeanette Kramer, carried Lillian's lunch in on a tray. She set it down on the table. "There's some soup and a sandwich for you. When you're done, I'll bring in dessert."

Lillian peered at her soup. "What kind of soup is this?"

"Chicken noodle," Jeanette said cheerfully.

"Oh, I never eat that. Take it away." Lillian pushed the bowl aside.

Emily noticed the nurse's surprised expression and felt sorry for her. Well, she needed to get to know her patient and decide if she would stick it out or not.

"But I found it in your cabinet," Jeanette said. "There were several cans. I assumed you liked it."

"There were several cans there because I *don't* like it. Now please, get this vile stuff out of my sight."

Jeanette picked up the bowl of soup. "Would you like some other kind of soup, Mrs. Warwick? Of course, if you do like it, you probably don't have any in the cabinet. Is that how it works?" she asked innocently.

Emily had to hide a smile. Jeanette Kramer wasn't the pushover she appeared to be.

"No soup today, thank you," Lillian said in a tone of exaggerated politeness.

Jeanette disappeared back into the kitchen. Lillian picked up half of her sandwich with her good hand and took a small bite. She set the sandwich on the plate again and looked around at her family. "Are you all going to sit there and stare at me while I eat?"

"We're keeping you company, Mother," Jessica said.

"I feel like a creature in the zoo."

Sam had lifted Tyler up to Jessica, and the boy now sat on her lap. As she turned to take a cup of coffee from Emily, Tyler began to smack the table in a quick, energetic rhythm, making the silverware and glasses shake.

"Tyler, stop that." Jessica gently took his hands off the table.

Lillian sat back in her wheelchair, startled. "What in the world is he trying to do, knock down the house?"

Sam laughed. "I don't think he's big enough for that, Lillian. Give him a year or two."

"He's just playing, Mother."

"Babies have no business at the table. I've told you that

before. Bring him back when he can carry on a proper conversation."

"Here, I'll take him. Come on, Tyler." Sam scooped up the little boy and carried him into the living room.

"Don't let him touch a thing, do you hear me?" Lillian called after Sam.

"Sam knows how to watch him, Mother. Don't worry."

Lillian took another bite of her sandwich and tossed the rest back on her plate. "Dry as dust. I suppose she found the tuna in the cupboard and assumed it was my favorite."

Dan glanced at Emily and rolled his eyes. Emily steeled herself, knowing that the next topic of conversation was not going to be any easier. "Mother, Sara is coming tonight to stay with you, as we planned."

"I remember." Lillian patted her mouth with the napkin. "It will be something to look forward to after spending the day with . . ." Lillian slanted her head sharply toward the kitchen. "Where did you ever find *her*?"

"Jeanette was very highly recommended. I hope you won't make her miserable working here."

"What me? Make *her* miserable? I have no rights in my own home anymore. Like those babies. Don't mind me. Do as you please. Let those children run wild and break everything."

"Calm down, Mother, nobody has broken anything," Emily reminded her.

"Give them a minute or two, they just got in there," Lillian pointed out.

Jessica rose. "I'll go in with Sam and watch Tyler." She looked pointedly at Emily. "Call if you need me."

Lillian watched the look exchanged by her two daughters. "What's up?" She peered at Emily. "Did the doctor tell you something you haven't told me?"

Emily shook her head. "Nothing like that, Mother. You're perfectly fine. Except for the broken bones, I mean."

Emily glanced at Dan. Jane stood on his lap, pulling his hair. Dan sat stoically, like a big friendly bear, tolerating his daughter's abuse. No help there. She turned back to her mother.

"I have some news for you. Some news about Sara . . ." She took a breath, not daring to look at her mother while she spoke. "She and Luke are married now, and—"

"They're *what*? Did you say *married*?" Lillian pressed her hand over her heart. "How could that be? They *can't* be married. Don't tell me she threw herself away on him. When did this happen? Why wasn't I informed?"

"They eloped over the weekend," Dan explained. "Nobody knew about it. They just told us last night."

"I'm sure you're surprised, Mother," Emily said in what she hoped was a soothing tone. "We were, too."

"Surprised? I'm appalled. How could you let this happen, Emily? Right under your nose. You had plenty of time to talk her out of that engagement. How could you have let her marry that ragged, lost soul? Some ex-policeman turned do-gooder. What kind of life will she have with him? No life at all, that's what I say. She could have done much better than Luke what's-his-name!"

"McAllister," Emily reminded her. "Mother, I have no problem with Sara's decision. I like Luke. I respect him and the work he's done. Some people would say it took tremendous courage and dedication to leave the police force and start up New Horizons in this town."

"Oh, poppycock! Some people don't have to stand back and see their granddaughter married to him."

Emily was momentarily taken aback. It was the first time she had ever heard Lillian acknowledge Sara as her granddaughter, but she didn't want to make a big thing out of it and excite Lillian even more.

"Mother, please try to calm down. Luke has a good head on his shoulders and a good future."

"Besides all that, they love each other." Dan had Jane sitting on his lap again, playing with a cloth napkin.

"Love! What do they know about love? They've been swept away by hormones. Believe me, I know."

Emily glanced at Dan, hiding her laughter. She couldn't imagine her mother swept away by anything, even a hurricane.

"I see you laughing, Emily. Well, I was young once, too." Lillian let out a long, exasperated sigh. "I need to go back to my room now. This has all been too much for me."

Dan put Jane down and rose to help Lillian. He turned the wheelchair and steered Lillian back to her room. Emily followed, holding Jane by the hand as she toddled down the hallway.

Jeanette came out of the kitchen and followed the parade. When they arrived in Lillian's room, Jeanette dropped the side of the wheelchair and maneuvered Lillian onto her bed. She took off her shoes and covered her with a blanket. Lillian waved her good hand at them and closed her eyes, clearly a signal that she wished they would all go away.

Emily realized that the situation with Sara hadn't been resolved. Would Lillian allow Luke to come tonight with Sara? She hadn't gotten a clear answer and realized she wasn't going to get one. She would tell Sara that Lillian knew about the marriage—and Sara could come tonight with Luke at her own risk.

### Newburyport, August 1955

THE WARWICKS WERE OVERWHELMING. EVERYONE SPOKE quickly and out of turn. Lillian could barely keep up. Oliver seemed quiet and sedate in comparison. Which was saying a lot.

Lillian's family was well off; her parents employed a housekeeper, a cook, and a maid. But the Warwick family employed a large staff of servants. The meal was served by two housemaids and a butler in a large dining room with a long banquet table. French doors on the far end opened to a beautiful view of the gardens behind the house and farther on, the sloping property and water.

Lillian had grown up in a fine home on Boston's Beacon Hill, but Lilac Hall was in another class altogether. It was like a castle out of a picture book—or like one of the great houses she had once visited in England's Lake District.

It was hard to imagine Oliver growing up amidst all this luxury. On one hand, he seemed the cliché of a spoiled, wealthy bachelor but on the other, he often seemed so natural and unpretentious that she could almost mistake him for a "regular guy."

"So, you have family in Newburyport, Lillian?" Oliver's mother, Alice, smiled across the table. Petite, with a youthful face and figure, she wasn't what Lillian had expected. She looked nothing like Oliver, except for her dimples. She dressed well, Lillian thought, save for some pieces of jewelry—several large rings and a diamond and emerald pin—that Lillian found ostentatious.

"My father's brother and his family live in Newburyport. On Camden Street."

"Camden Street? Oh, yes, nice neighborhood." Oliver's father, Harrison Warwick, looked like an older, stockier version of Oliver, though bald on top and without the dimples.

"I met a fellow named Merchant once, down in Pittsburgh. Dealt in scrap metals. I was doing some business there during the war. No relation to you, I suppose?"

*Pittsburgh? Scrap metals? Not very likely.*

"Not that I know of," Lillian said quietly. "My uncle is a banker. My father is, too," she added.

"Banking. There's a racket for you. Don't tell me about bankers—"

"Harry, please," Alice Warwick said. "Lillian doesn't want to talk about the business world, do you, dear?" Alice nodded at her before she could answer. "Tell us about yourself, Lillian. Oliver said you work in a museum?"

"At the Museum of Fine Arts. I work with Egyptian art. I help plan exhibits and evaluate private collections, or I might be asked to study a piece and write about it."

"How exciting," Alice practically trilled.

It wasn't really exciting work, Lillian thought. It was often very tedious and exacting, but she didn't bother to correct Mrs. Warwick's impression.

"She might be too smart for you, Oliver," Harry said with a sly wink.

"I can keep up so far," Oliver replied with a smile.

Despite the warm weather, the Warwicks had served a large lunch: cold cucumber soup, baked cod, potatoes au gratin, and steamed asparagus. Lillian couldn't even eat half of it. The entire situation made her so nervous, she had lost her appetite.

"I love museums, I love the arts," Alice said brightly. "We support the arts, don't we, Harry?"

Oliver's father nodded, like an obedient, old dog. "Yes, we do. Every chance Alice gets. I have the canceled checks to prove it."

"Oh, Harry. Don't mind him." Alice turned to Lillian again. "He's really very cultured. He doesn't like to show it though."

*He does an excellent job of hiding it,* Lillian thought.

"Someday I would love to sponsor a festival of the arts for our town. Right here, at Lilac Hall," Alice spoke excitedly, gesturing with her jewel-covered hands. "We could have dance and theater . . . and an exhibit of paintings, of course. Wouldn't that be lovely?"

"Yes, it would be. It's a beautiful setting." Lillian wondered if Alice Warwick was sincere or just a wealthy woman caught up in a momentary enthusiasm.

*Or perhaps she's trying to impress me,* Lillian thought. Though she couldn't imagine why that should be. If anything, it should be the other way around. Alice doted on Oliver. She probably thought that no woman was good enough for him.

The servants started clearing the plates.

"Just a moment," Alice said to the maid who was removing the platter of potatoes from the sideboard. "Ollie, would you like some more potatoes, dear? I had the cook prepare them your favorite way."

"No, thank you, Mother. I've had more than enough."

"Oh, all right. You can clear everything, Mary." Turning to Lillian, she added, "I have to keep after Oliver to eat right. He doesn't take care of himself. He needs a good wife to watch over him."

*A good wife? Good heavens, does she mean me?*

"When he came home from the army, he was skin and bones. It frightened me to death."

Oliver laughed. "Mother, that was ten years ago. I've put on a few pounds since."

"Yes, you've filled out nicely," she agreed. "That was a hard time for us. At least one of my boys came home—" Her eyes suddenly became glassy with unshed tears, and she covered her mouth with her hand.

Harry pulled a snow-white hanky from his pocket and handed it to his wife. He reached over to pat her hand. "We know you miss him, dear. We all miss him. That's the sacrifice we have to bear."

Oliver turned to Lillian. "My older brother, Harry, Jr. He was in the army, too. He died in Italy." He looked down a moment. "I didn't tell you that about Harry. I'm sorry . . . it's hard for me to talk about."

Lillian felt a shock of sadness. Oliver had told her his older brother had once pulled him out of the surf. But had never mentioned he'd died in the war. She saw him suddenly with his defenses down, and her heart went out to him and his family.

The maids served coffee from a silver service and small blueberry tarts on china dessert plates.

Alice composed herself. "These are fresh blueberries, gathered right here on the property. We have loads of blueberry bushes in the meadow. Oliver—and Harry—used to pick bucketfuls when they were little boys. They would come home with their hands and lips all stained purple, remember dear?"

"I remember, Mother. My manners have improved somewhat since," he assured Lillian. "I rarely graze out in the meadow anymore. Only when I'm very hungry."

Lillian had to laugh. "I hope not."

She took a bit of the pastry. The berries were tart and sweet at the same time. She could easily picture a young Oliver roaming this huge estate in summertime, barefoot and daring.

Finally the meal came to an end, and Alice encouraged Oliver to take Lillian for a walk around the property. Oliver led her out through French doors that opened to a brick patio, shaded by a large vine-covered arbor.

A path led down to a rose garden, enclosed by high stone walls. Long rows of rose bushes in every variety and color were in full bloom, their scent perfuming the warm, humid air. A beautiful stone fountain stood in the center of the garden.

"My mother spends a lot of time out here. She's a good gardener. Loves roses, but dahlias are her real passion," Oliver confided. "She's very competitive at the local flower show. You can hardly speak to her the week before. Do you like gardening, Lillian?"

"I like flowers. We don't have much of a garden at home, though. I can't say I ever tried."

"My mother will teach you. She'll be happy to," he added.

Lillian fixed him with a skeptical look. She wasn't sure when these horticulture lessons were going to take place but thought it best to let the comment pass for now.

The rose garden was hot and sunny. Lillian was relieved to pass through the far gate and onto a wide gravel path, bordered by high shady trees on either side.

"What do you think of my family?" Oliver asked.

"They seem very nice." Lillian wasn't sure what to say. "I'm sorry about your brother," she said sincerely. "That's a huge loss."

"Yes, it is. I looked up to Harry. I thought he was . . .

indestructible. It's hard to believe I was the one who came back and he didn't. I've often wished it had turned out the other way around."

"That's a very selfless wish."

Oliver shrugged. "It would have been easier for everyone that way. Harry was my parents' favorite, the good son. I'm not saying they don't love me; sometimes I think they love me too much. It's just that I've always been more trouble for them. Harry never gave them a moment's worry. He was more like my father, though even more conservative. He was going to take over the family business."

"And now?" Lillian asked, curious.

"I never planned on staying here, but now I feel obliged to. Even though my father has qualms about my aptitude to run things. So do I, for that matter."

His honesty and winsome smile moved her someplace deep inside. He took her hand and she didn't resist. They continued walking down the alley of tall trees, leafy branches arching high overhead, like a thick green canopy.

Lillian understood things a little better now. Oliver felt pressured to please his parents, to fill the gap left by his older brother. Maybe he even felt pressured to settle down and get married again.

They turned a bend on the path, and Lillian spotted Lilac Hall through a gap in the trees. It was set on a hill overlooking a sweeping meadow, the woods beyond and the dark blue harbor beyond that. It would be hard to imagine a more beautiful setting. Or a more beautiful home.

"How old is the mansion?" she asked Oliver.

"My father built it after the first war. It's a copy of a great house in Europe. He imported all the stones from Belgium—even those gargoyles peering over the rooftop—had them brought over on a ship. He brought the stone masons, too. My mother was the one who decided it would be called Lilac Hall, though. She had about a hundred lilac bushes planted on the main drive . . . over there, see?"

He put his arm around her shoulder and pointed. Lillian nodded, though she didn't really see what he was talking about. She was too conscious of his touch and his sudden nearness to care about a hedge of lilacs.

"It's quite a sight when they bloom in the spring."

"I can imagine."

He finally stepped away and took her hand again, and they continued walking. Lillian felt her head clear, but not completely.

He turned to her. "What do you think of the house, Lily? Does it meet with your approval?"

"It's stunning. I've always wanted to see the inside," she confessed.

Lillian had often seen the mansion from a distance and had heard about the grandeur of the house and estate. It was an unexpected thrill to see it all firsthand.

"I'm glad you like it. I thought we would live here once we're married. We'll have our own wing, plenty of privacy." He gestured with his hand, pointing out the section of the house he was referring to.

Lillian was dumbstruck for a moment then felt annoyed at him. "You have to stop talking like that, Oliver. It's just . . . nonsense, that's all."

Oliver didn't debate with her. "My parents like you, I can tell they do. Especially my mother."

"Your mother seems like a lovely woman. But whether she likes me or not is fairly . . . irrelevant." Lillian turned to face him. "We've been having a nice time the last few days, but that's all there is, Oliver. I'm sorry. It's just . . . just a little affair. Can you think of it that way?"

Oliver laughed. "I would be happy to show you what a little affair is, Lillian, but you're not that type of girl. You're the kind a man marries. If he's lucky. I would marry you in an instant. I would marry you tomorrow," he insisted.

"You know that's not true," she told him, crossing her arms over her chest and gazing out at the rolling meadow and blue sea and sky above it. "Why even say it? Are you trying to shock me?"

"It is true. Maybe if I say it enough, you won't be shocked anymore."

Lillian didn't answer. It was hard to keep his words from affecting her. He sounded so sure, so confident, so sincere. She knew it was all an act to win her over. Still, it confused her. She had feelings for him, strong feelings, but so far, she had been able to keep them under control.

Oliver put his hands on her shoulders and turned her around to face him. "I love you, Lily. I know it seems fast, but that's the way it is sometimes. I knew it from the first time I saw you, the first time I heard your voice. I haven't been able to get you out of my head for one minute."

Lillian tried to pull away, but he held her firmly.

"Please, Oliver. Please stop saying these things to me."

"I won't stop, not until I tell you everything. I'm sure of what I feel for you. It's not a whim. I know you don't feel the same right now. But I think someday you will. I'll do everything in my power to make you fall in love with me. I'll wait as long as I have to." He stared down at her. "What do you think? Is there a chance for us?"

Lillian was overwhelmed. She didn't know what to say and even if an answer had come to mind, she didn't feel capable of uttering a coherent sentence.

Once or twice, men had professed feelings for her. But nothing this sudden or passionate. She searched Oliver's dark eyes for the slightest trace of insincerity and couldn't find any. And that's what scared her the most.

Oliver didn't wait for an answer. He pulled her closer and kissed her deeply. Her arms twined around his neck and she kissed him back. She wasn't sure how long they stood there, kissing and holding each other. Then Oliver led her off the path to a shady spot under a tree. They lay down on the soft grass together, and Oliver pulled her close again. Lillian closed her eyes and felt suddenly and totally lost. She knew she should tell him to stop—or just push him away and go. But she couldn't will herself to do it. She felt as if everything were happening to her in a dream, a beautiful dream that she didn't want to end.

A strange and unprecedented thought came to her. What if, just this once, she told him what was in her heart? Without worrying about consequences, or the future, or what anybody would think. *This will be my fling, like Charlotte said,* Lillian decided. *Every woman who's been jilted by a fiancé is entitled to at least one.*

Oliver lifted his head. He kissed her softly on the lips again, then the nose and then each of her closed eyelids. He stroked her hair with his fingers. It had come totally undone. Lillian had no idea where all her hairpins had gone and, for once, didn't care. She opened her eyes as he kissed her again, wanting to see every detail and memorize it for the rest of her life.

Oliver stared into her eyes a moment, his face very close. Then he sighed and sat up. He pulled out his silver case and lit a cigarette. "I had better take you back to Newburyport. It's getting late. I don't want your aunt and uncle to be worried about you."

"I'm sure Charlotte's made up some story," Lillian said. "But you're right. I should go."

She sat up slowly and pushed her hair to one side with her hand. She felt . . . different. She wasn't sure why. She never felt this way after George had kissed her, no matter how long and athletic their tussles.

Oliver had been a perfect gentleman. Well, not too perfect. But he had been very respectful. He had said she was the kind of girl a man marries, and that's how he had treated her.

Still, she felt different. More knowing somehow.

She glanced at Oliver. He really was so handsome. It took her breath away. She reached over and touched his shoulder, almost to make sure she wasn't just imagining all this.

He turned his head and smiled at her, then kissed her fingertips.

He stubbed out his cigarette in the grass, jumped up and tugged her hand. They followed the path to the front of the house. A shiny black sedan and a white convertible were parked in the circular drive. Oliver chose the black sedan. He opened the door for Lillian and helped her into the passenger side then got behind the wheel.

"I never got to say good-bye to your parents and thank them for lunch," Lillian said as they pulled away from the house.

"Don't worry. They're not stuck on formality. I'll thank them for you."

They didn't talk much on the drive back. Oliver put his arm around her shoulder and Lillian sat close to him. When they pulled up in front of Charlotte's house, Lillian felt nervous. It was nearly seven. The sun was starting to set. She had been gone all day. She couldn't imagine what Charlotte had told her parents and was afraid they were going to be angry with her, maybe even call her parents.

"I'll walk you to the door," Oliver said.

"No, don't." Lillian shook her head. "It's better if you just go."

Before he could argue, she leaned over and quickly kissed him on the cheek. "Good night, Oliver."

Without looking back at him, she ran up to the front door of Charlotte's house. The door was open and she let herself in. She looked back at the street through the screen door. Oliver lifted his hand and drove away.

Lillian pressed her head against the screen for a moment. Then she turned and listened. The house seemed empty. She hadn't noticed a car in the driveway, but someone must be home if they left the door open.

Charlotte appeared at the top of the stairs. "Lily, you're back. Thank goodness you beat my parents home."

Lillian started to climb the stairs. "Where are they?"

"They went to a barbeque and were playing bridge after. I told my mother that we ran into Penny outside of church and she took you to Rockport, to look in the galleries."

"That was a good excuse."

"I thought so," Charlotte said proudly. "I had a dreadfully boring day. Lunch with Muriel Granger's dull-but-successful son. I bet you had an interesting day, though." Charlotte's eyes widened. "So? Tell all."

Lillian glanced at her cousin then passed her at the top of the stairway and walked into the bedroom. She wasn't sure she wanted to tell all. Not even to Charlotte.

# CHAPTER EIGHT

~

*Cape Light, Early December, Present-day*

"OF COURSE, YOU THINK YOU LOVE HIM. YOU'RE barely twenty-five years old. You're liable to think a lot of things." Lillian sat stiffly in her wheelchair, her gaze fixed on her granddaughter. "I thought you had some sense in that pretty head. Or you would at least, at some point, wake up and smell the coffee."

Sara crossed her arms over her chest. "I did wake up and smell the coffee. Just this morning. Luke makes wonderful coffee. He uses fresh beans."

Lillian made a sour face. "Please! Spare me the details of your honeymoon. Too much information, as the teenagers say."

Lillian appeared to have recovered her energy for arguing, despite her casts and the bruise around her eye that had turned an amazing shade of bluish purple.

Sara forced herself to look at the bruise, reminding herself that her grandmother was still a frail, injured old woman whom she shouldn't be upsetting. "Are you finished yet?" she asked quietly.

"Finished? I've barely begun. He pressured you into this, didn't he? Tell the truth. He used to be a policeman. And given the age difference between the two of you, I'll bet he used all kinds of psychological manipulation."

"What are you talking about?"

"You know what I mean. Or are you so brainwashed by this . . . this Svengali that you aren't even aware of what's happened to you?"

"Who in the world is Svengali?"

Lillian peered at her through narrowed eyes. "Why don't you goo-goo it later and find out for yourself?"

"You mean Google it?" Sara fought hard not to laugh.

"You have grounds for an annulment. I should have told your mother. She could have started working on it. She knows people. She could pull some strings."

"Emily has no objections to our marriage. She likes Luke. She's always liked him."

"Of course she would say that. She's so naive about people. I blame her for this entirely. She should have broken up that relationship long ago."

"Emily would have never done anything like that." *That's more Lillian's style,* Sara thought. Even if Emily had doubts about Luke, she would have found some reasonable way to express them; she never would have confronted Sara with ultimatums.

"She doesn't realize how he's pressured and intimidated you. Go on, you can tell me. I've seen it on TV. It happens all the time."

Sara could have screamed with frustration. Her grandmother watched too many daytime talk shows; they put all kinds of crazy ideas in her head. Of course, Lillian would never admit to watching daytime TV; she claimed all she ever watched was the evening news and the History Channel.

"No one has been intimidated, Lillian. No one has been

pressured. We've been engaged for nearly a year. That's not exactly the case of a kidnapped bride."

Lillian pursed her lips and adjusted the afghan that lay across her legs. "I refuse to accept or recognize this hasty, ill-advised union." When Sara didn't respond, she added, "Can't you see what you've gotten yourself into? The man is a professed failure, a dishonored law officer whose greatest accomplishment is kicking a drug and alcohol habit. Of course, no one ever really gets free of that sort of thing. That's why they always say *recovery* and not *recovered*."

Sara felt the blood rush to her head. "That's it. You've gone too far!"

Lillian gave her an innocent stare. "Isn't it true?"

Sara was so angry she could barely speak. It was true in part, but not the way Lillian painted it.

Luke had hit a low point in his life after the shoot-out that damaged his leg and killed his partner. His fiancée had deserted him, and his family had lost their patience. He had been in deep pain, physically and emotionally, medicating himself with drugs and alcohol. But that had been only a phase.

By the time Luke came to Cape Light, he had cleaned up his act. He had realized he wanted to live, not kill himself in small doses. He told Sara everything about his past soon after they met. They had been together now for several years, and she had no reason to worry that such a thing would ever be a problem.

"Yes, Luke was a failure," she admitted to her grandmother. "He failed miserably at being a cop because he never really wanted to be one. That was his father's dream. But he had the courage to face it, to get up and try again, to find a purpose in life that is truly meaningful for him. If you ask me, Luke's greatest accomplishment has been building the New Horizons center, especially considering that he had to fight a lot of opposition to bring it here. You're totally wrong. Luke is anything but a failure."

"Oh, yes, a great success story. He renovated a bunch of

broken-down cottages and made a school for delinquents out of it. Just what we all needed around here. How did we ever live without that place? I'll never know."

Sara started to reply then stopped herself. There would be no winning this argument. Why had she ever thought she could?

She poured herself a cup of tea from the silver service Lillian liked to use daily. Her hand shook slightly as she stirred in a spoonful of sugar. She noticed the gold band on her finger and drew strength and courage from the sight of it.

She was married now. The time for debate was over. She didn't have to sit and listen to another word.

"If you want me to stay the night, I will. If not, I'll call Emily or Jessica. Maybe one of them can come and stay with you."

Lillian shifted in her chair. "What about him? Where will he be?"

"Does *he* have a name?" Sara asked mildly. "Or shall we call him . . . Nemo?"

She set the cup down on the table and picked up a cookie. Her grandmother was one of the few people Sara knew literate enough to understand that quip, knowing that Nemo meant *no one* in Latin.

Lillian's eyes narrowed. "You know very well who I'm talking about. Your . . . husband." She said the word so softly, Sara could hardly hear it.

"My husband, Luke, is home. I thought you and I should have this conversation alone. I didn't think you were ready to see him."

"You were wise not to bring him. I would have told him to leave."

That was not the answer Sara had hoped for. She had hoped to smooth things over with Lillian then call Luke and have him meet her here. Luke had been less optimistic. He wouldn't be at all surprised when she told him the coast wasn't clear.

"All right. I'll stay over with you tonight. But Emily will

have to call around tomorrow and arrange for a nighttime attendant."

"As you wish."

"No, Lillian, as *you* wish," Sara corrected her.

Lillian gripped the armrests of the wheelchair. "I would like to go back to my room and get in bed. This fruitless argument has exhausted me."

"All right. I'll take you into the bedroom if you like."

As Sara rolled Lillian's chair toward the bedroom, she felt a twinge of guilt. Maybe she shouldn't have argued so strenuously. She didn't want to cause a high blood pressure episode. But Lillian was so stubborn and insistent. She made the most outrageous comments. It was hard for anyone to hold their temper with her.

In the bedroom Sara helped Lillian change into her nightgown and then helped her into bed. Her grandmother opened a book and dismissed Sara with a curt nod.

"If you need anything, I'm right outside," Sara reminded her.

"I'll be fine. Good night." Lillian spoke without looking up from her book.

Sara turned and left the room, leaving the door ajar.

She was sorry that her grandmother had such a block against Luke. Her marriage was causing a huge rift between herself and Lillian, and that thought made her sad.

*Boston, September 1955*

THE INTERCOM BUZZED. LILLIAN GLANCED AT THE flashing light, but didn't stop typing to answer it. Her desk was covered with slides and notepads and stacks of art books flung open to color plates.

Her Underwood typewriter sat on a compact metal typing table just to one side of the desk. Lillian had to concentrate to strike the right keys. She was not a good typist. Unlike most of the young women she knew, she had never taken a typing course. She felt it was below her. She was determined to reach a position where someone else would be doing the typing for her, though she hadn't quite reached that point yet.

She was composing a lecture on early Egyptian ceramics that she would deliver next week at a special museum luncheon. The senior curator in her department needed to review it on Monday, and Lillian was only halfway through the first draft.

She could tell from the intercom's flashing light that it was the receptionist calling. She hoped it wasn't more flowers. Oliver had been sending them daily to her home and to the office, for the past two weeks, ever since she had left Cape Light.

He had been calling, too. But she hadn't spoken to him since the night he'd dropped her off at Charlotte's house. The next morning, she had packed up and taken an early train back to Boston. Her aunt and uncle were surprised that she cut her vacation short, but she explained she was needed back at work.

On the train ride home, she had written Oliver a letter. Actually she had written him several letters but kept tearing them up and writing them over again, unable to get the message right. In the end, she had never mailed any or sent him any explanation.

She felt guilty for treating him coldly but thought that in the long run, it was for the best. He would be hurt but also angry and would get over her sooner that way.

She was sure his attraction was a whim; he was bound to lose interest if she ignored him.

After a brief pause, the intercom buzzed again. Lillian couldn't avoid it.

Lillian pressed the button to be heard. "Yes, what is it?"

"There's someone to see you, Miss Merchant. He doesn't have an appointment . . ."

Lillian thought it was going to be more flowers. Now she wondered if it was Oliver himself. He had told her his family had an apartment in Boston and he came into the city frequently. She wouldn't put it past him. She pressed the button again, her heartbeat racing.

"Did he give you his name?"

"Dr. Elliot."

Lillian sat back. Not Oliver after all. That was what she wanted . . . right?

But Ezra Elliot? What was he doing here?

"Miss Merchant? Did you hear me?"

"Yes, I heard. I'll be out in a minute. Please ask Dr. Elliot to wait."

Lillian smoothed down her skirt and put on her suit jacket. She wasn't sure why Ezra Elliot was here to see her but hoped he hadn't come as Oliver's emissary.

She stepped out to the reception area where Ezra stood, hat in hand. He was shorter than she remembered but gave off an air of vitality and warmth as he smiled and stepped forward to greet her. She knew that he lived and worked in the city, but there was still something vaguely country about him. She couldn't quite put her finger on it.

He wore a charcoal-gray suit, a white shirt, and a burgundy bow tie with white polka dots, which was not at all in fashion. Somehow the style suited him, Lillian thought.

"Lillian, good to see you again. I wasn't sure you would remember me."

"Of course I do, Ezra."

She had nearly forgotten what he looked like. Or maybe she hadn't been paying much attention when they met. His straight brown hair was parted high on one side and combed back flat with hair tonic. His small blue eyes peered out from behind gold-rimmed glasses above a long, straight nose and a sharp chin. She did remember his look of keen intelligence and his quick wit.

"I was in the neighborhood and remembered that you worked here. I thought I would drop by and say hello."

"Oh . . . I see. Hello." Lillian smiled at him.

She could tell he wasn't a smooth talker like Oliver. But that was probably a good sign.

There was an awkward silence. Ezra took off his glasses and polished them with a handkerchief. He had very nice blue eyes, she thought, lively and kind.

"It's a beautiful museum. I don't get here often enough."

"We have an interesting exhibit right now of seventeenth-century Dutch painters."

"Is that so? I'll have to take a look one day when I have more time. I'm due back at the hospital soon." He glanced at his watch. "I only wanted to say hello," he repeated.

He smoothed the brim of his hat between his fingers, looking as if he were about to leave. "Say, Lillian, I was wondering, do you like the opera?"

His question took her by surprise. "Yes . . . I do."

"I thought you might. A friend gave me two tickets this morning for *Turandot*, orchestra seats." He cleared his throat. "Would you be interested in joining me?"

Ezra Elliot was asking her out on a date. That was why he happened to be in the neighborhood. He wasn't as shy as she had thought.

"I would be happy to go to the opera with you. When is the performance?"

"Well . . . tomorrow night actually. You probably already have plans."

Lillian didn't answer for a moment. If she had any second thoughts, he was giving her a perfect chance to reconsider.

"No, I have no plans," she answered finally.

Ezra's face beamed with relief. Lillian was almost embarrassed for him.

"That's wonderful. The performance is at eight o'clock. I can pick you up at six. We'll have time for dinner."

"That would be fine."

Lillian gave him her address and phone number and then walked with him through to the museum's front entrance.

"I'll see you then," he said. "I look forward to it."

He settled his hat on his head and waved good-bye and walked out into the bright sunshine.

Lillian watched him for a moment, studying his jaunty walk. She headed back to her office to finish her work for the day.

So Ezra hadn't come as Oliver's emissary but on his own behalf. The realization was disappointing, but she brushed the feeling aside. Ezra hadn't mentioned Oliver. Perhaps her impression had been right about them; they weren't so much friends as friendly rivals. She knew Oliver would feel hurt if he heard she had gone out with his friend while all this time she had been refusing his calls. She felt bad about that then decided it was probably a good thing. Maybe Oliver would realize he had no chance with her and would find some new girl to fixate on.

When Lillian got home from work Nancy, their housekeeper, met her at the door. "Your parents are in the library, miss. They asked to see you when you came in."

"Thank you, Nancy." Lillian left her hat and handbag on the hall table and walked up the long, curved stairway to the second floor.

She wondered what her parents wanted to talk to her about. Probably some new worry about her younger sister, Elizabeth. Beth was sixteen and swept up in all the current fads. Their parents didn't approve of any of it, not the poodle skirts or the tight sweaters, bobby sox, and saddle shoes.

Last week a neighbor had seen Beth and a girlfriend talking to a boy wearing a leather jacket. Her parents still hadn't quite recovered from that, though Lillian had done her best to explain that all the teenage boys dressed that way these days. They all wanted to look like James Dean.

There had been daring styles and swing music causing a stir when Lillian was a teenager, but now a singer from down South, Elvis something or other, was causing an uproar. They said he made obscene gestures when he sang on stage. Lillian knew Beth had bought one of his records and hid it in her bedroom. Maybe her parents had found the record and that's what this was all about.

Lillian walked into the library and found her father reading the newspaper in his favorite chair. Her mother was sitting at the secretary, writing a letter. Low lamps were lit on the side table and desk, casting her parents in amber shadows. The room smelled of books and seemed airless and still.

"Nancy said you wanted to see me?"

Lillian sat on the small couch that faced the long, shuttered windows. The walls were lined with floor-to-ceiling bookcases, and the long windows framed a view of the small square at the center of their quiet, private street.

Her mother folded her letter and slipped it in the envelope. It was undoubtedly a letter to her younger brother, Lawrence, who was at Princeton. Her mother wrote him twice a week without fail. Her parents seemed far more interested in Lawrence's life, even at a great distance, than they ever did in her life or Beth's.

Her mother turned in her chair and gave Lillian her full attention. "We need to speak to you, Lillian. It's important. Albert, can you put the newspaper down a minute?"

Her father emerged from behind the newspaper. "Oh . . . hello, Lillian. When did you get home?"

Before Lillian could answer, her mother started talking again. "More flowers came today. From that man you met on vacation."

Lillian felt her heart beat harder. "Oliver Warwick?"

"Yes, Warwick." Her father nodded, looking suddenly serious.

"How did you know they were from him? Did you read the card?" Lillian asked.

"Who else would they be from?" Her mother gave an uncharacteristic shrug, and Lillian knew she had read the card but wouldn't admit it.

"Your father had a long talk with your uncle Joshua today," her mother went on. "Your uncle and aunt had no idea you were going around with this Warwick fellow while you were visiting them. If they had known, they would have stopped it immediately."

Lillian felt the blood rush to her face. She was sure Charlotte hadn't given her away. But Newburyport was a small town, and her aunt and uncle were bound to have heard something about her meetings with Oliver sooner or later. They weren't exactly inconspicuous, flying around town in that little red car.

"Your uncle was very concerned," her father said. "Did you purposely keep these outings a secret from him?"

"No, of course not." Lillian tried to keep her voice calm. "I never even really dated Oliver. We met at the party at the yacht club. Then he ran into a group of us on the beach, Charlotte and her friends. And the next day, I ran into him again by accident in Newburyport, outside of church."

"So, he followed you around town? Even to church? That's even more upsetting," her mother said.

"A man could be arrested for harassing a young lady that way!" Albert Merchant declared. "It shows he has a bad character and is morally corrupt."

"I don't know, Father. He's persistent . . . but I wouldn't call him *corrupt*."

"Of course you wouldn't," her mother snapped. "You're very naive, Lillian. Your uncle says you narrowly missed getting yourself into a great deal of trouble."

"Did you know this man is divorced?" her father demanded. "Did you know he also got a girl into trouble . . . or at least ruined her good name? The family paid her money, and she moved out of town."

Yes, she did know all that, but Lillian didn't bother to admit it. She had never asked Oliver about that rumor; she remembered Charlotte saying that it was all exaggeration. The girl was never pregnant; she was just trying to get money out of the Warwicks.

"No, sir." Lillian's father slapped the arm of his leather armchair. "You will not associate with this man ever again.

His family may have money, but he's a bad apple. A very bad apple."

"He'll ruin your reputation, Lillian," her mother predicted. "What does a woman have after that? Who will want to marry you then?" Her mother raised her eyebrows, clearly questioning whether Lillian had already risked her good name.

"I promise you, I'm not involved with Oliver Warwick. I have no plans to see him ever again. You've seen the way I've refused his calls. I can't help it if he keeps sending me flowers."

"I threw them all out," her mother said.

"You did?" Lillian felt upset but tried not to show it. She didn't think her mother had the right to throw out all her flowers, no matter who had sent them.

"The next time he calls, your father will tell him in no uncertain terms that he's never to call here or try to see you again."

"If he dares to bother you, I'll have the police after him."

"Dad, please. Let's not get carried away. Oliver Warwick is not a monster. There are many people in Cape Light who respect him. He's a decorated war hero. He won the Purple Heart."

Lillian didn't dare mention that he had also saved her life at the beach. Or how charming and clever he could be. How generous he was to his friends. How his vitality and humor lit up a room when you were around him.

Her father sat up straight in his chair, his back suddenly rigid. "Don't you understand? The Warwicks own that town and just about everyone in it. What do you expect people to say? The Warwicks are their bread and butter." He turned to his wife. "Talk some sense into her, Ruth."

"Lillian, I'm sure this man flattered you and filled your head with lots of sugary lies and promises. That's the way these seducers work. They find an innocent, trusting girl, one who's unaccustomed to attention, and they flatter her and sweet talk her until they get their way."

"Unaccustomed to attention" was her mother's way of saying that Lillian rarely had men interested in her. So of course she was naive and vulnerable.

Lillian felt stung, unable to help wondering if her mother's charges were true. Had all of Oliver's compliments and words of affection been an act, part of a scheme to take advantage of her?

She had thought so at first. Then later, she started to think he was actually sincere. Now she just didn't know.

She never would know, she reminded herself. After her father got finished warning him off, Oliver would give up on her. He didn't like her that much, Lillian decided, no matter what he said.

Lillian smoothed down her skirt. "Is that all?"

Her mother nodded. "For now. Remember, we're doing this for your own good."

"While you're living under this roof, we must look out for your welfare," her father added. "Once you're married, you'll be your husband's responsibility."

Lillian rose. "Yes, Father, I understand."

She had decided not to see Oliver again on her own, long before her parents' interference. But she still balked against having them dictate to her. She was disappointed in some strange way. It was hard to figure out exactly why.

Maybe it was the way her mother had thrown out all his flowers, without even asking her. *Maybe that's all it is,* Lillian told herself.


LILLIAN WAS RELIEVED TO HEAR THAT HER PARENTS were going out on Saturday night to a banquet, some bankers' dinner that her father was obliged to attend. They left the house at five in formal dress, a full hour before Ezra was due to pick her up for their date.

Lillian had explained to her parents that she was going out with a young man she met on vacation, who was a doctor at Children's Hospital. Her parents liked the idea of Lillian dating a doctor and didn't ask too many questions. Of course she didn't add that she had met Ezra through the depraved, morally corrupt Oliver Warwick.

Lillian wasn't sure how formally she should dress. She chose a black silk crepe dress that fell just below the knee and long black satin gloves that stretched above her elbow. She wore her hair up with pearl drop earrings.

Her younger sister, Beth, lolled on Lillian's bed, watching her get dressed. "Where are you going, Lily? To a funeral?"

Lillian glanced at her and smiled. "To the opera, *Turandot*."

"Oh, same difference. Everybody's moaning and crying and killing themselves. For love, of course. I thought *Turandot* was a kind of fish," Beth added, sounding puzzled. "Didn't Cook make that for dinner last week?"

Lillian had to grin. She dabbed some perfume on her wrists and behind her ears. "Do you mean turbot?"

"That's it." Beth jumped off the bed and grabbed at Lillian's perfume bottle. "Can I try some?"

"This is French perfume, Chanel. I don't want to waste it." Lillian pulled the bottle away, then seeing the disappointed look on Beth's face, gave in. "All right. Just a drop. I'll put it on for you."

She touched some perfume to her sister's wrist then watched her sniff. "Eeew. That smells awful."

"It does not. But I told you it wasn't for you." Lillian laughed at her. "What are you going to do tonight?"

"I'm going to the movies with Annie Arden. Mother said it was okay as long as Mrs. Arden brings us there and picks us up."

Lillian was glad to hear her little sister wasn't going to be alone tonight. Even Nancy had the night off and was going out soon.

"Lily, is something bothering you? Ever since you came back from vacation, you seem sad."

The question took Lillian by surprise. "Of course not.

Nothing's bothering me." She glanced at her sister and forced a smile. "Why do you say that?"

Beth shrugged. "I don't know. Is it because of that man, the one who sent all the flowers? The one Mother and Dad don't want you to see again?"

"How do you know about that?" Lillian felt herself blush.

Beth picked up one of Lillian's bracelets and admired it on her arm. "I'm not deaf. Are you sad you can't see him anymore?"

Of course she had overheard everything. Lillian shook her head. "Don't be silly. I'm just tired and very busy at work. I don't think of that man at all. Mother and Father are right, he's not a nice fellow."

That was a lie. She thought of Oliver all the time. And thought he was perfectly wonderful.

They heard a light knock on the door. "Dr. Elliot is here, Miss Merchant," Nancy announced.

"Thank you, Nancy. Tell him I'll be right down." Lillian checked her appearance one last time in the mirror, then grabbed her shawl and handbag and headed for the stairs.

Beth followed her out into the hallway but stopped at the top of the stairway.

"Would you like to meet my date?" Lillian asked her. "Mother and Father aren't here to ask him a million questions. Maybe you would like to represent the family?"

Beth grinned and shook her head. "No, thanks. I'll just stay up here and spy on you. Besides, I believe you have a good head on your shoulders, Lillian. You're a good judge of character," she added in a perfect imitation of their father's pedantic tone.

Lillian laughed and kissed her sister on the cheek. "Behave yourself tonight. Make sure you're home by twelve. No hanging out with boys in leather jackets, either," she warned her. "I'll see you later."

Ezra looked very dignified in a dark blue pinstriped suit, white shirt with French cuffs and gold cufflinks, and his signature bow tie. He had thoughtfully brought Lillian a wrist corsage, a single white gardenia on a white satin ribbon.

The gift was a far cry from the armloads of roses Oliver had sent all week, but it was a thoughtful, tasteful gesture, Lillian decided.

Ezra brought her to a small French restaurant, not far from the hall where the touring opera company was performing. She was curious to know more about him, and over dinner Ezra told her that he had grown up in Cape Light in a family of six children. His father had worked for Harry Warwick, in the front office at the cannery. The family was comfortable but by no means rich. Ezra had always wanted to be a doctor but knew he couldn't manage it without scholarships or going into debt.

"Then I got drafted. The main priority was surviving the war and coming home in one piece. Which I did, thank God. When I got out of the army, Uncle Sam paid for college all the way through med school. So that solved all my problems," he explained.

"So you enjoy being a doctor?" Lillian sipped her coffee, peering at Ezra over the rim of her cup.

"Oh, yes, I do. I was born to it. I have no doubt about that. Now all I need to do is find a woman who can put up with a doctor's scattered hours, and I'll be set."

He smiled at her. Lillian smiled back, but didn't say anything more.

Ezra was loquacious once he got started, Lillian found, but not boring. Not as charming and irreverent as Oliver . . . but she quickly brushed aside that comparison.

The seats were as good as Ezra had promised, and the opera was Lillian's favorite. Ezra mentioned that it was among his favorites, too, though *Carmen* was still his first choice.

It was obvious to Lillian that they shared many of the same interests, and Ezra was clearly an intellectual match for her. She felt comfortable seated next to him and they often exchanged glances, sharing the pleasure of a particularly well-performed aria.

But for all Ezra's attentions, the story itself was a constant reminder of Oliver. The icy, virginal princess Turandot decrees that her suitors must pass a test, solving three riddles to win her hand. A perfect metaphor for herself, Lillian knew. Turandot remains unmoved, until she encounters one man who falls in love with her on sight and willingly puts his life in her hands, even after he's met her demands. Lillian had seen the opera many times before, but that night, despite Ezra's proximity, all she could see on stage was herself and Oliver.

Oliver's larger-than-life personality and wild claims of affection were as romantic as any opera—and just as seductive. She might never see him or hear from him again, but Lillian knew it was going to be a long time before she would forget him.

Ezra drove her home and walked her to the front door. Taking the key from her hand, he unlocked the door for her then handed back the key.

"Thank you, Ezra. It was a lovely evening."

Ezra took her hands in his. His blue eyes twinkled behind his glasses. He wasn't movie-star handsome, but he certainly was attractive.

"I can't remember when I've had such a fine night out, Lillian. Or such a beautiful companion to share it with."

"Thank you," she said. "I enjoyed it, too."

"I've been meaning to ask you something. Maybe I should have brought it up before I even asked you on this date. . . . But it's a bit awkward. . . . I wanted to know if you were seeing Oliver Warwick. He warned me that he saw you first, remember?" Ezra laughed but she could tell his concern was serious. "Oliver and I are old friends, and I don't want to step on anyone's toes or create a difficult situation for you."

Lillian had expected him to mention Oliver sooner or later, but now that he had, she felt unnerved—upset and emotional. It was the opera, she decided. It always got her emotions stirred up. She would probably have trouble falling asleep tonight.

She shook her head quickly. "No, I'm not seeing Oliver. We're not even in contact with one another. Does that answer your question?"

Ezra looked pleased and relieved. "Yes, it does. That was all I wanted to know." He smiled warmly at her. "I hope we can go out again soon. May I call you?"

"Yes, of course. I look forward to it." Lillian forced a smile. She didn't know what was wrong with her. She liked Ezra and enjoyed his company. He had no great fortune to offer, but he had a promising future. He was definitely the kind of man her parents would approve of.

Ezra leaned over and kissed her good night, a gentle, sweet touch on the lips. "Good night, Lillian. I'll call you soon."

Lillian opened the door and stepped inside. "Good night, Ezra."

Lillian slowly climbed the steps to the third floor. She peeked into Beth's bedroom, making sure that her sister was safe and sound. Then she went into her own room and began to undress.

Before she met Oliver she would have thought a relationship with Ezra had a chance. But now she knew differently. She knew there was something more that a woman feels when a man kisses her. Something she felt with Oliver, but didn't feel with Ezra and most likely never would feel again.

She pulled off her long gloves and tossed them on her vanity along with the crumpled program from *Turandot*. Then she stepped out of her dress and carefully hung it back in the closet.

She would continue seeing Ezra. She would "give him a chance," as her mother might advise. But she knew in her heart that there wasn't much future in it.

She felt angry for a moment—angry at Oliver Warwick

for doing this to her. For changing her in some fundamental way when she never wanted to be changed.

She washed off her makeup, put on her nightgown, and got into bed. She shut off the light but lay wide-eyed, staring at the shadows on the ceiling.

What was going to happen to her? Should she resign herself to the fact that no man would ever meet the mark Oliver had set? Or should she simply step back from the game and focus on her career, resigned to spending the rest of her life alone?

LILLIAN CAME HOME FROM WORK EARLY ON TUESDAY. Her lecture had gone well but she was tired from all the preparation and the stress of performing in front of the museum's board of directors and wealthy patrons.

As she passed through the foyer, she noticed the dish on the side table that held the day's mail was still full. Usually her mother got to it first and sorted it into piles for each member of the family. But it looked as if the mail had not yet been sorted, and Lillian sifted through the envelopes, wondering if she might find a letter from Charlotte.

There was a letter for her in a plain white envelope. It wasn't Charlotte's handwriting, though. The words "Miss Lillian Merchant" were written out in a square, masculine hand, an unfamiliar hand. Lillian checked the postmark. It had been mailed two days ago from Cape Light.

Lillian felt a shiver of intuition and knew instinctively the envelope was from Oliver. Thank goodness she had come home early today before her mother. The letter would have never reached her. She was sure of that.

She stared at it, wondering what Oliver must think of her now, after her father had ranted at him over the phone last Sunday night, making all kinds of threats.

He might have heard about her date with Ezra. It had only been a week ago, but gossip had a way of traveling.

Lillian suspected that Ezra himself might have made sure Oliver knew about it.

Lillian found herself reluctant to open the letter. If Oliver was angry with her and had sent a bitter tirade that canceled out all the sweet sentiments he had professed, she didn't want to read it. If it was the opposite, restating his love and determination to win her heart, she didn't want to read that either.

She slipped her finger under the seal. Her hand shook as she tore it open.

Just behind her a key turned in the lock and she heard voices—her mother and Beth.

Lillian tucked the letter into her pocket and drew a deep breath. She would have to wait until later to read it.

# CHAPTER NINE

❦

*Southport Hospital, Present-day*

WHEN LUCY RETURNED TO THE HOSPITAL ON FRIDAY, Helen Carter was gone. She asked Margaret what had happened to her.

"This is a hospital, Bates. Patients come and go. They get better and they go home. We don't keep them here."

Lucy didn't appreciate the sarcasm. She got plenty of that at the diner from Charlie. Come to think about it, Charlie and Margaret had a lot in common.

"I think she declined any further treatment and went home," Margaret added as they walked down the hall together.

Decided against treatment? Lucy couldn't fathom it. Did that mean Helen Carter was just giving up? Lucy knew patients had the right to determine their own course of action, but to ignore a doctor's recommendation for cancer treatment seemed like the act of a person without any hope at all.

Lucy went about her work for the day, feeling distracted

and upset. Her first assignment was an elderly lady named Mrs. Spivak who needed a bed bath. Margaret supervised for a while then went off to oversee another student in the room next door.

The bath was not a particularly hard job, but Lucy had to admit that it was harder washing a live human being than one of the rubber dummies in the nursing lab at school.

She concentrated, remembering the sequence she had been taught and how to keep flipping the sheets around to keep the patient warm and protect their modesty.

Mrs. Spivak was probably close to eighty. She seemed used to hospital care and didn't say much at all during the process. Lucy changed her into a clean gown, combed her hair, and rubbed lotion on her hands. Finally, when Lucy was done she asked, "Have you ever done that before, dear?"

"No," Lucy admitted. "Why? Was there some problem?"

"No, dear. It was fine. You could go a little lighter with that sponge though. You nearly wore my skin out."

"Oh, I'm so sorry. I wish you had told me."

"That's okay." The woman laughed and patted Lucy's hand. "I got a bath and a massage rolled into one."

Lucy smiled and gathered up the basin and sponge. She was about to leave the room when Margaret returned.

"So, how did you do in here, Bates?"

"Fine." Lucy wondered if Mrs. Spivak would complain, but the elderly lady was already working the remote on her TV, seemingly absorbed in channel-surfing.

"Bates . . ." Margaret shook her head and marched over to the bed. "Look at this."

Lucy felt a chill in her gut. What had she screwed up now? She stared at the bed, not sure what she was supposed to be looking at. Had she made the bed incorrectly?

Margaret yanked on the guardrail at the side of the bed and quickly pulled it up. "You forgot to put up the guardrail. This woman could have fallen out of bed."

"Oh . . . I . . . I'm sorry."

The guardrail. It was one of the first things they taught

in nursing school. Countless accidents are caused simply because the guardrail is left down. Patients, especially older patients, fall out of bed and injure themselves. Then there are hours of paperwork and sometimes even lawsuits. Rule number one: Always pull up the guardrail.

And Lucy had forgotten.

Lucy followed Margaret out into the hallway, her chest tight with dread.

"I'm going to have to give you an F for the day. You know that, don't you?"

"Yes, I understand."

It was her third bad grade in two weeks of training. How had that happened? First the F for spilling water on Helen Carter, then an absent grade for missing the day when Jamie was home sick, and now this. Lucy almost asked Margaret how many F days you were allowed before you got one for the entire course. But then she decided she didn't really want to know.

Lucy felt so frustrated, she wanted to cry. Again.

She steadied herself with a few deep breaths and focused on the next tasks assigned: checking lungs, blood pressure, and temperature. This time, she promised herself, she was going to get it right.

LUCY FELT A LITTLE BETTER BY THE TIME SHE ENTERED the cafeteria for lunch. She had managed to get through the rest of the morning without further mistakes. So she treated herself to a yogurt, some fruit and tea, and a packet of celebratory cookies, then looked around for a table.

A group of nursing students sat together in one corner. One of the young women saw Lucy but didn't invite her over. Lucy had a feeling they didn't like her very much. There was no room at the table anyway.

Lucy wandered in the other direction, looking for an empty seat. A man at a table waved at her. Jack Zabriskie. She wanted to pretend she hadn't seen him—she felt cranky and tired and wasn't wearing any makeup—but it was too late.

*Why would Jack care about my makeup?* she asked herself as she reluctantly moved toward him. *He probably thinks I'm old enough to be his mother . . . or at least his older sister.*

She sat in the empty chair beside him and forced a cheerful smile. "Thanks, Jack. I thought I was going to have to eat standing up."

"That trick is only for interns. Sometimes they have to eat while they're asleep."

"Sometimes they have to work in the ER when they're asleep, from what I hear." Lucy flipped open her yogurt and stirred it.

He watched her curiously. "What's the matter? Hard day?"

She glanced at him, surprised he was able to read her mood so easily. Charlie never seemed to notice that she was upset unless she burst out crying.

"Yeah. I don't mean to complain but—"

"Go on, complain. I won't tell Margaret Sherman on you."

"It's no secret to her, believe me. The thing is, I thought I would do much better at this working-with-the-patients phase." Lucy brushed a loose strand of hair out of her eyes. "I was great in the course work and nursing labs. Straight A's except for organic chemistry. But I'm striking out in the real world. I've gotten three bad grades already, and I'm not even through my second week."

He gave her a sympathetic look. He had such nice blue eyes—dark blue, a perfect match to the deep blue shirt he wore today. He really was very good-looking. She was sure the other nursing students all had crushes on him.

*Eat your hearts out, ladies. He saved a seat for me. So there.*

"Maybe you're nervous. Sounds like you've lost a little confidence in yourself, and now you're just waiting to make a mistake. It's a self-fulfilling prophecy."

"I'm not nervous," Lucy protested. "Well, I wasn't nervous when I started. I was calm as toast. That Margaret Sherman breathing down my neck every minute, she makes me nervous."

"She makes me nervous and I'm a doctor," he confided with a grin.

Lucy smiled back at him. "I can't criticize her too much. She's an awesome nurse. She can walk into a room and just look in a patient's eye, and *boom*, she knows: Something's wrong." Lucy shook her head. "I'll never be able to do that, not in a million years."

"Sure you will. I mean, in a million years." He gave her a serious look that slowly softened. "Margaret Sherman wasn't born being able to do that. She learned it, one day at time. It's just like anything else, Lucy. You have to put the time in. Are you willing?"

"Of course I am. If I don't flunk out by next week."

"You won't. You know your stuff. It's all in here." He pointed to his temple. "Focus, concentrate, and relax. It's not going to fall together for you unless you lighten up a little. Believe me, I've been there."

Lucy sighed, knowing he was right. She had gotten herself tied up in knots. No wonder she had forgotten a stupid thing like raising the bed rail.

"All right. I'll try." She took a sip of her tea and glanced up at him. "Listen, how did you get to be such a smart guy?"

He shrugged and smiled at her. "I don't know. . . . How did you get such pretty red hair?"

The comment took her by surprise. She felt herself start to blush and then felt even more self-conscious. Good heavens, she was too old for this. Jack didn't mean anything by it. He was just trying to cheer her up.

"It's just genetic. Like everything else, right?" she said quickly. She picked up her tray and stood up. "Thanks again for the pep talk."

"You'll do the same for some nurse in training someday. I'm certain of it."

"I hope so. I'll see you."

"See you around," he said as she walked away.

Lucy dumped her tray and headed back upstairs. She always felt better after talking to Jack. She didn't know why he was so nice to her, but it certainly helped.

She had heard once that God can't always send an angel when you need help, so sometimes he sends a friend who does an angel's job. Jack was certainly her angel at this place, a cute one, too.

*Maybe this is a sign,* Lucy thought. Maybe God didn't want her to give up so easily.

SARA DIDN'T ATTEND CHURCH EVERY SUNDAY, AND LUKE hadn't been a churchgoer at all when he first moved to town. Then little by little, he had gotten to know Reverend Ben and started to come to hear his sermons. Now Luke came every week, bringing any of the kids at New Horizons who wanted to attend. Sara came with him when she could.

Sara glanced at Luke, sitting down the row from her, separated by four of his students. He smiled at her over their heads and woolen hats, and their eyes met. She felt that special sense of connection, as if he were sitting right beside her, holding her hand.

Reverend Ben had started the announcements. "This being the first Sunday of Advent, we begin our preparations for the holidays. Work on the Christmas Fair is well under way, and committees will be meeting after the service in Fellowship Hall. Please see Sophie Potter if you would like to volunteer.

"Next Sunday, there's our annual Advent Party and potluck dinner, and on Saturday December seventeenth, the Christmas Fair. Mark your calendars, everyone. Or Palm Pilots," he added with a grin.

Reverend Ben then called the congregation to worship, and the choir began the first hymn. Sara stood up and held out the hymn book to share with the little boy beside her. She caught sight of Emily a few rows ahead, bouncing a fretful Jane in her arms as Dan balanced the hymnal between them.

Sara wondered how Lillian was doing. She hadn't gone back to visit since last week, when Lillian had argued with her over Luke. Emily had understood why Sara wouldn't stay there again. She didn't even try to persuade Sara otherwise. She had just sighed, as if she expected something like that to happen and told Sara not to worry—she would hire some help at night and Lillian would just have to put up with it.

After the readings of the scripture, Reverend Ben took the pulpit and began his sermon. "It's that time of year again, holiday time. Preparations begin. Time to make our lists and pull out those boxes of decorations from the attic or the basement. Bake cookies, put up the tree, decorate the house. Don't forget the inflatable lawn Santa. I've heard you can get them fairly cheap this year at that big garden place up on the highway." A few people laughed and Reverend Ben smiled.

"But what are we preparing for? It's easy to get confused about it. It's easy to lose the real meaning of the season when we get so caught up in all the shopping and cooking and gift wrapping. It starts to seem so much like work and rather joyless, doesn't it?

"I have a trick for you. This works for me and I'm going to pass it on. Did you ever get the house ready for a new baby? You know how that is. It's more work than Christmas, but it's a different attitude, a different mindset. Yes, there's a lot of shopping and gadgets to deal with. There's also cleaning up and clearing out. A sense of creating a peaceful, pure space for that new life to thrive. A safe, warm, loving place. Not just in our home, but in our hearts.

"There's a deep, abiding sense of anticipation. A deep excitement about this new life coming into our world, this new person. So many possibilities. A sense of joy and wonder and hope. We are open and accepting. We are forgiving and thankful." He paused to push his glasses a bit higher on his nose.

"We are humble, too, standing in awe of a tiny being, the innocence that will touch our souls and make us somehow innocent again. We anticipate this new life that will give our lives a new beginning.

"Those are the thoughts you might hold in your hearts as you prepare your home and your family for Christmas. That's the perspective that can help make this season more meaningful for you. What are we preparing for and celebrating on Christmas Day but the birth of a baby, our Lord, Jesus Christ? The mystery and the joy at the very center of that day.

"Let's move forward into the season of Advent, with joy and anticipation for the great gift God the Father will soon bestow on this world."

Sara listened closely to the sermon. She liked Reverend Ben's analogy. It helped her focus on the true meaning of Christmas, which she agreed too often got lost in the sauce. And she realized that was the exact same way she had felt about planning a big wedding. The real meaning of joining her life with Luke's seemed to get lost in a burbling chocolate fountain. She had been unsure about eloping but now felt they had made the right choice.

The service moved on to "Joys and Concerns," when the congregation shared their joys of the week and also their problems. Sara saw a hand pop up in the back row and recognized Digger Hegman, sitting next to his daughter Grace.

"Yes, Digger," Reverend Ben said.

Digger rose and slowly straightened out. Sara could almost hear his bones creak under his thick wool jacket, heavy turtleneck sweater, and baggy trousers. "On Thanksgiving Day, my daughter Grace drove me up to Vermont, and we had a family reunion with my other two daughters, and all my grandchildren, who I don't see very much, living down here. And that was a great joy to me." He nodded and smoothed his long beard with his hand. "And the dinner was very tasty. I brought the oysters for the stuffing."

Everyone laughed and Reverend Ben smiled. "I'm glad you had a good visit with your family, Digger. I hope you get to see them all again very soon."

Emily raised her hand next and Reverend Ben nodded at her. "I have a joy and a concern today," she began as she stood up. "I'm very happy to announce that my daughter Sara Franklin and Luke McAllister were married in a private ceremony last weekend."

The congregation applauded, and Sara felt her cheeks get warm and red. She glanced at Luke, who was looking at her, beaming. Typical Emily. She would do something like that.

"And my concern is for my mother, Lillian. She's had a bad fall and is confined to her house with two broken bones. We ask for your prayers for her recovery."

Lillian probably wouldn't get many visitors or get-well cards, Sara thought, but she would get her fair share of prayers from the generous hearts gathered here today.

The service ended, and Sara and Luke had barely left the pew before they were swamped with well-wishers. Sophie Potter was first to enfold her in a big hug. "I'm so very happy for you, dear! So happy for both of you." Sophie turned to Luke next and hugged him as well.

Reverend Ben's wife, Carolyn, was next in line. "What wonderful news! Every happiness to the both of you."

Sam's sister Molly Willoughby and her husband Matt had already heard the news through Jessica and Sam, but they were eager to offer their congratulations. Sara had never realized that news of her marriage would bring so many smiles to so many faces. Even Digger, who was a special friend of Luke's, stood by looking almost teary-eyed with happiness.

"You picked a fine girl. Great happiness to you." The old fisherman shook Luke's hand as if pumping a well.

By the time everyone had offered their good wishes, Sara was nearly exhausted. She finally reached the church vestibule and looked around for Emily.

"Now, don't be mad at me," Emily said as she approached. "I know I should have asked you first. But it just slipped out."

"It's all right. Everyone's been so sweet. Besides, I should have guessed you were going to do that. How is Lillian holding up? Has she found anyone she likes for the night shift?"

"To tell the truth, she's fired everyone we found so far. Thursday, Friday, Saturday . . . she's batting a thousand. Oh, wait," Emily corrected herself. "She was going to let the Saturday night hire come back, but the woman quit. Someone new is coming this evening. I'll have to go over and get them started. I hope they come early enough to beat the snow. It's supposed to start early this evening."

"Well, I hope this one works out," Sara said.

"Me, too," Emily admitted. "Actually, Lillian was wondering how your marriage was working out—whether you had 'come down off your cloud yet.' "

Sara laughed. "At least she didn't ask you if I woke up and smelled the coffee."

"What?" Emily looked genuinely puzzled.

"Never mind." Maybe it was being in church this morning, or just having had time to cool off and get perspective, but Sara felt more forgiving of her grandmother.

"Listen," she said, "I'm still willing to stay with Lillian but only if she'll change her attitude about Luke. I mean, we're married now. I don't understand her problem."

"I know, honey." Emily touched Sara's arm. "I'm not sure if she's ready to give in yet. You know your grandmother. Give her time, she'll come around."

"Right." Sara knew Emily was only saying that to make her feel better. Her grandmother was a champion grudge holder. Time had no meaning when it came to Lillian to holding on to ill will.

"WHO LET YOU IN HERE? I TOLD THAT NURSE I WASN'T up to seeing any visitors today." Lillian leaned back in her wheelchair and glowered at Ezra Elliot who stood in the doorway of her living room, hat in hand.

"I told her I was your doctor. Those seemed to be the magic words to grant me entrée to the kingdom."

"Very funny. You're not my doctor and haven't been for many years," she reminded him.

"If I wait for you to be in the mood for guests, I'll be visiting you in a graveyard, Lillian."

"How touching. Just don't bring carnations."

Ezra laughed. "Aren't you going to invite me in?"

"You are in, as far as I can see. What's the difference what I say?" She exhaled and spun her chair around. "You may sit in the living room for a few minutes, I suppose. But you can't stay long. I'm very tired and out of sorts."

Ezra sat down on the camelback sofa. He had taken off his coat and muffler and laid them down neatly on the armchair beside him. "So, how do you feel, Lillian? Are you still in pain?"

"Only when I laugh," she said with a serious face.

He smiled at her. "Quite a black eye. I never could have pictured you with one."

"Well, here it is. Not very pretty, is it?"

"Oh, it isn't so bad. After a few moments, you hardly notice it anymore," he consoled her. "It will go away in a few days."

"I hope so. It's getting uglier every day, turning all kinds of hideous colors."

"Is that why you didn't want to see me? Are you self-conscious about it?"

Lillian glared at him. "Don't be ridiculous."

"It hardly matters. I was just relieved to hear that you

hadn't hurt yourself more seriously. A fall like that at our age . . . well, it could have been much worse."

"The end, you mean. Don't mince your words, Ezra. I've never liked that."

"All right. You could have killed yourself. Happy now?"

Lillian sighed. "It does give one pause. It does cause one to . . . reflect." When he didn't say anything, she added, "Do you ever think about the past, Ezra?"

"Oh, yes, all the time. Is that what you've been doing, Lillian? Strolling down memory lane?"

She nodded. "Too much, I think."

"Typical for people our age. I suppose you look back and have your regrets. Is that it? Do you regret that you and I never got married?"

She suddenly looked up at him. "It never would have worked. We're too much alike. You've never understood that."

"So you say. We'll never know, will we? There are so many questions we'll never have answers to, I hardly see the sense in trying. Especially at this stage of the game."

"I'm not searching for any elusive answers," Lillian said curtly. "I'm not searching for anything. Sometimes I feel as if I'm really alive back there"—she tilted her head to one side—"and all this is just a dream. Just a waiting room."

"A waiting room? What are you waiting for?" He paused. "Oh, I get it." He removed his glasses and wiped them with his handkerchief. "You have plenty of life left in you, Lillian. More than some people half your age. I'm a doctor, remember? I know about these things."

"Thanks for the diagnosis."

"Don't mention it." He picked up a deck of playing cards from the pedestal coffee table. "How about a hand of gin rummy? Feel up to it?"

Lillian frowned and he expected her to say she was too tired, but she nodded reluctantly. "All right. Just a hand or two. Shall we pick up the points from our last game? I believe the score pad is still in the secretary."

"Excellent idea." Ezra jumped up and retrieved the pad. "I was ahead, as I recall."

"Perhaps, but not by much. I can't remember the last time you beat me at this game, Ezra."

"Gives me something to live for, Lillian. We all need something to make us get out of bed in the morning."

Ezra chuckled but Lillian just scowled as he dealt out their cards.


The snow began earlier than anyone had predicted. It fell steadily, in a thick white curtain. Sara and Luke had left New Horizons right after lunch and gone into town to Sara's apartment. They had plans to see a movie later in Newburyport. Sara wanted to clean up the apartment first, to get ready for the workweek. Her place was a mess, and she felt as if her belongings were scattered all over town.

They still weren't sure where to live and had been moving between their two homes: Luke's cottage out at New Horizons on Beach Road and Sara's small apartment. Neither place seemed quite right. Sara was trying hard to make more closet space for Luke's belongings, though there wasn't much there to begin with.

"I think we need a new place altogether." She lugged a carton of old shoes and books out of her bedroom. "Maybe we should rent a house. Did you throw out the real estate section already?"

"I can expand the cottage, build out. I already talked to Sam about it. We'll make the bedroom bigger and build you a small study for your writing."

Sam Morgan was her aunt Jessica's husband and an excellent carpenter and builder. Sara knew if Sam was in charge of expanding the cottage, it would be a showplace. Luke would help, of course. He knew enough carpentry to follow Sam's directions. Together they had done just about all the work of renovating the old Cranberry Cottages into the New Horizons Center.

Although Luke was capable of doing construction work, Sara couldn't imagine when he was going to fit it in. He barely had time for all his responsibilities now: running the center, taking part in meetings up in Boston, and whatever new training he was asked to complete.

Sara didn't relish the idea of living in a construction site for the next few months. Or camping out in her tiny place.

"Why don't we just live in a big RV? Then we can take a cross-country trip anytime we like."

"Good idea. As long as it's solar-powered." Luke got up from the kitchen table and helped her with the box. He peered inside. "Why am I always helping you carry boxes of books, Sara? Ever since we met. Is this my destiny?"

Sara grinned. It was true. It seemed she was always moving, and Luke was always helping her. "I really don't believe in destiny. I believe in free will. But in your case, it's probably true. You were born to lug my stuff around."

He smiled and dropped a kiss on the top of her head. "You are my destiny, I know that much."

Sara smiled back at him, feeling completely happy despite the chaos of their living situation.

He put the box down and put his arms around her then gave her a real kiss. Sara melted against him, savoring the feeling of Luke's arms holding her tight.

The phone rang. "Don't answer it," he whispered.

"All right, just let me hear who's calling." They stood very still, listening.

Emily's voice came on the line. "Sara? If you're around, could you pick up, please? I really need your help—"

Luke quickly released her, and Sara ran over to answer the phone. "I'm here. What's the matter? Is something wrong?"

"It's your grandmother. Can you run over and check on her? She's all alone and I'm not sure when the new night nurse is coming."

"Alone? How did that happen? She's not supposed to be left all alone." Sara didn't mean to sound as if she were blaming Emily, but she was alarmed.

"I'm not really sure. She called me a few minutes ago and said the day nurse had left early. I'm not sure if the woman wanted to get an early start home because of the snow, or if she had some conflict with your grandmother and maybe just quit. She was supposed to wait until the next shift arrived before she left. But apparently, Mother's all alone right now." Emily paused and let out a breath. "Meanwhile, I can't even get in touch with the nurse who was due to start tonight. I was hoping she could come earlier, but she's not answering her phone. I would go over there myself," Emily added, "but Jane's not feeling well. She has a bad cold and Dan's gone out for the day. He won't be back until late."

"I understand. Don't take Jane out in this weather." Sara glanced at Luke, who was listening to the conversation. "We'll take care of everything. Lillian's house is only a few blocks from here. We'll be there in five minutes."

"Thanks, Sara. I knew I could count on you." Sara could hear the relief in Emily's voice. "Call me later, will you?"

"Sure, I'll call you in a little while and let you know what's going on."

Sara and Luke dressed for the snow with hats, gloves, boots, and down jackets and climbed into Luke's truck. Sara found a snow shovel on her porch and tossed it into the back. The snow was much deeper than they had expected. Over six inches had fallen during the afternoon and it was still coming down steadily.

The neighborhood between Sara's house and Lillian's looked still and quiet, the houses, cars, and wide front lawns were covered in a soft, white blanket of snow. It was growing dark outside, and the twilight cast a bluish tint on the scene. Sara didn't see anyone out on the street, though windows glowed with warm yellow lights, making the houses look cozy and warm.

Not Lillian's house, of course. The tall, gray Victorian was dark, as usual. Worse, it was forbidding and eerie-looking compared with the other houses on the street, which all looked like pretty little gingerbread cottages.

Sara felt sorry for her grandmother, stranded in her bed and unable to get up to even put a light on. She hoped Lillian hadn't gotten frustrated and maybe even fallen trying to fend for herself.

Luke parked the truck and they waded through the snow to the front door. Luke had brought a flashlight, which made it easier to find the spare key and fit it in the door. Sara unlocked the heavy door quickly and pushed it open.

Luke stood behind her, but didn't follow. "Maybe I should wait out here."

"Don't be ridiculous. You'll freeze. Come inside. She's lucky we've come at all."

Luke followed Sara into the foyer. He switched on a light, and Sara walked back to the spare room that had been turned into Lillian's temporary bedroom.

"Who's there? Who is it?" Lillian shouted from her bed. "Identify yourself immediately! I have a gun!"

"You don't have a gun, Lillian. What are you talking about?"

Lillian pressed her hand to her chest. "You scared me half to death. I thought someone was breaking into the house!"

"Didn't Emily call and tell you we were coming?"

"She probably did call. I dropped the phone and couldn't reach it." Lillian peered at her. "Who's *we*? Your husband is here? Is that what you mean?"

"Yes, Luke drove me over. He's out in the living room." Sara spotted the cordless phone on the floor and picked it up. She would have to call Emily right away; she was probably worried sick by now. "Should I tell Luke to wait out in the snow when he was kind enough to run over here to help you?"

Lillian grunted and turned her head to one side. "That obnoxious woman who was here today, calls herself a private duty nurse, she ran out on me. Just like that." Lillian snapped her fingers. "Left me high and dry. I'm going to call that agency first thing in the morning. She should have her license taken away for that."

"She just walked out? You didn't have an argument with her or anything like that?"

Lillian gave Sara a wide-eyed stare. "Of course not. What would I have to argue with her about? I barely said two words to her. I'm at the mercy of strangers, a prisoner in my own home. I've barely had a thing to eat or drink all day. I'm so hungry I could faint. I'm going to waste away in this bed. No one will even know or care."

Sara sifted through the drama to the facts: her grandmother was hungry and thirsty, though she suspected there was some exaggeration to this report, since a tray of food from a recent meal was sitting on the bed table.

Sara picked up the tray. "I'll fix you something to eat."

"Yes, but first I would like some tea. In my pink flowered cup, the bone china one. Those ugly mugs these nurses choose have such thick rims, I can hardly drink from them."

Lillian was so particular. Even under the most trying circumstances, she still maintained her high standards. Maybe that's what kept her going all these years, Sara thought as she left the room.

Sara called Emily from the kitchen and calmed her fears.

"I'm so glad you're over there with her," Emily said. "I finally got in touch with the night nurse. She's got car trouble and can't get down here. I've called the agency emergency number, but it's Sunday night. I'm not sure they can find anyone on such late notice."

"I understand. Luke and I can stay. It's not a problem." She would explain it to Luke. She was sure he would understand. He could go back to the apartment and get them a few things to stay over.

Sara fixed the tea and found Lillian's special cup and saucer. She headed for her grandmother's room, bracing herself to break the news.

But when she walked in she found Lillian asleep, her chin resting on her chest as she dozed. She was holding something in her hand—it looked like the pages of a letter.

Sara set the teacup down. She slipped the letter out of her grandmother's hand and set it beside the tea on the table. Then she cleared off some books and newspapers from her grandmother's bed and tried to pull the blanket a little higher on her chest. But the blanket wouldn't budge. It was stuck. Something was holding it down.

Tucked beside Lillian and hidden under an afghan, Sara found an old shoe box. She recognized it immediately. It was the box of photographs from the attic, the one she had seen on the stairs the day Lillian fell. Sara picked it up and opened the lid. A musty smell of old paper and dust floated up and made her nose feel stuffy.

Sara glanced at her grandmother, softly snoring, her reading glasses sliding down her nose. It was tempting to go through the contents of the box. Lillian would never know.

No, Sara decided quickly. It wasn't right. Not without Lillian's permission. Her grandmother was feeling her privacy invaded enough lately. Sara put the lid back on and placed it back where she found it, cuddled next to Lillian on the bed, hidden under the afghan.

*Boston, September 1955*

LILLIAN WAITED HOURS TO READ THE LETTER FROM Oliver—partly because it was hard to slip away from her family, and partly because she was afraid to see what it said.

After dinner, she went up to her room and closed the door, locking it just in case Beth decided to breeze in.

She sat on her bed and pulled the letter out and unfolded it. She felt so nervous that she could barely focus her eyes to read. Yet, when she read the words, it was as if she heard his voice. It was as if he were standing right there, in her room.

*Dear Lily,*

*I've tried very hard to respect your wishes. But the idea of never seeing you again or holding you in my arms is more terrifying to me than any danger I've ever faced. I need to see you again, just one more time if that's all you will allow. But please don't send me away without a final word of good-bye or one final chance to look into your beautiful eyes and tell you again how much I love you.*

*Ezra is a fine man and if you prefer him over me, I'll have to respect that. But I'll never accept it. No matter what you say, I believe you do have feelings for me, feelings that are as deep and powerful as what I feel for you. Don't be frightened, Lily. To find real love, the kind I feel for you, changes everything. Please let me see you one more time, even for a few minutes. I'll wait for you in the Public Garden, by the swan boats, on Saturday afternoon at two o'clock.*

*I put aside all pride and beg you, Lily. Take pity on me. I'm nothing now without you and never will be. If I don't see you there, I'll know I've been sadly mistaken and it was only my wishful thinking that made me believe you love me, too. I'll accept that and I'll never bother you again.*

*With love everlasting,*
*Oliver*

Lillian's hand shook. She read the letter a second time, hardly able to believe Oliver's words. What should she do? What in the world was she to do?

She couldn't go to meet him. That would be . . . impossible. But how could she ignore him? How could she ignore this letter, this desperate plea from the heart? She would have liked to believe that she was not moved, not persuaded by his dramatic expressions of emotion. But she knew she was. She felt loved. She felt wanted by someone. Desperately. No one had ever felt that way about her before.

Oliver Warwick loved her. For that fact alone, even if she didn't return his feelings, didn't she owe him at least a few words of explanation? A few kind words to soften the blow and a respectful parting? Even George Tilles had given her that.

She thought maybe she did owe him that much. She thought maybe she should go to meet him on Saturday. They would sit somewhere public, in a coffee shop perhaps, and have a talk. It would be the decent thing to do.

As the week wore on, Lillian changed her mind a thousand times. She carried the letter in the bottom of her purse and slipped it out and read it over and over again. She didn't know what to do. She felt sorry for Oliver but also didn't want to encourage him any further. And if her parents ever found out she had gone to meet him . . . she didn't want to imagine the consequences.

Every night before she fell asleep, Lillian thought only of Oliver. His face floated above her as she drifted off to her dreams.

LILLIAN'S MOTHER WAS SURPRISED TO SEE LILLIAN dressed in a good suit on Saturday afternoon. "Where are you going? Do you need to go into work today?"

That would have been a good excuse, Lillian realized. Why hadn't she thought of it? But then her mother may have tried to call the museum and she wouldn't have been there. She was already nearly an hour late, having patiently sat with her father as he went through his Saturday ritual of recording her expenses for the week. She hadn't quite dared to try to slip out of that.

"I'm going shopping . . . and out to lunch, with a girl-friend. I'm meeting her downtown. We might go to the movies later, too," Lillian added for good measure. She wasn't used to lying. She hoped she wasn't overdoing it.

"Oh, that's nice," her mother said. "Well, call later if you're not going to be home for dinner."

"Yes, I will." Lillian draped a silk scarf around her neck, grabbed her handbag, and left the house quickly before her mother could ask any more questions.

It was a bright day but cool. Fall was in the air. Lillian hailed a taxi and hopped in.

"Where to, miss?"

"The Public Garden, please." Lillian sat back and stared out the window, suddenly feeling misgivings over what she was about to do.

The streets flew by, bringing her closer and closer to Oliver. The thought unnerved her. She nearly opened the door and jumped out. Finally, the cab pulled up to the park. Lillian paid the driver and climbed out.

She glanced at her watch. She was over an hour late. She wondered if Oliver would even be there. She didn't have to do this at all. She could turn around and go home, she told herself.

But she knew in her heart, she didn't want to do that. She took a breath and walked into the garden, taking the path that led to the swan boats. The boats were still running and the park was filled with people, couples walking together and families with children and young mothers pushing prams.

Lillian silently practiced the little speech she had prepared for Oliver. She would be sensible but kind. She would explain how she was deeply flattered by his attentions, that she respected and even admired him. But she would also remind him that she had always been very clear that they had no future together. He had to grant her that. She couldn't be blamed for his feelings, could she? She was sorry, very sorry.

She looked up and he was there. Standing right in front of her. He walked closer. His face lit up as he gazed down at her. His dark eyes burned with a strange, amazing light, as if he couldn't believe that she had actually appeared.

She couldn't look away. She couldn't even speak.

He put his hands on her shoulders, and she stepped into his arms and tilted her head back. Then she closed her eyes as he kissed her. Kissed her as if he were a drowning man, finally breaking the surface and finding a breath of air.

# Chapter Ten

### Southport Hospital, Present-day

WHENEVER LUCY FELT RATTLED, SHE TRIED TO REmember Jack's advice. She concentrated but also tried to relax and stop worrying about making another mistake.

On Wednesday morning, she and Margaret Sherman were attending a patient who was recovering from an appendectomy. A man in his mid-forties, he also suffered from diabetes. Margaret pulled his chart out from the box on the room's door, glanced at it, then handed it to Lucy.

Inside the room, Lucy's supervisor watched as Lucy checked his temperature, blood pressure, and listened to his lungs.

"All right, Lucy. I'd like you to start a new IV, please."

Margaret stepped back and Lucy knew that she was on her own. Lucy felt a rush of nerves. Her mind went blank. She walked toward the IV pole, and started to untangle the line from the IV bag that hung there, all the while unable to remember what to do next.

She was doing this to herself, she realized. Why was she sabotaging herself like this? Did she want to fail? Did she think someplace, deep down inside that she didn't deserve to be a nurse and the best she could do was serve burgers at the Clam Box for the rest of her life?

"Lucy?"

Lucy took a deep breath, willing herself to calm down before she turned. "Yes?"

Margaret held out the chart with the doctor's orders scribbled on them. "You need this?"

"Yes, absolutely. . . . The line is all twisted. I wanted to straighten it out first."

"Very good."

Lucy scanned the doctor's notes and found the orders for the IV, the rate of insulin drip for the patient. The routine she had learned cold in the nursing lab and the medical principles behind it came back in a rush, as if she had suddenly hit the right key on a computer.

She left the room briefly, returned with a fresh solution, and quickly changed the bag. Then she watched the rate of flow on the monitor, double-checking that it was at the level prescribed by the doctor. Too much or too little could cause severe problems, even a diabetic coma.

"Are you done?" Margaret asked.

Lucy already knew that was a trick question. "Not quite. I just want to check the catheter."

Margaret nodded. "Very good," she said quietly.

"I need to check your catheter, Mr. Cordova. Could you show it to me, please?"

The patient held his arm toward her and Lucy checked that the catheter was functioning correctly, there was no infection, and it didn't need any fresh tape. Everything looked fine.

Margaret walked over and took a look for herself. "Okay. That looks good to me."

Lucy glanced down at the bed and had to smile to herself. "Mr. Cordova, someone left the guardrail of your bed down.

We need to keep that up at all times, please. It's for your own safety."

The patient looked up at her. "Oh, sorry. I didn't know."

"That's okay. Good thing I caught it for you." Lucy yanked the guardrail up, locked it in place then glanced at Margaret.

Was she trying not to smile? It was hard to tell.

Margaret left the room and Lucy followed. She knew she would get a decent grade today and maybe even a little extra credit.

### Cape Light, Present-day

"HERE YOU ARE, TEA AND TOAST, LILLIAN. AND A TWO-minute egg with orange marmalade. I put it in a little dish, see? Sara said you don't like jars on the table."

Luke emerged from the kitchen, carrying Lillian's breakfast tray. She leaned back in her wheelchair, her mouth agape.

"Where's Sara? Who said *you* could serve me my breakfast? Did you stay over here again last night? The snowstorm was an emergency. I didn't agree to a regular situation."

Luke set the tray down in front of her and wiped his hands on the towel he had slung over his shoulder.

"Sara had to leave early. She's covering an early meeting in Gloucester for the paper." Luke shrugged. "If you don't want the breakfast, that's fine. I'll take it back to the kitchen and eat it myself."

Lillian sat up straighter in her chair. "You'll do no such thing. Get your own breakfast."

"I will. In a minute." Luke sat down at the table where he had left a mug of coffee. "I think it's time you and I had a little chat."

Lillian peered at him. "Really? Are you ready to admit that you strong-armed my granddaughter into marrying you?"

"She told me that you called me . . . Svengali." He drew out the word, giving it an extra mysterious sound.

"That was extreme. But you get the idea."

"Do *you* get the idea is the question."

Lillian picked up a slice of toast and nibbled the corner. "What idea is that, pray tell?"

"The idea that Sara and I love each other and are married now. Period. If you don't like it, fine. I'm not asking for your blessing. But Sara wants to help you out while you're stuck in that chair and that means I help you, too. We're a package, a two-for-one deal. Where she goes, I go."

"Very sweet," Lillian sneered. "You're nearly as devoted as a Labrador. If Sara was lonely, she should have gotten herself a dog instead of marrying you."

Luke laughed. "Maybe, but you wouldn't have liked having a dog around here any better than you like me."

"You always were a gate crasher," Lillian muttered.

"Yes, I've crashed your gates again," he admitted easily. "I've been sleeping here for the past three nights. Didn't you know that?"

Lillian avoided his eyes. "I knew. But I didn't want to make a big thing about it. Out of sight, out of mind."

Sara had kept him and Lillian separated. Not in an obvious way, but it wasn't very hard in the big house with Luke upstairs and Lillian confined to the downstairs.

"Of course you didn't want to make a big deal about it. Especially since you can't abide any of the help Emily brings to stay with you overnight."

Lillian pursed her lips in distaste. "I don't know where she finds these women. They scare me. She tells me that they're bona fide private duty nurses, but who's to say, really? They could be robbers. They could kill me in my sleep. There was a news show the other day that showed how easy it is for these grifters to impersonate any type of profession they please. Why, when you board an airplane you don't even know if a real pilot is flying it."

Luke sighed, hiding a smile. "You like having Sara here, don't you?"

"I trust Sara. I know she's not going to run off in the night with the silver flatware." She stared straight at Luke. "I can't say the same for you, however."

He stared right back at her. "The silverware must be hidden pretty well. I haven't found it yet."

That got her. Lillian choked on a bite of egg and had to wash it down with her tea. "That egg is like rubber," she informed him, regaining her composure. "I'm sure it wasn't two minutes."

"Two minutes and eleven seconds. Sorry."

She put down her spoon and rested her hands on the table. "So, what do you want from me? What are you driving at?"

"I want a cease-fire. Even countries at war take a break every once in a while. So let's agree to disagree. I want you to accept my presence in Sara's life, period. For her sake, not mine."

"Very noble."

"I have my moments."

"So I've heard." Lillian crossed her good arm over the one in the cast. "By accepting your presence I suppose you mean staying over in this house when she does, without me raising the roof about it?"

"That's the idea," he said encouragingly. "You know, I have some influence with Sara, too. If I told her it was uncomfortable for me to be here with you, or to have her stay here alone, she would listen to me."

"So, you're threatening me?"

Luke shrugged. "Not at all. I'm just giving you the big picture. Sara loves you, Lillian. Heaven only knows why . . . but she loves me, too."

"Don't fool yourself, the powers above are equally baffled on that one," she said dryly. She sighed and smoothed back her gray hair. "I suppose I'm in a losing position, sick and weak as I am. You are taking advantage of that. Doesn't that bother you?"

"No, not much," he said lightly. "So, was that a yes?"

Lillian's chin trembled. Finally, she nodded.

Luke's smile widened. Victory was sweet, sweet as orange marmalade.

He thrust out his hand. "Okay then, let's shake on it."

Lillian looked appalled for a moment, then when she saw he was serious she offered her good hand and he gently shook it.

"I'm doing this for Sara's sake," she said. "It's like abstaining from a vote. I still haven't given my blessing."

"I understand. Once you get your casts removed and you're back to your fighting weight, we can go at it again. I promise." He stood up. "I'd better get ready for work now. Your day nurse will be here any minute, but I won't go until she arrives."

"What a comfort," Lillian murmured.

"By the way, Sara wants you to look at these." He reached into his pocket and tossed a pile of paint chips on the table.

Lillian held one up and examined it. "What am I supposed to do with these?"

"Sara wants me to paint the room you're staying in. She says it's depressing. She was thinking of light blue or maybe yellow."

"The room *is* dreary," Lillian agreed. "Yellow would be nice. Nothing too bright," she added in a fearful tone. "A soft yellow, more of a vanilla color. Something English-looking, with white trim."

"That's the spirit." Luke patted Lillian on the shoulder, ignoring how she flinched at his touch. "There are going to be some changes around here, Lillian. Brace yourself."

"Oh bother. That's just what I didn't want to hear."

ON SATURDAY MORNING LUCY WAS SURPRISED TO FIND Charlie in the kitchen, cooking eggs and bacon for the boys' breakfast. He had gone out early to open the diner, and she expected him to stay there most of the day.

"Charlie, what are you doing home?" She poured herself a cup of coffee and sat at the table.

"I just went in to take care of the rush. Jimmy can handle the rest. I'll go back later; I'm on tonight anyway. The boys want to put up the Christmas tree now. Don't you remember?"

No, she didn't. The last thing Lucy wanted to do was put up the tree. She just wasn't ready. All the boxes up from the basement, all the decorations all over the place. She didn't need that mess today. She already had a huge one all over the house.

She had been working all week, either at the hospital or the diner, and in between that, going to classes. There was housecleaning, laundry and food shopping to do. How in the world could she stop everything and put up the tree?

"Do we have to?" she asked quietly. "I have to go into the hospital this afternoon, and I have a lot to do around here this morning."

Charlie dished eggs and bacon onto plates. "The hospital? On Saturday?"

"Margaret said if I made up the hours I missed when Jamie was sick, she would take away the absent grade, which is almost like an F. Which I don't need."

Charlie shook his head. "All I know is I paid a fortune for that tree. The boys had to pick out the biggest one on the lot. It's sitting in a bucket in the backyard and if we don't put it up today, there's going to be needles everywhere."

"Mom, we need to put the tree up. It's almost Christmas," Jamie reminded her.

It was already December ninth, Lucy realized. Christmas was closer than she wanted it to be.

"I made an ornament in art, see?" Jamie held up a tangle of red and green pipe cleaners, covered with glue and sparkly stuff that was falling on his eggs.

"Very nice, honey. What is that, a snowflake?" Lucy asked vaguely.

"It's a star."

"Oh, right. Nice." She glanced at Charlie. "Okay, we'll start right after breakfast. I'll go down to the basement and get everything."

"I'll help you." Jamie jumped up from his seat and followed her. He was happy, at least. His older brother sat hunched over his food and just rolled his eyes.

Lucy liked to decorate the tree at night. She would put on Christmas music and make hot cocoa, and Charlie would make a fire in the hearth. When the tree was all decked out, they would shut off the lamps and look at the Christmas tree lit up in the dark.

It didn't feel right to be doing this in broad daylight, but she couldn't stop to worry about the ambience. Charlie secured the tree in the stand and strung the lights while she sorted out the ornaments, placing the open boxes all over the room.

Each member of the family liked to hang certain ornaments. Her favorites were the angels and a set of ice skaters. Jamie was in charge of the nutcrackers, some animal ornaments, and Santa flying a helicopter.

Charlie had a set of round "Clam Box Diner" ornaments he liked to hang in a prominent spot, at about eye level. Every year he'd put them up and say, "Aren't these great? They're going to be collectors' items one day."

C.J. also had some ornaments that were his domain, but he just stood there with hands shoved into the pockets of his jeans, acting too cool to fool around with the Christmas tree. Then Jamie found the box of Red Sox ornaments—a bat and baseball and the official World Series Champions ornament—and they started to argue over who would hang them.

Lucy was quietly but quickly pulling the ornaments out of the boxes and hanging them one after the other, like a tree decorating machine. She had never decorated the tree this fast, but she didn't have time to waste, figuring out just the right spot to put everything. She would get everything on the tree and fiddle around with it later.

"Lucy, for pity's sake, don't you see what you're doing?" Charlie came out from behind the tree, where he had been adding an extension cord for the lights. "You've got everything bunched in one spot. The whole thing is going to tip over."

"Oh . . . I didn't realize." Lucy stepped back and took a look at her handiwork. He was right.

She started to unhook a few ornaments and move them around, but the hooks were stuck in the soft pine branches and that was even more time consuming. What a mess. She wished she hadn't gotten stuck with this job today because now she felt guilty for feeling so stressed and joyless about Christmas.

Most of the boxes were empty, and Lucy was ready to put the empties back in the basement when Jamie found the crèche.

"Mom, the manger. Where should I put it?"

Lucy could tell he was eager to set up the manger scene. Sometimes they put it under the tree and sometimes on a little side table. Lucy wasn't sure what she wanted to do with it this year. She hadn't given it any thought and didn't feel like she had time to deal with it now.

"Oh . . . just leave the box under the tree, honey. We'll do it some other time."

Jamie stared at her, looking confused, and Lucy felt embarrassed. Reverend Ben's sermon last Sunday had hit home, and she had promised herself to take his advice to heart—to try to cultivate a better attitude toward the holiday and keep herself and her kids focused on its real meaning. For Lucy the crèche had always represented the heart of Christmas.

But she just didn't have the time this morning to maintain that mind-set. She had to clean up around here, start the wash, get some groceries, and then get over to the hospital.

She didn't have time to fiddle around with the crèche right now.

"I'm sorry, honey. Just put the box under the tree. We'll do it later, I promise." She watched Jamie close the box and place it under the low branches, looking confused and disappointed. "I need to get some fresh cotton for the snow anyway," Lucy added, reaching for an excuse.

Jamie didn't seem to hear her. He took a stack of empty boxes and carried them out of the room.

Lucy glanced at Charlie and C.J. "Does anyone want hot chocolate?"

C.J. shook his head. "No, thanks. I just had breakfast."

"I don't want any." Charlie folded up the stepladder. "Guess I'll get back to the diner. You'll be in tonight to work, right?"

Lucy felt a cold fist in the middle of her stomach. "I told you I couldn't come in tonight, Charlie. I have to be at the hospital from two to six, to make up my course hours."

Charlie's eyes took on a familiar, resentful expression. "I thought you were going to be back in time. I didn't know you had to stay until six. That means you won't get to the diner until seven. That's too late."

"I didn't plan on going to the diner at all."

Lucy was sure she had mentioned her change in plans several times during the week. Sometimes Charlie only heard what he wanted to hear.

"What am I supposed to do now without a waitress? Close down on a Saturday night? Lucy, how much money is this nursing business supposed to cost me? Can you tell me that?"

Money again. It always came down to that. Charlie always managed to make her feel guilty about this luxury of hers, going back to school to learn a real profession.

"I can't miss my hours or I won't get the course credit. That would be a waste of money, too, Charlie."

Charlie pulled his cap on. "Do what you want. You always

do anyway. I guess you'll have to drop Jamie off on your way to Southport."

"I guess," Lucy agreed. C.J. was going to a basketball game with a friend this afternoon, and the other boy's parents would pick him up. Jamie would probably want to see a friend today, too, but Lucy would have to arrange it. Of course, she had to figure out the boys' social plans and driving arrangements on top of everything else.

Still, reflexively, she found herself wanting to make peace. "I'll ask Margaret if I can leave at five. That way I can come to the diner and help you, okay?"

Charlie nodded but didn't meet her gaze.

Lucy raced through her housework, accomplishing as much as she could in the few hours before she had to leave. Tomorrow was another day, but she had other items on her to-do list: Christmas shopping, writing a term paper, and studying for a test. She had volunteered to help with the Christmas Fair but hadn't made any of the meetings.

She hoped her life would be different once school was over and she got a real nursing position. She hoped she would be organized and wouldn't feel so stressed all time, but somehow she couldn't imagine it.

THE HOSPITAL WAS A WELCOME RELIEF FROM HOME ON Saturday afternoon. The floor was very quiet. By midafternoon, most of the patients were dozing and their daytime visitors had left. Even Margaret Sherman wasn't around to make Lucy nervous. Another nurse, Nora Martin, was there to supervise her. Nora was a few years older than Lucy and very calm and friendly. Although she watched Lucy carefully, Nora didn't make Lucy feel she was always on the brink of harming a patient or causing some disaster, and she didn't try to trip her up with trick questions, the way Margaret did. She even agreed readily when Lucy asked if she could leave early, suggesting that

Lucy make up the hour during the week. Best of all, she gave Lucy a good mark for the day.

Lucy found that she actually regretted leaving the peaceful, orderly atmosphere of the hospital. She dreaded working at the diner that night. But she had promised Charlie.

Unfortunately, her old car had different ideas. The car hadn't been working right ever since the snowstorm. Charlie thought there was water and ice in the gas line, but he hadn't had time to check it for her and didn't want her to spend money at a garage when he was sure he could fix it himself.

Meanwhile, Lucy had found herself stuck a few times this week. Just as she was at that moment, trying to make the engine turn over and hearing only a dull whirring sound.

She sat there in the cold, not knowing what to do. Charlie was going to be furious when she called him.

Lucy got out of the car and put up the hood. She peered inside at the engine. She didn't know what she was looking at, but thought it was worth a try.

"Having trouble with your car?"

Lucy turned around to see Jack walking toward her. He wore a dark blue down vest with a tan sweater underneath, jeans, and heavy boots. He looked like he had just walked off a ski slope.

"Oh . . . hi. Yeah, it won't start. I'm not sure what's going on. It's been sort of moody all week, ever since the storm." She looked up at him. "Do you know anything about cars?"

He shook his head and grinned. "Sorry, I only work on human beings. I could give it a shot of adrenaline."

Lucy laughed. "I'd better wait for a mechanic. But thanks."

"Do you need a ride? I'm going in to do rounds. But it shouldn't take too long. I could drive you home if you need a lift."

Lucy was sure he had better things to do on a Saturday

night than be a Good Samaritan and drive her around. "You must be busy. I don't want to ruin your plans."

"It's okay. I don't have any plans. Is there someone who can pick you up?"

"Well, not really. My husband is working tonight. He won't be able to get here until much later."

She knew Charlie wouldn't be able to leave the diner to pick her up, and she didn't know who else to call. Southport was a good forty miles from Cape Light.

"If it's not too much trouble for you . . . I really would appreciate a lift."

"It's no trouble." He glanced at his watch. "Why don't I meet you in the hospital lobby in about an hour?"

"Great. I'll look for you there."

Jack started off toward the hospital, and Lucy lowered the hood, removed her handbag and other belongings, and locked the car. Then she headed inside to call Charlie. Charlie wasn't going to be happy, but at least she had a ride home. That was one problem solved.

Lucy found a quiet spot in the hospital lobby and took out the books she had stashed in the backseat of her car. She started working on her paper, making notes from the textbook.

Nearly an hour later, Jack found her scribbling away, totally oblivious of his arrival. "You don't like to sit around and waste time, do you, Lucy?"

She smiled at him and began to stick her books and pad back in her bag. "I don't have any time to waste."

"What are you studying?" He glanced at the textbook she was holding.

"Microbiology. It's not so bad, or not nearly as bad as organic chemistry. I barely made it through that one."

"Me, too," he confessed. "Luckily patients don't get to see their doctor's transcripts from medical school. Or maybe that's not so lucky."

Lucy smiled at him. She had a feeling he was a good doctor, who was caring with his patients.

They walked out into the parking lot, where Jack led her over to his SUV. She noticed the ski racks on top and realized her impression had been right—he was a skier.

Jack started the engine and pulled out of the parking lot. The SUV's seats were roomy, soft leather and even heated. It was so different from Charlie's truck. Lucy felt as if she were driving around in her living room.

She glanced over at Jack, feeling a little strange. She had rarely been alone with an attractive man since getting married. It felt oddly intimate, alone in the car at night like this. It felt a lot like a date, she realized. Would she feel this way if someone else had come by to give her a lift? Reverend Ben, perhaps? Or Charlie's pal, Tucker?

Of course not. The truth was she found Jack attractive. She had a little crush on him. *These things happen,* she told herself. It wasn't the end of the world, but she really ought to feel silly for feeling this way.

"Are you okay?" Jack glanced over at her, and she turned from the window to look at him.

"Oh, sure. I'm fine. I was just thinking . . . about something." She cleared her throat, not knowing what to talk about. The funny thing was, it seemed they always had plenty to talk about at the hospital.

"Do you ski?" she finally managed to say. "I noticed the racks on top of your car."

"When I get a chance. My hours are pretty crazy. But it's actually better to go out on weekdays when the slopes are less crowded. Do you ski, Lucy?"

"Uh, no. I used to do a lot of ice skating. When I was younger." Wow, did that sound bad. He must think she was ancient. "Before I got married, I mean. Then I got too busy. Charlie doesn't like to ski or ice skate. He likes to go ice fishing once in a while."

"Ice fishing. That's pretty intense." She noticed his eyes and his strong profile as he concentrated on the road. Jack Zabriskie was handsome.

"Doesn't make much sense to me," Lucy admitted. "Give

the poor fish a break, for goodness sake. Don't they deserve a little time to hibernate or whatever?"

Jack laughed. "I totally agree."

It was quiet again and the silence made Lucy feel self-
conscious. "I bet you did have plans tonight, but you're too
nice to tell me. Am I right?"

He smiled but kept his eyes on the road. "I was going to
catch a movie later. No big deal."

Lucy wondered if he was going alone or with someone, then told herself it really wasn't any of her business.
Jack was young and unattached. He could do whatever he
pleased.

They passed a mall that was packed with shoppers, the
parking lot filled to the edge of the highway. "Everyone's
out Christmas shopping tonight. I haven't bought a thing,"
she confessed. "We put up our tree today. Maybe that will
get me in the spirit."

Lucy remembered Jack was recently separated from
his wife. Had he put up a tree on his own? She somehow
doubted it.

"Do you have plans for the holidays?" she asked.

He shook his head. "I grew up in Pennsylvania, near
Pittsburgh. My family is all down there. I guess I'll visit for
Christmas if my hours work out." He glanced at her. "I
might just skip it though, go skiing instead."

Lucy was quiet for a moment. "The holidays can be hard.
You feel as if you should be happy, but not everyone is."

"Yeah, that's it," he said. "I think I told you that my wife
and I split up. My family knows about it, but it's still hard
to go down there alone. I guess I'm not really in the mood
for Christmas this year."

"I'm not either," she confided. "I just feel too busy. But
you can't skip it when you have kids. Christmas is such a big
deal for them. So I try to make an effort for them, to give
them a nice day."

He smiled at her. "I bet you give them a great day. Do
they still believe in Santa?"

"They're both too old for that. But they still wake up early and rush downstairs for their presents. Jamie, the younger one, asked for these boot things with wheels on the bottom. So he can roll around town and break his neck—Rollies, I think they're called. I bet I'm going to be standing on some long line tomorrow for those."

"Get me some while you're at it. I'm a size eleven." Lucy laughed at him. "I'm not kidding. Can you imagine doing rounds in Rollies? I'd be done in no time."

"I'll look for your size, but I'm not promising anything."

"I would like to have kids someday," Jack said quietly. "I feel like I'm getting older and I'm missing out."

Lucy was surprised by his confession. She had often heard women say they wanted children, but rarely men.

"You have lots of time, Jack. Don't worry. You'll have kids. I'm almost sure of it."

"Thanks, I hope so." He glanced at her. "I bet you're a great mom. I bet your kids adore you."

Lucy felt herself blush and was thankful for the dark.

"I wish I had more time to do things with them," she confessed. "They grow up so fast, it's amazing."

He smiled at her and she smiled back. She felt a special connection to him, a spark that was more than friendship. It made her feel attractive and interesting . . . and guilty, too.

Jack turned off the main road, and they were soon in Cape Light. The harbor came into view and the snow-covered village square, a perfect backdrop for the town Christmas tree.

Main Street was decorated with garlands of white lights swooping over the avenue and pine wreaths with red bows on all the streetlights. The shop windows were filled with holiday displays, with golden ribbons on miniature trees, and miniature train sets, circling them.

"I forgot how pretty this town is," Jack said. "I don't get here very often."

"It's a nice place to live all year long. But it really shines at Christmastime," Lucy agreed.

They drove a bit farther down the street, and Jack parked in front of the Clam Box.

"You must be hungry," Lucy said. "Would you like to come inside and get a bite to eat? On the house, of course."

"Thanks, but I'd better head back. Maybe another time."

"Anytime at all. Bring a friend," she added. "I can't thank you enough for helping me."

"It wasn't anything, Lucy. That's what friends are for."

So, he thought she was a friend. She would have to think about that. Later.

Lucy gathered up her handbag and book bag, got out, and said good night to Jack. Then she turned toward the diner. Charlie had hung a Christmas wreath on the door and some twinkling lights across the window. She would have to do more decorating here, but it was a start. Lucy felt in a better mood about the holidays. Maybe shopping tomorrow wouldn't be that awful. Maybe she would look for some little token for Jack. To thank him for helping her out tonight. That wouldn't be too much, she thought. Would it?

# CHAPTER ELEVEN

~

*Cape Light, Present-day*

"Emily, thank goodness you've come. They're taking over, I tell you! They're turning this place into . . . Santa's Workshop!"

Sara looked down from the ladder at her grandmother who sat stiffly in her wheelchair, waving her good arm over her head, as if signaling for help on a desert island.

Sara was sorry that Lillian was so upset. Then again, she had warned her that they were going to decorate.

Emily walked in and kissed her mother's cheek. Emily had promised to come straight from church, but after the service she told Sara and Luke she needed to stay for the Christmas Fair meeting. Lillian was not happy to hear that and had interrupted with several frantic calls. Finally, Emily was here. Sara thought she might be almost as relieved to see her as Lillian was.

"Calm down, Mother. The place looks beautiful." Emily turned to look at the living room, which had been remarkably changed in only a few days. Luke had painted, and

Sara had taken down the heavy damask curtains and replaced them with some golden sheers she found in the attic.

"I don't know what you're complaining about. You should be grateful to Sara and Luke for going to all this trouble for you."

"Grateful? Who ever asked them to decorate my house like some department store window? I certainly never did!"

Lillian made a sour face and tugged at the crocheted shawl tucked around her shoulders. "All this light, it hurts my eyes. I liked the heavy curtains. They kept the sun from fading the furniture."

Sara finished tacking pine boughs around the carved wooden mantle and started to climb down from the ladder. She had already secured garlands above the arched entrance ways that separated the large rooms and then had wound wide ribbon around all the columns and the long banister on the stairway.

Luke was outside decorating, as per Sara's orders. She had sent him out with yards of icicle lights, more pine roping, and a huge wreath for the front door.

"Everything looks beautiful, Sara," Emily said, ignoring her mother. "Are you going to put up a tree?"

"Right over there, by the bay window." Sara showed Emily the spot that had been cleared for the Christmas tree. "It's out on the porch. We picked it up last night."

"A tree? You mean a large tree?" Lillian rolled toward them, using her good hand to move the chair.

"Lillian, I told you we were going to buy a tree. I even told you where we wanted to put it. Don't you remember?"

"I thought you meant some tabletop decoration, the kind you always get for me. That's enough trouble as it is."

Every December since Sara had moved to Cape Light, she brought her grandmother a tiny Christmas tree and decorated it for her. Lillian always acted as if she didn't care one way or the other, but Sara knew their little ritual was important to Lillian.

"Oh, Mother, it will be good for you to have a real Christmas tree for once," Emily said. "I can't remember the last time you had one in here."

"And for good reason," Lillian snapped. "The needles get all over the house, stuck in the carpet, in the upholstery. You find them in your food if you're not careful."

Emily bit back a smile. "It sounds as if Sara and Luke have already bought the tree. I suppose you'll just have to deal with it."

"We'll be very careful about the needles," Sara promised. "We'll certainly keep them out of your food."

Lillian frowned. "That's what you say now. Just wait until you find me choking to death. I've really never understood this strange tradition—chopping down a tree and dragging it into your house and making a positive fetish out of it. It's positively pagan. Next thing I know you and your new husband will be painting yourselves blue and dancing around a bonfire."

Sara had to cover her mouth to keep from laughing out loud. "Now there's an idea for a New Year's Eve party, Lillian. We did want to do something different this year."

Emily sat down on the couch near her mother. "It is their first Christmas together, Mother. It's a special time for them, and they want to make it memorable. Didn't you and Dad feel special about your first Christmas together?"

"What difference does that make? It's my private memory. It only has meaning for me," Lillian snapped, but Sara saw a strange expression cross her grandmother's face. Neither Emily nor Jessica mentioned their father often. Sara knew that he was a touchy subject for the Warwick women. On one hand, his memory seemed idealized; he was always portrayed as a larger-than-life figure who charmed everyone he met, including his two daughters. On the other hand, there were dark, unhappy memories of the family's disgrace and fall from fortune, and Oliver Warwick had been the cause of it all.

"Memories are all you have when you get old," Lillian

went on in a bitter tone. "The only place you feel alive again is remembering the past. The present is a sham. Everyone pretends to include you, but you're really only a bystander. You have no say anymore, not even in your own home. I'm much happier in the company of ghosts and shadows now. Ghosts and shadows . . . who understand me."

"Oh, Lillian," Sara said, suddenly feeling awful about everything she had done. She had thought she was helping, trying to clean and freshen up the old house. She hadn't realized that her grandmother felt as if she was being pushed to the sidelines, her wishes ignored.

"I'm so sorry," Sara went on. "I thought you would be pleased with the decorations and everything. We don't have to put up a tree if you don't want one."

Lillian sighed heavily, met her granddaughter's remorseful gaze, and looked away. "Christmas tree, no Christmas tree, what does it matter? You bought the thing, paid good money for it, I'm sure. Just put it up now and get it over with. I can stand it this once, I suppose. It won't kill me."

"No, it won't kill you," Emily agreed. "It might even cheer you up a bit, Mother. I think it's been good having Luke and Sara here. Look how much they've helped you."

Lillian didn't answer at first. She worked on the fringe of her shawl, smoothing it out with her long fingers. "He painted my room. Did you see it?" she asked Emily.

"No, I haven't. How did it come out?"

Lillian shrugged. "It looks cleaner. The color looked different on the little card from the hardware store. It's a bit brighter than I expected."

Sara and Emily exchanged a look. Of course it was. That went without saying.

"Let's go take a look. I want to see it." Emily got up and pushed Lillian's chair toward the bedroom. Sara stayed behind in the living room. She had brought down some boxes of Christmas decorations from the attic. Now she carried them over to the spot where she and Luke planned to put the tree, feeling deflated by her grandmother's anger. But what did she honestly expect? Maybe once the tree was up and decorated, Lillian would relent and maybe even take some pleasure in it.

Sara was sure that her grandmother had some special memories of Christmas that were precious to her, that cheered her. Even if she didn't want to share them.

## Boston, November 1955

LILLIAN FOLDED AN EXTRA SWEATER AND PLACED IT IN her bag, then took it out again. Did she have enough warm clothes? It would be colder up in Cape Light and Newbury-port, especially out on the beach. But thick sweaters and pants weren't very attractive. She knew it was an acceptable style for women now and very practical, but she wasn't used to wearing trousers like a man.

She felt confused and couldn't keep her thoughts straight. She was usually so quick and efficient at packing. But this was . . . different.

Beth lounged on Lillian's bed, paging through a copy of *Life* magazine. "I didn't know you were going away again this weekend. I thought we were going to the movies to-morrow night. Why didn't you tell me?"

Lillian bit her lip. She had forgotten her promise to take Beth and her girlfriend to the movies. Beth was grumpy because she didn't want Lillian to go away. She missed her and didn't like being stuck all alone in the house with their parents. Lillian couldn't blame her. In a few years Beth would be going away to college, and then Lillian would be stuck here alone—unless she got married.

"I'm going up to see Charlotte. She's having a party and wants me to be there. I thought I told you."

"Can I come?"

Lillian shook her head. "Sorry, I don't think so. Besides, you would be bored. There's no one there your age."

Beth sat up. "I can't imagine how you're not bored up there in the wintertime. What is there to do? You can't go to the beach. You never even liked it there when we used to go for summer vacation."

Lillian added the red sweater again and smoothed it down on top of the pile. "Of course I like it. It's very pretty. Besides, I like to get out of the city once in a while and go someplace quiet."

Beth flopped back against the pillows and watched her older sister move around the room. "It's a guy, right? And Mom and Dad don't know."

Lillian felt a little jolt. Beth had guessed so easily. Would her parents guess, too? "I told you, I'm just going to see Charlotte. I think you're reading too many of those *True Romance* magazines. I saw them hidden under your bed," she teased.

"Don't try to distract me, Lily. I think we have a true romance right here, a juicy one, too." Beth stood up and walked closer to Lillian. "Go ahead," she whispered. "You can tell me. I won't tell a soul, I promise." She stared at Lillian expectantly then drew an X over her heart.

Lillian felt a tender rush toward her little sister. Beth was so sweet, so dear to her. She knew her little sister would never betray her to their parents. In fact, she would probably do her best to help Lillian cover up if it ever came to that.

Lillian had been aching to take someone into her confidence. So far, Charlotte was the only one who knew. More than happy to help the romance along, Charlotte had invited Lillian up for weekend visits so that she could secretly see Oliver.

But Charlotte got so excited whenever Lillian tried to talk about Oliver rationally—the way she felt torn between her feelings for him and her loyalty to her family—that Charlotte hardly heard a word of it.

Lillian sat down on the bed and looked up at Beth. "Yes,

it's a man. He's very nice. He's wonderful, really. But don't tell Mom and Dad. Promise me?"

"Oh, Lily!" Beth sat down next to her, her eyes bright, her voice low and excited. "That's so romantic! Is he handsome? What does he look like?"

"Yes, he's very handsome. And very smart and charming. I think you would like him, and I know he would adore you."

"But why can't he come here? Why can't I meet him?" Lillian didn't answer right away. "Oh," Beth said softly. "It's that Oliver fellow, isn't it? The one father wants to have arrested."

Lillian gripped her sister's hands. Her own hands were like ice. "Yes, it is. But don't tell, Beth. Please? He's not at all the way they say. . . . You believe me, don't you?"

Beth nodded, her expression serious. "I'm sure he's a good person if you think so, Lily. You're so particular. Mom and Dad will just have to try to understand."

"I hope so," Lillian said.

"Don't worry. They will." Beth leaned over and hugged her, suddenly seeming older and wiser.

Lillian hugged her back, giving her a hard squeeze, then stood up and closed her suitcase. "I'd better go or I'll miss my train. Look, I'll try to get back early on Sunday. Maybe we can still do something."

"Promises, promises," Beth joked. She picked up a sweater Lillian had left on the bed. "Can I borrow your blue sweater this weekend? It goes perfectly with my poodle skirt, and I'm going to a dance tonight. Please?"

"But, Beth . . . that's cashmere." Lillian's resistance faded as she took in Beth's pleading expression. "Okay, just this once. Don't spill anything on it—or else!"

Beth hugged the sweater to her chest, looking pleased. "Don't worry. I won't." Then she added in a whisper. "Your secret is safe with me."

"Thanks. I hope my sweater is, too."

*Blackmail,* Lillian thought, smiling to herself. She knew Beth would never give her away, but a little insurance never hurt.


THE TRAIN RIDE FROM BOSTON TO CAPE LIGHT TOOK nearly two hours. Lillian had a seat by the window and a book open in her lap but her thoughts kept drifting. She had been meeting Oliver at least once a week, sometimes more often when he came into the city and stayed over in the apartment his family owned. This was the third time Lillian had gone up to see him under the guise of visiting Charlotte.

Her parents didn't seem to suspect anything unusual, though once they asked her if she ever ran into him in Newburyport. Lillian had assured them that she had not. She knew her uncle Joshua and aunt Rebecca were keeping close tabs on her, too. But with Charlotte's help it was easy to arrange meetings with Oliver all weekend long.

Although Charlotte had been good at keeping her secret, Lillian knew that sooner or later, the truth would get out. Secrecy and subterfuge were not her nature. She had always prided herself on being straightforward and honest, no matter what the cost. All this sneaking around and lying to her parents made her feel guilty and unhappy. Though once she was with Oliver, it seemed worth all the trouble, and more.

She wanted to bring Oliver home to her family; she just couldn't see how. They despised him, sight unseen, and had already forbidden her to see him. If they ever knew that she had been carrying on this romance, they would never trust her again. Lillian didn't know what to do. She felt trapped, painted into a corner. Her feelings for Oliver were serious—she couldn't deny them anymore—yet there didn't seem to be any way her parents would accept him, so how could their relationship ever lead anywhere?

She felt frightened and for the first time in her life, powerless to solve her problem.

The train track ran along the shoreline, and Lillian stared out at the gray-blue sea and a wintry sky with low, gray clouds. She pictured Oliver, the way his brilliant smile would light up his face the moment he saw her and the way his strong arms would feel hugging her close. For the moment, the vision eclipsed all her worries and misgivings.

When the train pulled into the Newburyport Station, Lillian was one of the only passengers who got off. Oliver ran up to meet her, greeting her with a long, tender kiss. He grabbed her bag, and they walked over to his car.

"How long do you have, Lily?" he asked as they pulled out of the station.

"About an hour and a half. Charlotte said she'll come pick me up. But you never know—my aunt might come instead, so I'd better get back there on time."

Lillian and Charlotte had worked out a scheme so that Lillian could spend time alone with Oliver. They pretended Lillian had taken a later train to Newburyport, and Oliver would drop her off at the station there just before it arrived.

"Only an hour and a half?" Oliver sighed, pushing the car into gear. "Beggars can't be choosers, I guess. Someday I'll have you all to myself. Every day, every minute."

Lillian glanced at him but didn't answer. She had stopped scolding him for his high-flown, romantic comments. Secretly, she had come to expect and even enjoy them.

Oliver drove into the village of Cape Light, and Lillian admired the decorations on Main Street. There were pine wreaths on doors and garlands across storefronts. The antique lampposts were circled with red and white ribbons, like giant candy canes. The town looked cheerful and inviting, a dusting of snow on the ground adding to the holiday feeling.

As they passed the Clam Box, Lillian said, "I notice your friend's restaurant is still in business."

"Yes, Otto's doing very well. You can hardly get a seat in there at times."

"I suppose you never know," she said, surprised to hear the restaurant was prospering.

He laughed at her. "No, you don't, do you?"

Oliver drove down to the village green and parked near the harbor. The dock was empty and quiet compared to the summer day when they had strolled around here. There were only a few boats moored in the water, which was a dark blue-gray, the choppy waves topped by white caps.

At the far end of the green, Lillian noticed the old stone church. "That's a pretty church. Do you go there?"

"My family does. My mother grew very close to Pastor Whitaker after my brother died. He's getting on now. I suppose he'll retire someday."

She glanced at him curiously. "Do you believe in God, Oliver?"

He gave a short laugh. "Yes, I do. I doubt you'll find a single man who lived through combat who doubts the existence of God."

"I don't mean at some awful moment when you're terrified. I mean, all the time. Like right now, for instance."

He turned to face her, his expression serious. "Yes, I do, Lily. I don't go to church, though. Is that important to you?"

She looked out at the harbor, choosing her words carefully. "Doing the right thing is important to me, Oliver. You know I care for you, but I don't feel right sneaking around like this. It seems very wrong. You might think it's silly but . . . I can't help but feel that God is unhappy with us and somehow, we're going to be punished for all this lying and sneaking around."

"Oh, Lily. Please. Don't say that." Oliver sat up straight and shook his head. "God knows I love you with all my heart. That must count for something, don't you think?"

She was silent for a long time.

Finally she said, "Oliver, I've been thinking. I feel . . . trapped. Trapped in a puzzle that has no solution, no happy ending." She turned and looked into his eyes. "I'm afraid, I don't know what to do. I'm not sure I can meet you like this anymore."

He put his arm around her. "Of course there's a solution, Lily. And there will be a happy ending—you and I, together. Always."

"How?" she asked bleakly. "I can't see how it will ever work out."

"Look around you. Look at this place. Don't you think you could be happy here? It's not that far to go in to the city for the theater and museums and all the things you like to do. I would never keep you from all of that. Listen, we'll keep an apartment in Boston. You could go there any time you like, do what you like, see your family."

"Oh, my family . . . yes, I suppose."

"What do you think? Tell me honestly now."

Lillian sighed. She knew what he was asking her. She knew what she felt in her heart. She didn't have to think it over for a second. Yet it seemed like such a momentous leap to say the words out loud—a leap from one side of a mountain chasm to the other. She wasn't sure she would really make it.

"Yes, I could be happy here," she said quietly. "It's quiet and rustic. Very rustic," she added, causing Oliver to chuckle. "But the place has its own charm." She turned her head on his shoulder and looked him in the eyes. "If I'm with you, I know I would be happy anywhere."

"Lily." He wrapped his arms around her and kissed her deeply. Then he pulled back a bit and dug his hand into his pants pocket. He pulled out a small blue velvet jeweler's case, and Lillian's heart beat wildly. She had never expected this. Never in a million years.

Oliver turned to her and took her hands in his. "Lillian, I've loved you from the first minute I set eyes on you. I love you with all my heart and soul and always will. I'm the luckiest man in the world to have found you, and I'll be luckier still if you would agree to share your life with me. I'll do everything in my power to make you happy. Will you marry me?"

Lillian was speechless. She didn't have to think twice. She didn't have to think at all. She nodded her answer, tears filling her eyes. "Yes, I will. I love you, Oliver. I will marry you."

Oliver opened the box and took out the ring, a large, round diamond in a simple platinum solitaire setting. Lillian held out her hand and he slipped the ring on.

"Well, I'll be. Perfect fit." He laughed, looking a bit teary-eyed himself. "Do you like it? Say something, Lily."

Lillian had been staring at the ring, unable to quite believe the object that now circled her finger. "It's stunning. But it's so big, Oliver. You didn't have to get me such a large diamond."

"You're a tall woman, Lillian. I couldn't get you some tiny speck of a thing. You're going to need lots of jewelry before we're through."

He smiled at her tenderly then drew closer for a kiss. Lillian closed her eyes and kissed him back, her heart and soul full of love and happiness.

A few moments later, though, Lillian returned to earth. She couldn't help it. Her happiness was shadowed by worries about her family. She looked down at her ring again. "I don't know if I should keep this yet. I won't be able to wear it . . . until we tell everyone."

Oliver folded his hand over her own. "Of course you have to keep it. Don't worry about your family, Lily. Once they get to know me, they'll like me. You'll see. It was the same with you at first, wasn't it?"

"My parents are different," she insisted. "They won't be won over that easily. I don't think they'll even let you in the house."

"Oh, Lillian, be reasonable. It's not the Middle Ages. They can't keep you under lock and key." When she didn't answer, he added, "What will they do? Disown you?"

Her voice broke as she answered. "Yes. They will. They've already said as much."

"Love will find a way, my love," he insisted, trying to cheer her up. "One way or the other, we'll be together."

Before she could answer, he pulled her close and kissed her again. Lillian lost herself in their embrace, almost able to believe what he'd said was true and that everything would work out just as Oliver promised.

## Cape Light, Present-day

EMILY HAD TO LEAVE WHILE LILLIAN WAS SLEEPING; DAN had called to say that Jane needed her mother. Sara and Luke finished putting up the rest of the decorations and had the tree all ready for the ornaments. It looked beautiful, Sara thought, but she was no longer certain how her grandmother would react.

She walked quietly to her grandmother's room. Finding the door open a crack, she peeked inside. Lillian was lying on the bed fully dressed, a light blanket covering her. Sara started backing out of the room when one gray-blue eye opened.

"Spying on me?" Lillian asked.

"Checking on you," Sara corrected her. She walked into the room and turned on a low lamp on the bedside table. It was late afternoon, and the sun was already setting. "Emily had to go. She said she'll be back tomorrow. She won't be able to bring you in for your checkup on Tuesday, so Luke and I will take you."

Lillian struggled to sit up, fending off Sara's offer of help. "I see everything's been arranged without consulting me, as usual."

"You were sleeping. We didn't want to wake you."

"As if it would make any difference if I were awake. I can tolerate your husband living in this house now, since it seems necessary. But must he be part of my every waking hour? Must he be escorting me to my doctor's appointments, as if . . . as if . . ."

"As if he was actually related, you mean?" Sara's tone was flat and sarcastic.

Lillian sighed heavily. "I think I've been very tolerant, under the circumstances. I have been trying to accept your questionable choice, but it's hard." She looked up at Sara. "I don't want to make a problem in the family, though."

Sara wanted to laugh. Since when did her grandmother ever avoid making a problem for anyone?

"This particular pill would have been easier to swallow if you had had a real wedding," Lillian added, leaning back on her pillows. "This running off and eloping, it's very romantic but too great a shock. It doesn't help one accept the situation."

"I suppose that's true," Sara said. "I never thought about it quite that way."

"All these elaborate, drawn-out marriage preparations are not just about the wedding. They help everyone get used to the idea of the couple being married, even if the match is not ideal. But you and . . . that man upstairs . . ." She avoided saying Luke's name, as if he were an anathema to her. "You and he skipped that step and I, for one, am having trouble playing catch-up."

Sara knew she had to take this with a grain of salt. She was sure that if she and Luke had had a real wedding, Lillian would have spent the months leading up to it objecting loudly—just as she had when Jessica had married Sam Morgan. So in a way, her elopement had spared a lot of hard feelings.

But her grandmother did have a point. "I think that's probably true," Sara agreed. "A wedding or any kind of celebration does make a marriage feel more real somehow."

Lillian nodded. "It's important to celebrate a marriage and for everyone to think positively, no matter the circumstances."

Sara sat on the edge of the bed. "I've been talking with Emily about having a party. There's a restaurant in Newburyport that she found. It's very pretty." She looked up at Lillian. "But we're not sure now when the party would be. I don't want to have any kind of family celebration until you're better. You won't be able to come with all those casts on."

Lillian looked surprised. "You're putting it off because of me?"

"You want to be there, don't you?"

"I can't be choosey about the parties I attend at my age. I accept all invitations. The next might be my last, you know."

Lillian always spoke as if she were at death's door, but Sara knew that was all talk. Lillian would probably outlive them all. Of course, she couldn't let Sara think being part of her wedding celebration was special to her in any way.

Sara glanced at her grandmother and took a breath. "I have another idea for a party, too. I was thinking about this while I was decorating. I was thinking, what if we had the party here—at your house?"

Lillian's eyes widened. "In this house? Your wedding party?"

Sara nodded. "Emily had her engagement party here. It was really beautiful."

"Oh, that debacle. I barely survived once those clumsy caterers got through with it. Jessica had to lock me in my room."

"Lillian, it wasn't that bad," Sara said with a laugh. "I just think it's such a beautiful old house. The rooms are enormous. There would be plenty of space for all the guests, and I know it could look beautiful with the right decorations and a little more fixing up."

"The fixing up is what I'm afraid of. You won't paint the dinner room Day-Glo orange, will you?"

"Of course not." Sara took heart. Was her grandmother seriously considering this idea?

"Does your mother know about this scheme? Is she in on it with you? She's been waiting for a good excuse to come in here and *renovate*." Lillian practically spat out the word.

"No, I didn't talk to her about it. I wanted to ask you first."

"Oh, there's a switch. It's usually a done deal by the time I get wind of anything important."

"So, will you think about it?"

Lillian glanced at her for a moment. "Yes, I'll take it under consideration. There will be limits, of course, to what I will allow to be altered, moved around, et cetera."

"Yes, I understand." Sara decided she would quit now while she was ahead. "Would you like to come into the living room? Luke and I are ready to put ornaments on the tree."

"Do you have the tree up already?" Lillian seemed surprised at their progress. "You must be very careful with the ornaments, Sara. They're extremely fragile—hand-blown glass from Switzerland and Italy—and valuable family heirlooms. I don't want anything broken—"

"Of course not. That's why we want you to help us. To tell us where everything should go."

Sara knew Lillian would direct anyway, but she wanted her grandmother to feel that she and Luke recognized her authority—even if they had turned her house upside down the last few days.

Lillian took a deep breath. "All right. I'll come out in a minute. Just let me get my bearings. Would you bring me a cup of tea?"

Sara nodded and rose from her seat on the bed. "That's no trouble. I'll be right back."

### Boston, December 1955

LILLIAN SAT IN HER USUAL PLACE AT THE LONG DINING room table. She couldn't eat a bite; her stomach was jumping with nerves. No one seemed to notice, though. Her younger brother, Lawrence, was home from Princeton on his holiday break, and all eyes were turned his way. Her father had picked Lawrence up at the train station last night, and this was their first dinner together as a family. Her father was drilling Lawrence about his term, how his exams went, and what grades he expected.

"The history final was harder than I expected," her brother admitted. "There were two essay questions, and I had to take the full two hours to finish."

"Take your time," her father advised. "You shouldn't rush through these examinations, Lawrence. This year is very important for you. You won't get into Harvard Law with less than an A-minus average."

"What about that fellow you know who's going to help him?" her mother asked. "That judge something or other. I thought he was going to write a recommendation."

"He will write a recommendation. He'll write a very persuasive one. But the boy needs the grades to back it up."

As usual, her father got very agitated whenever his son's future was discussed. Lillian wasn't sure what her father would do if Lawrence didn't get accepted to Harvard Law. Throw himself into the Charles River maybe? Or throw Lawrence?

She had done her undergraduate and master's studies at Wellesley and had been accepted to start her doctoral work at Harvard, but her father didn't seem to take much notice of it, except when he complained about the tuition bills.

The dinner plates were cleared and the maid brought out fruit and dessert. Nancy came to the dining room door then. She looked straight at Lillian, and Lillian felt her heartbeat race.

"There's a young man to see you, miss. Shall I show him in?"

Her parents both stared at her. "Are you expecting someone, Lillian?"

Lillian didn't answer. She nodded at the housekeeper. "Yes, show him into the library, Nancy. I'll be right up."

Then she stood up and slowly pushed her chair back under the table. Her legs felt like jelly, and she had to hold on to the back for support.

"You haven't answered us, Lillian," her mother said more sharply.

Lillian felt them all staring at her. Beth met her eyes then looked away. Even though Lillian hadn't told Beth about her secret engagement, she could tell her little sister had already guessed who their visitor was. Well, it was time they all knew.

"It's Oliver Warwick. He wants to speak to you, Father. To both of you," she added, glancing at her mother.

Her father sat back in his chair, looking red-faced and shocked. "Warwick? What the devil is he doing here? Did you know he was coming here, Lillian?"

She could see he didn't understand what any of this signified, and she didn't dare start explaining it to him. Not without Oliver at her side.

She turned and walked quickly toward the door. "Just come with me to see him, please? That's all I ask of you. It won't take very long."

Her father jumped up from his chair and tossed his napkin on the table. "You're darned right it won't take long. I'll have that bum out on his ear." He looked over at a baffled Lawrence. "Come with me, son. I may need your help."

The entire family paraded out of the dining room and climbed up one flight to the library. Lillian heard them a few steps behind her. She opened the library door and saw Oliver standing there, scanning the titles in the bookcase. He turned and smiled when she walked in. He held two bouquets of long-stemmed roses. He wore an elegant navy-blue suit and a burgundy silk tie. He looked perfect, she thought. She had to hold herself back from running into his arms.

"Hello, Lillian. I hope I'm not too early?" He glanced at his gold watch.

"No, you're right on time."

"Good. These flowers are for you." He handed her a bouquet. "And these are for your mother."

Lillian was too nervous to think about flowers and set them aside on the library table.

"Do you have your ring?" Oliver picked up her hand and looked at her blank finger.

She nodded. "Right here, in my pocket."

"I think you should be wearing it."

"You're right. I should." Lillian took out the diamond ring Oliver had given her and slipped it on her finger.

He watched as she did it, then met her eyes and smiled. "It's going to be okay. Don't worry, sweetheart," he whispered.

Lillian glanced at the door. She heard her family coming. "I need to warn you. My father is very—"

Her father burst into the room, his glance searing as he took in Lillian and Oliver, standing close together, talking quietly. Intimately. He couldn't have looked any more shocked or disdainful if he had found them kissing, she thought.

She quickly stepped to one side of Oliver, but he reached out and lightly touched her arm, giving her a moment of courage.

"Hello, sir. I'm Oliver Warwick. You must be Lillian's father." Oliver stepped forward and held out his hand.

Albert Merchant stared at his hand but didn't take it.

"What the devil do you think you're doing here? Didn't I make myself perfectly clear in our last conversation? Do you want me to have you removed by the police? Or will you go willingly?"

Oliver squared his shoulders, still wearing a small smile.

"The situation has changed since our last conversation, Mr. Merchant. I don't think there's any need to call the police, sir." He was speaking in a very dignified way, Lillian thought. Not like a nervous twit, shaking in his boots, but not arrogant and disrespectful of her father, either.

"I hope you will hear me out, Mr. Merchant. What I have to say is very important. In fact, it's crucial to your daughter's future happiness."

"There's nothing you'd have to say that would be important to me, young man," her father shouted.

Lillian saw her mother creep forward from the doorway and tug on her father's sleeve. "Let him speak, Albert. I want to know what's going on here."

"Very well," her father said reluctantly. "What is all this about? Do you want permission to see Lillian? Well, we won't allow that. I thought I made that clear to you weeks ago."

Oliver smiled calmly. "I want permission to marry her, sir." He looked down at Lillian and took her hand. "Lillian has accepted my proposal. We're engaged."

Lillian looked back at her parents' pale, shocked faces. Her mother put her hand to her throat and sat down heavily in a chair. Her father's face turned beet red, his eyes bulging.

"Engaged? You can't be engaged! That's impossible."

Oliver's expression grew serious. Lillian could sense him digging in, holding his ground. He wasn't the least bit cowed by her father's temper. She could see that underneath Oliver's casual, breezy attitude, there really was a steely backbone.

"We are, sir. I've given her a ring and she's accepted." He turned to Lillian, who held out her hand. Her father took a step forward and stared at the diamond.

Lawrence gaped over his shoulder. "Wow, that's some rock!"

"Lawrence! Behave yourself," her mother scolded. She was sniffling quietly into a handkerchief.

"So I see. A ring. So what? That doesn't mean anything," her father scoffed. "Lillian will just have to give it back to you. I suppose you two have been sneaking around behind our backs, lying to us all this time and betraying our trust. Haven't you, Lillian?" he shouted.

Lillian shivered and Oliver put his arm around her shoulder. "You left us little choice, sir, considering your attitude toward me, sight unseen. You've listened to a lot of rumors and hearsay. I'm not the man you seem to think I am.

"All I ask is the chance to prove that I'm worthy of your daughter. We can have a long engagement, as long as you like. I can give Lillian a good life, everything she's ever hoped for. If love counts for anything, she'll never find a man who could love her more than I do."

Lillian's eyes were locked on her father. Was he swayed at all by Oliver's plea?

"We want your blessing, Father," she spoke up. "We want both of your blessings," she added, looking over at her mother.

"Oh, Lillian! How could you do this to us?" Her mother was sobbing, covering her face with her hands.

"Over my dead body!" her father declared. "I've asked around about you, Warwick. I know all about you, and fine words can't change what you are and always will be. We may not be as wealthy as your family, young man, but we're decent people. I'm sure that you tricked poor Lillian into this secret romance—tricked and seduced her with your lies. She's a respectable young woman and will not be dragged into the gutter by the likes of you, a divorced, debauched . . . scoundrel!"

Her father moved toward Oliver, looking like he might deck him. Lillian stepped between them. "Dad, I love him. We want to be married."

"Don't be ridiculous! What do you know about love?" Her mother stepped up alongside her. "Come with me." She tugged on Lillian's arm, pulling her away from Oliver and toward the door. "Let your father handle this. And give back that ring!"

Her mother grabbed Lillian's hand and tried to pry the ring off her finger, but Lillian snatched her hand away.

"Lillian, are you all right?" Oliver started to follow her,

but as he walked across the room she saw her father and Lawrence grab him on either side and hold him back.

"Take Lillian upstairs, Ruth. We'll show Mr. Warwick to the door."

Lillian glanced over her shoulder as her mother pushed her out of the room, taking one last glimpse of Oliver, his wide, startled eyes and sad expression.

"All right, just don't hurt her," she heard Oliver say to her father and brother.

She stopped fighting. They had lost. She let her mother lead her up the stairs toward her bedroom. Beth followed slowly behind, sad and silent.

When they reached Lillian's bedroom, her mother practically shoved her inside. "Go on, get in there. I can't bear to look at you. Your father and I will come and speak to you when we're ready."

Lillian threw herself on her bed, muffling her sobs in her pillow. She felt as if she could cry for hours, until she was empty and hollow inside. There seemed no hope for her, nothing to live for, no reason to take another breath.

She wasn't sure how long she had been lying there when she felt a hand gently stroke her hair. "Poor Lily," Beth said. She knelt down beside the bed and Lillian turned to look at her. "So that was Oliver," she whispered.

"Yes, that was him all right."

"I thought he was wonderful—the way he stood up to Father and said how much he loves you. And he's so handsome."

He had been wonderful, Lillian thought, but it hadn't helped. "Oh, Beth, everything seems worse now than it did before." Lillian felt more tears welling up. "They'll never let me marry him. They won't even hear him out."

Beth stroked Lillian's hair again. "You can't give up now, not if you really love each other. That's the most important thing."

Lillian met her sister's gaze. "Yes, it is, isn't it?"

Her parents' recriminations and anger hurt her deeply,

but that was nothing compared to the heartbreaking despair she felt at the idea of never seeing Oliver again.

Beth gazed down at Lillian's hand as it rested on the blanket. "Is that a real diamond?" she asked quietly. "I've never seen one that large. His family must be very rich."

"Would you like to try it on?"

"Oh, can I?" Beth sat up quickly.

Lillian slipped the ring off her finger and slipped it on to Beth's hand. "It's so beautiful," Beth breathed. "It really sparkles." She twisted her wrist, letting the gem catch the light. "It's as if he's given you all these rainbows."

"It's a very high-quality stone," Lillian said, touched by her sister's reaction. Rainbows, indeed.

Beth took the ring off and handed it back to her. "It suits you, Lily. You sparkle when you're with Oliver. I never saw you like that before. You probably don't realize it, but you do."

Lillian smiled at her. "Thank you, Beth. You're right, I had no idea."

She did feel different at Oliver's side. Was that because she was sparkling?

"That's what it's all about, don't you think?" Beth asked.

"Maybe." Lillian gazed down at the ring then back up at her sister. "What would I do without you, Beth?"

Her sister shrugged. "Oh, you would get along. Once you marry Oliver, you won't even think about me."

"Of course I will. I'll always want to spend time with you, no matter who I marry." Lillian smiled bleakly.

If she ever married Oliver, she would be forced to give up a lot of things. She would be forced to make some very big choices.

# CHAPTER TWELVE

*Southport Hospital, December, Present-day*

THE FLOOR WAS VERY BUSY WHEN LUCY ARRIVED ON Friday morning. She was late, as usual, and rushed to catch up with her supervisor and the other students who were on morning rounds.

Lucy had not been to the hospital since Wednesday, and there were several new patients on the floor. That meant she had to read their charts and quickly learn what was going on with each one and what kind of care they required.

She found Margaret in a room with two patients, behind the drawn curtain that surrounded the bed near the window. From what Lucy could tell, the woman was recovering from abdominal surgery, and Margaret and another student nurse were checking the incision.

Finally Margaret pulled the curtain back and saw Lucy. "We've got our hands full this morning." She indicated the patient in the other bed, who was watching TV. "I need you to give Mrs. Geiger a bed bath, Bates. Then she needs to get out of bed and do some walking in the hall."

Mrs. Geiger looked alarmed. "I can't walk around. I just had surgery. I need to rest."

"A stent, laproscopic," Margaret said to Lucy, indicating that the woman had surgery to open an artery in her heart, but the surgeon had performed the procedure through a very small incision.

"It's better if you can get up and move around a little," Lucy said to the patient quietly. "You can go home sooner. If you lie in bed, you could wind up with complications like bedsores or pneumonia."

"Pneumonia?" The woman sat up, looking much more energetic. "I don't need that."

"Of course you don't," Lucy said kindly. "Let me get you cleaned up and I'll change your gown. And then we'll take a little stroll."

The woman smiled at her. "All right. I'll try."

Margaret watched as Lucy prepared the bed bath. Then another student nurse came in. She looked worried and the rubber gloves she wore had blood stains on them. That didn't look right, Lucy thought.

"I'll be right back, Bates. Keep going," Margaret said as she went to help the other student.

Lucy nodded and kept going with the bed bath. "I'm not scrubbing too hard for you, am I?" she asked, remembering her last complaint.

"Not at all. Feels good. I'm covered with that iodine stuff on my chest, see?" Mrs. Geiger pointed to the orange-brown stain that showed around her bandage. "That comes off, right?"

"Of course it does. You can probably take a shower tomorrow. This is just a quick clean up."

"Well, I appreciate it. My daughter and my grandchildren are coming this afternoon. I don't want to scare the kids."

"Don't worry. You'll look just fine for them," Lucy promised.

She knew she would be wildly busy today but made a mental note to come back later and see if Mrs. Geiger needed some help fixing her hair or putting on some makeup. It seemed silly and superficial, but when a patient felt as if they looked more like their "normal" self, they tended to feel better faster.

Mrs. Geiger was soon washed and wearing a clean gown. Lucy wondered if she should wait for Margaret to return before getting the patient out of bed. Margaret was really supposed to be watching everything the students did but, of course, she couldn't be in six places at once.

Lucy took a look around the bed and cleared some garbage off the bedside table. She noticed two IV bags hanging from the pole. One was very low and needed changing. She checked Mrs. Geiger's chart. She was a diabetic and taking insulin and also electrolytes for her heart condition.

"I'll be right back," Lucy said. "I need to find my supervisor, then we'll get you up."

Mrs. Geiger nodded and turned on her TV again, flipping through the channels. Lucy soon found Margaret a few doors down. Another student had been changing a bandage and a few of the stitches on the incision had come out. Not a grave matter, but the doctor had to be called, and Margaret and the student were with the patient, applying pressure to the wound while they waited for him.

Margaret glanced up at Lucy. "What is it, Bates?"

"Mrs. Geiger is ready to get out of bed. And her IV is very low," Lucy added.

"All right. I'll be right in."

Lucy nodded. She had noticed fresh IV bags left by the bed, so she went back to the room.

Margaret came in and gave Lucy an impatient look. "Can you do this quickly, or should I?"

"I can do it," Lucy said. She picked up the IV bag and made sure it was the insulin and not electrolytes, which were not needed yet. She attached the fresh bag, then checked the doctor's orders for the rate of the flow. She checked the meter on the line and then looked over the catheter on Mrs. Geiger's arm.

Margaret watched impatiently. "Yes, yes. That looks fine. All right, get her up carefully. First the chair, then see if she can do a few laps in the hallway."

"A few laps, that's a good one." Mrs. Geiger looked at Lucy and rolled her eyes. Lucy helped her over to the chair, and her supervisor disappeared.

Lucy cleaned up from the bed bath. One sheet felt wet, and she went to the linen closet to get a fresh one and a dry blanket.

When she returned she found Mrs. Geiger slumped over in her chair, her head on her chest. Lucy ran over to her, her own pulse racing. "Mrs. Geiger? What's wrong?"

Lucy leaned over and lifted her chin. Mrs. Geiger's mouth hung open and her eyes rolled back in her head.

"Oh no! Oh my . . ." She reached over and hit a button by the bed, signaling a patient emergency.

Within seconds doctors and nurses came running into the room, instantly followed by a huge medical cart. Jack was one of the doctors. Lucy was grateful to see him . . . and mortified.

He bent over and quickly examined Mrs. Geiger then looked at the IV bags and the meter on the line. Then he pulled the line out of the catheter. "Get her on the bed. She's gone into shock."

Margaret came up beside Lucy. "Wait outside, Bates. At my desk."

Lucy nodded. She felt the tears fill her eyes as she walked out into the hallway. She was such a screwup. Whatever made her think she could be a nurse?

She waited at Margaret's desk for what seemed like an hour, though when she looked at her watch she realized only ten minutes had passed.

Lucy wanted to leave—just walk out the door and keep going. But first she had to find out what had happened to Mrs. Geiger.

*Please, God. Please let her be okay. Please don't let her die. I couldn't live with myself if that happened. . . .*

At last Margaret emerged from Mrs. Geiger's room. "Over here, Bates," she said, steering Lucy to a quiet corner of the nurses' station.

"Did she come out of it? Is she going to be all right?" Lucy asked anxiously.

"She's come around. We caught her just in time."

"Oh, thank God." Lucy felt so relieved, she thought she was going to collapse. She looked up at her supervisor. "What happened? What did I do to her?"

"The insulin drip, didn't you check the doctor's orders? I saw you reading the chart."

"I set it to ninety, exactly as it said."

"It said forty, Lucy. You must have read the order wrong." Margaret rubbed the back of her neck wearily. "I should have checked, but I thought you could read a chart by now."

Lucy took a breath, fighting hard not to cry. "I did read the chart. It said ninety, as clear as day . . . well, as clear as I could see. I can't help it if these doctors have such horrible handwriting!"

Now she was crying and shouting at her supervisor. Margaret touched Lucy's arm. "Calm down, Lucy. It's over. The patient will be okay. *I* might get carpal tunnel from all the paperwork I'll have to do to report this, but *she'll* be fine."

Lucy thought of poor Mrs. Geiger, how she had pulled through her heart surgery so well and was looking forward to seeing her grandchildren today.

*Meanwhile, I come along and nearly kill her.*

Lucy wiped the tears from her cheeks. *Thank you, God, for letting her survive. Don't worry, I'm taking the hint. I'm not going to push my luck any further.*

"Lucy, why don't you take a break and compose yourself?" Margaret suggested.

Lucy shook her head. "I can't do this anymore. It's just not working out for me."

She pulled away and started walking quickly toward the elevators.

"Lucy? Where are you going?" Margaret called after her.

Lucy turned and looked at her briefly over her shoulder. "Back to the diner. I didn't quit my day job."


"IT'S ALL FOR THE BEST, TUCKER. THE BOYS NEED HER at home, and I need her here. Sure, I know she had her heart set on being a nurse, but she was never cut out for that type of work. Better she learned it now than later." Charlie leaned over the counter and spoke to Tucker Tulley in a near whisper, his eyes fixed on Lucy who was on the other side of the diner, taking an order.

Tucker, one of the village's finest, was also Charlie's best friend since childhood. He stopped in the diner every morning on his way to the police station, or for a coffee break if he was walking the beat.

He poured sugar into his coffee and stirred it. "That might all be true, Charlie. But it's a bitter pill to swallow, don't you think?"

"Sure, she's upset. It's only been, what, three or four days? She'll get over it, you'll see. Lucy never broods very long over things." Charlie flipped a burger onto one half of a roll and covered it with the other. "I bet she forgets all about this nursing school business by New Year's."

He set the plate on the shelf for outgoing orders but was careful to ring the bell lightly. It was late afternoon, the lunch rush was over, and the Clam Box was practically empty. There wouldn't be much action until dinnertime. Charlie wasn't sure if he was going to stay open that night with more snow predicted.

"So she's quit for good after all that school work." Tucker sipped his coffee. "That's a shame."

"That's what she says. I heard her on the phone this morning, talking to her school advisor. The woman wanted

Lucy to come back after the holidays and start over. But Lucy said, no, don't bother, she wasn't coming back." Charlie wiped the counter with a damp cloth. "I'm not pleased about her wasting all that tuition money but the truth is, I was glad to hear her say she was giving up."

Tucker frowned. "Poor thing. She must have had some scare."

"She read something wrong off a chart, and the patient went into a coma. Well, not a coma exactly. It was more like a fainting spell, I think. I bet it happens all the time, you just never hear about it."

"Doctors are only human. Nurses, too . . . even cops. I could tell you stories, believe me."

"Tell them to Lucy. Maybe it will cheer her up."

"Maybe she'll brood about it a while and change her mind." Tucker had always liked Lucy. He admired her for putting up with Charlie all these years and for having the guts to go for what she really wanted.

"Maybe," Charlie replied slowly. "But not if I can help it."

Lucy walked over and picked up the hamburger. "This had fries on the side, Charlie, lettuce and tomato on top." She handed the dish through the shelf to him, and he took it back to the grill.

"Hello, Tucker, how are you today?"

"I'm good, Lucy. How's it going?"

Lucy tilted her head to one side. "You must have heard from my husband that I dropped out of my training."

Tucker licked his lips. "Yes, I have. Sounds rough. Maybe you need a break."

"It's not as simple as that, Tucker. I wish it were."

"It's not that easy to give up your dream, Lucy. Not after all the work you've put into it."

"It is when you're a flop at it," she said bluntly. She glanced at him, her expression softer. "Thanks, Tucker. Nice try, but . . ." She shrugged and took the plate back from Charlie. "I'll see you later."

Tucker turned to Charlie. "I don't think I helped her very much."

Charlie scowled at him. "You didn't have to encourage her, Tucker. Just treat her normal, like good old Lucy. Like she never even tried to be a nurse, okay?"

"Okay, okay. You don't have to bite my head off. I was just trying to say something nice to her, that's all."

Charlie shook his head. "This is hard for me. Lucy is always the one bucking me up, you know? I'm not used to things being the opposite. It makes me nervous," he confided.

"That's marriage for you. You think you got it figured, and one day you get home and all the furniture's rearranged. You don't know what's what anymore."

Charlie looked out at Lucy, delivering the order, grabbing a pot of coffee and hurrying back to fill the customer's cup. The familiar sight should have been comforting to him. He'd gotten what he wanted. Everything was back to normal.

But Charlie felt a tightness in his chest. It didn't sit right. Lucy didn't look right. Her smile for one thing, it looked stiff and forced. Or her face held this blank expression. She was going through the motions. The light was on but nobody was home.

A SHORT TIME LATER, THE DINER WAS EMPTY. LUCY SET out clean place mats and silverware. Charlie stood by the big front window. "Hey, Lucy, come here. Look, the snow's starting."

Lucy walked over and looked out the window. She always got excited when she saw snow, like a little kid. She stared outside a moment but didn't say anything. Charlie saw that flat look in her eyes and felt his heart twist a little.

"Looks like we might have a white Christmas this year."

"Looks like it," she agreed.

Christmas was only a few days away, this coming week-end. He wondered if Lucy was ready, had done all the shopping for the boys. He put a hand on her shoulder. "Maybe we should close up early. Nobody will come in to-night with this weather. You probably have things to do for Christmas, right?"

"I could start wrapping the presents, I guess. And maybe do some baking."

"I might go up to the mall. I didn't get your gift yet," he confessed.

Lucy took a step forward, just far enough so that his hand no longer rested on her shoulder. "You don't have to buy me anything, Charlie. It's all right. We don't need to spend the money right now."

"Don't be silly. Of course I need to get you a present. I bet you got me one."

He knew for a fact that she had gotten him a new watch. A real nice one, too, with a lot of dials and gadgets on it, the kind he really wanted. Lucy had a knack for gift giving. She always seemed to find exactly what a person really wanted.

Lucy turned back to him and touched his arm. "Honest, Charlie. I can't think of anything I need. You've spent enough money on school. I'm going to put it back in our savings account, I promise."

How would she ever pay it back? She worked at the diner and hardly drew a salary. Unless she took a second job. He didn't want her to do that.

"Hey, don't worry about that now. We'll figure it out." Charlie put his arm around her. "Let's just try to enjoy Christmas. Jamie's getting so worked up, I think he's going to bust."

She smiled slightly, but didn't answer.

They stood together looking out the window for a mo-ment. There was hardly a soul on Main Street or even a car passing by. "Something about the snow makes everything so quiet, you know?" he said finally.

Lucy nodded and sighed. "I know what you mean. It covers over everything for a while."

### Boston, Christmas Eve 1955

IT WAS SNOWING, HEAVY WHITE FLAKES THAT FELL LIKE feathers. Lillian could hardly see across the street. There was a lot of traffic downtown, people hurrying to get home and start their holiday and last-minute shoppers marching through the snow with shopping bags.

She spotted Oliver standing in front of City Hall. He wore a long gray overcoat and a black Fedora. He stood very tall, turning his head from side to side, watching for her. He didn't seem to notice the snow at all.

Lillian nearly turned around and went the other way. She knew he hadn't caught sight of her. Finally, she forced herself to cross the street and waved to him.

Oliver met her as she stepped up on the sidewalk. He took her suitcase and kissed her on the cheek. "I was afraid you weren't coming."

"Here I am." She forced a bright note into her voice. She had had so many misgivings at the last minute, she nearly hadn't come.

"Are you ready?" He bent his head, trying to catch her eye. "No, don't answer that," he said suddenly. He took her arm and led her through the big plate glass doors.

It was an ordinary municipal building. Very dreary, Lillian thought. She sat on a wooden bench in a long, cold hallway while Oliver showed some papers to a woman at a window.

There were a few other couples waiting, too. Lillian didn't look at them. She looked down at her hands, covered in black leather gloves. She had always imagined herself getting married in a white gown and veil, not an overcoat and leather gloves.

She had always pictured herself getting married in a

church by a minister, surrounded by her family. Her father, walking her down the aisle, giving her away. Dressed in a long white gown and veil, wearing the pearls that brides in her family had worn for generations.

There was no one here but strangers. And Oliver.

Lillian felt like praying, but she didn't know what to say to God. *I'm sorry*, she started off. *I'm sorry to hurt my family this way. I hope someday they'll understand. Please bless us, dear Father. Please bless our marriage.*

Oliver came to sit beside her. He took her hand in his. She could tell he was nervous, though he was smiling.

They were called quickly and were soon standing in front of a judge or justice of the peace; Lillian wasn't sure what the man's exact title was. He went through his litany quickly. Lillian heard her voice falter when she spoke her vows. Oliver's voice was loud and clear.

Suddenly, they were married. She couldn't believe it.

Oliver swept her into his arms for a deep, soulful kiss. Then he hugged her close, practically knocking her off her feet.

"Congratulations," said the man who had married them. "Now would you step to the side, please? You just need to sign that paper and you're all done."

Lillian signed her name and then Oliver did, too. He led her outside and hailed a cab with his free hand. A large taxi pulled up right away and Oliver helped her inside.

"Well, where to? We can go see your family. I'm not afraid." He slipped his arm around her shoulder, pulling her close.

"Not yet," Lillian said.

Oliver leaned toward the driver. "The Ritz Carlton, please." As the cab pulled away he said to her, "We'll stay over tonight at the Ritz. Tomorrow we can go back to Cape Light and spend Christmas Day with my family. They'll be very pleased to hear we're married. What do you think of that?"

"All right." Lillian thought of her family, how she would

miss having the holidays with them. She had even left presents under the tree, though she doubted anyone but Beth would open them.

She would have to call soon and tell them she was married. She pictured her parents getting the news and how the house would be like a wake over the Christmas holiday, mourning her downfall. She felt sad again to have caused her parents so much unhappiness. She wished it could have been different.

But she didn't want to say anything about that to Oliver and spoil things. "Do your parents know we eloped?" she asked.

He grinned at her. "Of course not. What fun would that be, Lily? I can't wait to see the look on their faces tomorrow. They think the world of you. Actually, they think you're too good for me. I told them I was coming in to Boston to have dinner with some old army buddies. They'll be thrilled to hear I really came to marry you."

Lillian hoped so. She dreaded to think both of their families would be displeased by their marriage.

"Maybe we should hire a photographer to come with us, to capture the look on their faces when we tell them the news," Oliver suggested. "We didn't take any pictures back at City Hall."

"Oliver, that's ridiculous."

"Why not? We need some photographs to look at when we're old and gray, don't you think?"

When Lillian didn't answer he said, "You won't be sorry, Lily. Not for one single day. Not for one hour."

Lillian knew that could not possibly be true. Of course somewhere along the way, she would have her misgivings. She had some now that she wouldn't admit to. But when she looked in Oliver's eyes, she knew she had made the only choice she could make. Whether it was right or wrong, whether it would lead to her happiness or unhappiness, seemed beside the point.

"I reserved the honeymoon suite at the Ritz, just in case you wanted to stay in town," he confided. "Remember that day you came to meet me in the Public Garden? Our room looks right out on that spot. I made sure."

"Did you really?" Lillian asked with a laugh. "Don't you think that's being overly sentimental?"

He hugged her closer. "And what's wrong with that, Mrs. Warwick? We're married now. I can be as sentimental as I please."

He kissed her tenderly, starting their honeymoon, Lillian realized. She kissed him back, knowing at that moment she was happier than she had ever been.

### Cape Light, Christmas, Present-day

"LUCY? COME ON DOWN, WE'RE ALL WAITING FOR YOU." Charlie called her from the bottom of the stairs.

Lucy tied the belt of her robe and found her slippers. They had spent Christmas Eve with the Tulleys and had come home late. Lucy felt sleepy. Lately all she wanted to do was sleep. But she couldn't just loll around in bed while everyone waited to open their presents.

Charlie handed her a mug of coffee as she came into the living room. Jamie was already kneeling beside the tree, sorting out the presents and handing them around. C.J. sat on the couch, wearing a T-shirt and sweatpants and looking as groggy and grumpy as she felt. She could hardly tell his regular clothes from his pajamas anymore, she realized.

Usually Lucy handed out the presents. She knew what was in each package and got a little thrill waiting to see if the kids or Charlie would like what she chose for them. But she didn't have the energy for it this year. Jamie seemed excited to be given the job, and she was content to sit back and watch.

"Can we start opening these?" C.J. shook a small box. "Or are we waiting for a whistle or something?"

"Go ahead," Charlie said. "You go first, C.J. Let's take turns. I want to see what everyone got."

C.J. opened a small square box. Lucy saw his eyes bug out of his head as he realized what was inside. She and Charlie had bought him an iPod. That was all he really wanted, so they splurged.

"Wow, this is awesome! Thanks, both of you." C.J. hopped up and gave them each a kiss. How rare was that? Lucy couldn't help chuckling.

"You can change it for another color if you want," she said.

"That's okay. This is perfect." He was already hooking it together and fiddling with the controls.

Charlie looked at Jamie. "Okay, Jamie boy, your turn. Go for the big one, that's my advice."

Jamie grabbed his biggest box and tore off the paper. "Rollies! Aw-right!" His face beamed as he looked up at Lucy. "I really wanted these."

"Yeah, I know." Lucy nodded, feeling warm inside to see him so pleased with his present. The first two stores she had tried had been sold out. In the third she waited on line almost an hour to finally get her hands on a pair. But it had been worth it.

"No wearing those in the house or to church," Charlie said.

"Can I wear them at the diner? I can bus tables for you."

Lucy laughed. "Let's see how that works out. Maybe I'll get a pair, too."

"I got you a present I think you'll like a whole lot better," Charlie said to her. He pulled a small box out of his bathrobe pocket. Lucy was surprised. In the past when she told him to skip her Christmas gift, he had taken her at her word.

"Go ahead. Open it," he urged her.

Lucy felt a little nervous. She could tell from his expression that Charlie was excited to see if she liked his gift. She didn't want to disappoint him, but he wasn't that good at picking out gifts for her.

She pulled off the paper and found a small gold box.

She lifted the lid and could hardly believe what she saw inside. A diamond heart on a white-gold chain. Tucker had given his wife, Fran, a similar one for her birthday months ago, and Lucy had mentioned how much she liked it.

Charlie had remembered that? She would have never guessed he even heard her. And this one, more delicate than Fran's, was even lovelier.

"Well . . . do you like it?" He leaned closer, trying to read her expression.

"I love it. It's beautiful, Charlie. But you didn't have to get me such an expensive present. I thought we agreed not to spend a lot of money on each other this year."

"You need something nice once in a while, Lucy. Everyone does. Here, let me put it on for you."

Lucy handed him the box. She hadn't planned on wearing it right away. She still had a feeling it might go back to the store. This was really too extravagant a gift, and she didn't feel right accepting it. Not when she had made them waste so much money the last few years on her going back to school.

Charlie took the necklace out of the box, and Lucy turned so he could put it on her. She lifted her hair away and he fastened the clasp.

"There. Looks perfect," he said, admiring her. Lucy felt the heart with her fingertips. "Go ahead, go look in the mirror. Don't you want to see it?"

"Yes, of course." She walked over to the mirror in the dining room and looked at her reflection. It was a very pretty piece of jewelry. Very simple. Just the kind she wanted. Still, it didn't feel right to her to keep it. She didn't feel as if she really deserved it. She kept it on, though, for Charlie's sake.

Charlie opened his gift from her next, a Swiss Army watch with all the trimmings. He seemed thrilled with it, and she knew she had made the right choice.

The boys had been opening their other gifts, and there was paper and ribbon all over the living room. Jamie was already playing with a "make your own" motorized race car and had all the parts out on the coffee table. C.J. lounged back on the couch with his headphones on, leafing through a big book of sports photos.

Lucy smiled at the happy chaos. "I'm going to get breakfast ready," she told Charlie. "Then we'll see if we can get these two to put their presents down long enough to go to church."

THE CHURCH WAS PACKED ON CHRISTMAS MORNING. Just about every seat in the sanctuary was taken when the Bates family arrived. They found a few spots in a rear pew, and Lucy tried to collect her thoughts. It was going to be a full day. After the service she would cook dinner for her family and her mother. The Tulleys were coming over later for dessert and coffee. There would be more socializing and more presents to open, too.

Reverend Ben had started his sermon. Lucy hadn't been paying much attention. He was talking about the joy of giving, how that was the real gift of Christmas. "The way we find ourselves taking such pleasure in bringing happiness to others, with a gift specially chosen for each of them, with a card or a visit. Or even a fruitcake . . . okay, maybe not a fruitcake," he added, making everyone laugh.

"On a scientific note, there have been studies of something called 'do-gooders' high. Scientists have confirmed that when we help someone else or do a good deed, it actually changes our brain chemistry. It sets off certain chemicals that make us feel good, happy, and worthwhile. It boosts our self-esteem." He hesitated, then added, "I understand you can get the same effect from eating a bowl of ice cream, though you'll have to worry about working off those extra calories."

Lucy smiled. Reverend Ben had a way of communicating his spiritual messages in everyday terms. She always got something useful out of his sermons.

"I don't think we need a scientific study to tell us that it makes you feel good to do something nice for someone else, that it's truly better to give than to receive. We experience it most acutely on Christmas morning, watching the people we love open the gifts we've chosen for them. The trick is, to make it last all year long. To start giving outside the Christmas box. There are so many ways for us to give to each other throughout the year—to visit a friend, or take time to call a parent or some senior who might be shut in and lonely. To lend a helping hand to a neighbor, or even a stranger through some community project.

"We read in the Gospel of Matthew, chapter twenty-five, verse forty: 'Verily, I say unto you, Inasmuch as ye have done it unto one of the least of these my brethren, ye have done it unto me.' That is at the spirit, at the very heart of our faith.

"Let the spirit of this day carry you forward, with a giving heart throughout the year to come."

Lucy knew what Reverend Ben said was true. Maybe that was why she had wanted to be a nurse in the first place, why it had mattered so much to her. That feeling of helping made her feel good. It made her feel she was making a useful contribution to the world.

She would have to find something else now that made her feel that way. She wished she could shake off the heavy weight she had been carrying around inside, just for today. But she felt it deep inside, like a stone lodged where her heart should be.

She stood up when the chorus did and started to sing a Christmas carol she knew by heart. Somehow, she promised herself, she would get through the day.


SARA HOPED THAT HAVING EVERYONE OVER THIS AFTER-noon after church wouldn't be too much for Lillian. But without the visitors, her grandmother wouldn't have much of a holiday.

That morning, before church, Sara had set the table and gotten everything ready for the Christmas brunch. She had worried that Lillian wouldn't have anyone with her during the service and wondered if she should stay home.

"I can manage on my own for an hour," Lillian had scoffed. "I'm not going to spontaneously combust."

Luke started laughing. "Stay away from the stove and the microwave, just in case, Lillian."

When the service ended, Sara and Luke rushed out of church, and drove back to Providence Street. Sara found Lillian in the living room, just where she had left her. She was wearing a new sweater, a light blue shade that suited her white hair and blue eyes. She had somehow managed to put on her pearl earrings and some lipstick. She looked better than she had in weeks.

"So, where is everyone?" she snapped. "Let's get this over with. I hope you removed all the breakables from the end tables in the living room, Sara. Those boys are like a wrecking crew. I hope they don't knock that tree over."

Sara translated this to mean that Lillian was actually looking forward to her company.

Before Sara and Luke could assure her there would be no such disasters, the front door opened and everyone arrived at once.

"Wipe your feet, everyone!" Lillian shouted from the living room. "Sara, make sure they wipe their feet! They should all take their shoes off. All that mud and salt from the sidewalk is going to ruin the carpets."

Dr. Elliot came in first, looking dapper as usual in a gray tweed sports coat, dark blue wool vest, and striped shirt underneath. His red bow tie was imprinted with tiny Christmas trees, Sara noticed. He kissed her lightly on the cheek and handed her a gift-wrapped box, then did the same to Lillian.

"Merry Christmas, Lillian," he greeted her jovially.

She seemed surprised by the show of affection. "Merry Christmas to you, Ezra," she echoed, her eyes wide.

"Oh, excuse me. I thought you were sitting under the mistletoe. I see now that's only pine garland. My eyesight must be going on me."

He glanced at Sara and winked, making her smother a laugh.

Jessica and Emily suddenly appeared, walking into the house in stocking feet.

"Oh, my goodness. Isn't that tree gorgeous? Sara, this is all just wonderful," Jessica crooned.

"And look what she did around the mantel. Isn't that perfect?" Emily said, drawing her sister's attention to the far side of the room.

Carrying platters of food and boxes of cakes and cookies, the two sisters made their way into the kitchen and dining room. Dan and Sam followed with their children, baby bags, shopping bags of gifts, and some large, new toys that looked very noisy.

"Lillian's going to hate those toys," Sara whispered to Luke as the kids ran into the living room to check out the tree.

Luke shrugged and crunched down on a gingerbread cookie.

"What can you do, babe? That's why they call it Christmas."

# CHAPTER THIRTEEN

❦

*Cape Light, December 31, Present-day*

$\mathcal{L}$UCY WAS RELIEVED WHEN CHRISTMAS WAS OVER AND she didn't have to pretend anymore that she felt happy. She took down the decorations at the diner the day after, even though Charlie liked to keep them up until New Year's Day.

The week between Christmas and New Year's was always quiet at the Clam Box. Lucy hardly knew what to do with herself. She had grown accustomed to catching up on her schoolwork at the diner during the downtime, with textbooks stashed beneath the counter or spread out at a booth in the back. Now she didn't have any studying to do. She wondered if she should take up knitting.

She sat at the counter, paging through *The Cape Light Messenger,* the town's local newspaper.

Charlie came in from his daily run to the bank, kicking snow from his boots.

She looked up at him. "Quiet here today."

"It's school vacation. People go away. Maybe we should take a few days off, take the kids skiing or something."

He had been trying to cheer her up lately, though he never said she should return to school. She knew what his attitude was about that: it was all for the best that she dropped out. Soon she would shake it off and get back to their old routine.

"We don't ski," she reminded him.

"We could try it. C.J. went on a school trip last winter, he loved it."

"He wants to go snowboarding, that's different." Lucy looked back at the newspaper. "Listen, since it's so dead in here, I'm going to leave a little early. I have to run over to the mall and return a few things."

"Oh? What do you need to return?" She could tell from the tone in his voice, his antennae were up. She folded the newspaper and set it aside, deciding to deal with this head-on.

"I appreciate that diamond heart you gave me, Charlie. I really do. But I want to bring it back. Do you have the receipt?"

Charlie's expression grew serious, his jaw set. "Don't bring it back, Lucy. I know you love it."

"Yes, I do. That's not the problem. It was much too expensive. We can't afford to spend so much on extras right now. You know that."

He shrugged. "What the heck. I just wanted you to have something nice, something to cheer you up."

"I know that. And I'm touched by your thoughtfulness, Charlie, how you went out of your way like that to please me. That's the best part of the present. You can't buy that in any store and I'll have it forever. The rest is not that important, and you know what I'm saying is true about the money."

He nodded slowly, then stepped up to the stool she sat on and put his arms around her. "Lucy, you're a gem. That's all I have to say."

"Oh, stop." She shook her head and tried to pull away, feeling embarrassed.

"No, no. Come on now. I'm not done. . . . I just want to see you back to your old self again. I know I complained a lot when you started working at the hospital. But I'm starting to think maybe I shouldn't have made such a big deal about it. That didn't help things any, did it?"

Lucy sighed. "No, it didn't," she said honestly. "But it wasn't that. It wasn't anything you did. I'm not cut out to be a nurse. You were right. And I was wrong."

"Oh, Lucy, I hate to hear you talk like that. What are you listening to me for? You never did before. When was I ever right about anything?"

Tucker and Charlie had a favorite joke they liked to tell. They called it their Zen husband joke. *If a man says something in the forest, and his wife isn't there to hear him . . . is he still wrong?*

They cracked up with laughter at it every time, though Lucy could never see what was so funny.

"You have to be right about something once in a while, Charlie. It's only statistical probability."

She slipped off the stool and out of his reach. It was good of him to encourage her. Lucy was surprised and touched by his concern. But she didn't want to talk about it anymore.

SARA WORKED AT THE NEWSPAPER THE DAY AFTER Christmas. It was quiet and slow, nothing newsworthy happening in town or anywhere else in the area. She wound up leaving the office early and went back to Lillian's where the daytime nurse, Jeanette, met her at the door.

"How was Lillian today?" Sara asked as she hung up her coat.

"Tired, but I think having a Christmas party here lifted her spirits." Jeanette slipped her coat on and grabbed her handbag and canvas tote. "She's resting now. You ought to wake her soon, or she won't sleep well tonight."

Sara thanked the nurse and said good night. She walked back to Lillian's room and slipped inside. The lamp on the night table was on, but her grandmother was sound asleep.

Sara noticed her secret box was sitting open on the bed, letters and photographs scattered on the quilt. Lillian stirred and Sara thought she would crush everything if she rolled over. She didn't like to touch Lillian's private belongings without permission, but this seemed an emergency. The old photos looked fragile as dried autumn leaves.

Sara scooped up the photos and sheets of yellow-edged paper and put them back in the box. She couldn't help glancing at the handwritten pages, wondering what they were and why they meant so much to her grandmother.

She picked up the top page. It was dated December 31, 1955. *New Year's Eve*, Sara thought. Her eyes skimmed the thin, curling handwriting. It looked like a diary entry—Lillian's diary? Some pages that had survived?

Sara sat in the chair by the table and began to read the words her grandmother had thought so important to preserve:

> . . . *It's a lot to get used to, living with the Warwicks. They are so very different from my family. It's almost like visiting a foreign country, with strange customs that I don't understand. I'm still not accustomed to the idea that I am actually married to Oliver and will live here forever. Well, quite possibly.*
>
> *My parents still hang up when I call and haven't answered my letters. I don't know what to do. Oliver says maybe we should visit them. But I'm afraid. I couldn't stand another scene like the time he came to call. It would be even worse, I'm sure. I know I've hurt them, but they've hurt me as well. Is it so wrong to have fallen in love with Oliver? I don't understand why they punish me this way* . . .

*Cape Light, December 31, 1955*

OLIVER HAD JOKED THAT HIS FAMILY THOUGHT SHE WAS too good for him. Lillian had to admit that hadn't been much of an exaggeration. They had accepted her gladly, laughed off the elopement as typical of their impulsive son, and then gone on to plan a huge party to celebrate the wedding and introduce Lillian to local society.

The preparations for the party were a whirl. Oliver's mother, Alice, was in her element, Lillian thought, and Oliver's father seemed content to see his wife engaged in a project that made her happy, no matter the expense.

Alice insisted that they travel down to New York to buy gowns for the party. They visited Saks Fifth Avenue and Bergdorf Goodman then took a break at the Plaza Hotel.

"I always go to the Palm Court when I'm in town. It's so pleasant." Alice sipped a cup of tea. A tiered silver cake stand filled with finger sandwiches and delicate pastries had been set between them. A woman in a long golden gown played the harp, accompanied by a tuxedoed violinist.

Lillian's family had taken her on weekends to New York. Although the Merchants could well afford tea at the Plaza, Lillian had never been here before. She sometimes wondered if Oliver and his family weren't too open-handed. Her family considered their money a burden, a grave responsibility, as if they were standing guard over a vault, protecting it for someone else.

"I want to buy your trousseau, Lillian," Alice was saying. "You'll need a new wardrobe for the cruise." Oliver had surprised Lillian with a trip to Europe for their honeymoon, an extended cruise that would stop in England, France, Spain, and Italy.

"It's a mother's role, really," Alice continued, "but I would be honored if you would allow me to do this for you."

"That's too generous, Alice. I have plenty of clothes." Lillian had secretly packed a trunk right before her elopement and shipped all her best things to Cape Light. She really did need some new clothes for the trip but felt awkward having Alice buy them for her.

"It's not about the clothes, dear. You dress beautifully, but you're a married woman now. You want to dress in a different way than a career girl. You're starting out a new life, and so everything should be new. Now please don't argue with me. I know you've given up enough to marry Oliver. Let me do something nice for you."

Lillian had given up a great deal, though she had never mentioned it to Alice—or to any of the Warwicks, including Oliver. She knew she wouldn't be able to continue in her job at the museum and would probably never start her doctorate. The greatest loss though, by far, was her family. When she had called to say that she and Oliver were married, her mother sobbed into the phone and then her father yelled at her and slammed down the receiver.

She had tried calling again and again. Each time, they hung up as soon as they heard her voice. Finally, she stopped calling and sent a long letter, begging for their forgiveness and understanding—and inviting them to come to the party that was planned for New Year's Eve.

So far, except for a hurried call from dear Beth, she hadn't heard a word from them. Lillian missed her sister most of all; she wasn't sure when she would get to see Beth again.

Charlotte's parents had also been appalled at the marriage, and though her cousin lived only a few miles from her now, Lillian had not yet managed to see her.

Charlotte had begun dating Peter Granger during the summer, and Lillian expected that her cousin would be engaged soon. It hurt to know that she would miss that special time with Charlotte, the engagement and planning her wedding. They had promised each other they would be in each other's bridal parties. Now she wondered if she would even see Charlotte get married.

As the day of the New Year's Eve party approached, Lillian waited for a call, a letter, or a telegram. But there was no word from her family.

Workmen swarmed over the great house all week long

and by the day of the party, Lilac Hall was beautifully transformed with garlands and exotic flowers and fantastic decorations constructed of yards and yards of gossamer-like tulle. Every room was decorated and lit with thousands of candles. Pink and red petals were strewn about, as if it had rained down roses.

Elegant cars, one after the next, pulled up to the door, and white-gloved servants escorted the guests inside the great hall, the women dripping with furs and jewels, the men in tuxedos.

Lillian wore a silver lamé dress with a heart-shaped neckline. Her hair was upswept, as usual, but arranged in a looser style, with a bit more curl, and Alice had insisted on giving her a pair of long diamond and sapphire earrings to wear.

Lillian's hand trembled as she put on the earrings, moments before the party was to begin. She was about to be presented to all of the Warwicks' family and friends and all of Harry's business associates. Oliver swore she was a knockout, that he would be the envy of every man in the room, but she was having trouble taking comfort in that.

"Ready, Mrs. Warwick?" Oliver stood behind her as she took one last glance in the long, oval mirror in their bedroom.

"I suppose. I can't get used to this dress. I usually don't wear anything this . . . revealing." She twisted and checked her rear view again.

"Don't worry. You've got the perfect figure to reveal, dear." Oliver stepped up behind her and kissed the back of her neck. "You seem so nervous, Lily."

"I suppose I am. I'm not comfortable with strangers. I'm not very good at meeting new people."

"I'll be with you every minute, and they won't be strangers for long." When she didn't answer, he added, "I'm sorry about your family, Lily. Perhaps one of them will surprise us—Charlotte, maybe?"

Lillian shook her head. "No, Charlotte won't be allowed

to come. Her parents probably have her under lock and key tonight."

She forced a calm expression. She didn't want Oliver to see her unhappy. She didn't want to cast a shadow over the party, after all the trouble his family had gone to to plan this celebration and make her feel welcome in their home.

"It will be fine," she promised him. "I'm not surprised that my family didn't answer my letter. They're very stubborn. I probably won't hear back from them for months."

Despite those brave words, all that night Lillian secretly waited for her parents to come, for anyone from her family. But no one appeared to share her happiness and wish her well in her marriage.

The next morning Lillian found a letter in a silver tray beside her place at the breakfast table. "That came for you early this morning, miss," a maid said. "Special Delivery. It must be important to be sent on New Year's Day."

Lillian recognized her father's handwriting immediately. Oliver had not come downstairs yet, and she went into a small study to read it.

She tore the envelope open. It was a short letter, surprisingly brief, she thought, looking over the single page before she began to read it.

She didn't need to read much. The first few lines told the entire story.

*. . . You have deceived and disgraced us. Your betrayal has cut us to the heart. We don't even recognize the person you've become. This ill-advised union will end unhappily, we have no doubt. We cannot find it in our hearts to forgive you. It is best for us if we consider the daughter we knew lost to us forever, so we ask that you never try to contact us again. . . .*

Oliver found her with her face covered by her hands, sobbing quietly. Wordlessly, he put his arms around her.

"Lily, sweet Lily. Don't cry. At least we'll always have each other."

## Cape Light, Late December, Present-day

LILLIAN WOKE UP TO FIND THE CURTAINS OPEN AND Sara sitting beside her bed. She squinted at her granddaughter, unaccustomed to the light. "What do you have in your hand? What are you doing with that?"

"I'm sorry. Everything had fallen out of the box onto your bed. I picked it up and . . . I couldn't help reading it."

Lillian pushed herself up and sat back against the pillows. "There's no excuse for reading other people's letters and private papers. You had no right to do that."

Sara carefully placed the brittle pages on Lillian's bedside table. "Yes, I know. I wouldn't want anyone reading my journals, not even fifty years from now."

Lillian leaned back and scowled. "Maybe I need a little metal safe under the bed."

"I'm sorry. I won't do it again." Sara sat forward and tried to catch her grandmother's eye. "But Lillian, since I did read it, I was wondering . . . what happened with your family? Did you ever make up with them?"

Lillian glanced at her, then stared straight ahead. "They never forgave me. After a while, I gave up asking. I was for the most part, happy in my marriage, content in the life I made with your grandfather. After a while . . . it didn't hurt nearly as much.

"I saw Charlotte occasionally, until she moved to California. I saw my little sister Beth, too, every once in a while. I missed her the most. She was the only one in my entire family who really loved me. And I loved her."

"What happened to her?" Sara had heard some of this story, but not much about Beth.

"She died when she was a little older than you are now.

Car accident," Lillian said sadly. "I didn't find out until it was too late to attend the funeral. There was no way to find out if she ever left word for me. I will always miss her."

"How sad for you. The whole story is very sad," Sara said.

"I missed my family terribly at first. But I made my choice. I was very happy in my marriage for many years and enjoyed a privileged life as Oliver's wife—until our big disaster struck. But that's another story," she added.

Lillian shook her head, as if clearing her thoughts. "I have no regrets, really. People have fared much worse than I. I've lived a full life and I knew true love. I have two daughters whom I'm proud of . . . and now you," she added quietly.

Sara smiled, surprised and pleased at her grandmother's rare moment of recognition.

"And your other grandchildren, too," Sara said. "The little ones. It's quite a crew."

"Yes, quite a crew. Well, only time will tell about the little rug rats. I don't find children very interesting until you can have an intelligent conversation with them. It's a lot of whining and nose wiping until then."

Sara grinned at her grandmother's typical honesty. Lillian would never pretend to be the doting grandma, that was for sure.

"I was wondering, are there any pictures in your box of that party at Lilac Hall?"

"How do you know what's in that box?"

"I don't. I'm only asking. I saw some pictures on the bed and put them back in there. I thought maybe you had one of the party."

With a great show of reluctance, Lillian opened her secret box. She rifled through it a moment, then produced a photo which she handed to Sara.

"That's Oliver and me, in the entryway. Those are all exotic flowers. His mother had an arbor built inside the house. She even had a flock of doves released at midnight, at the champagne toast. She had an artistic streak, you might say. It was quite spectacular."

Sara had to agree. Even from the small, faded photo she could see that the party had been lavish and truly spectacular.

"Lillian, have you thought any more about letting us have our wedding celebration here, in your house?"

Lillian sat back and sniffed. "Yes, I have, as a matter of fact. I think it would be a great deal of trouble, a great wear and tear on this house and my possessions, Sara. Not to mention, a great wear on me, personally . . ."

"Oh. Well . . . I understand." Sara nodded, feeling her heart fall.

"But if it means that much to you and the others, I suppose I can agree," she concluded. "Reverend Ben's been encouraging me to be a kinder and gentler person. I suppose it would be some effort in that direction."

Sara jumped out of her chair and hugged her grandmother.

Lillian sat stiffly, barely tolerating the physical contact. "Now, now. I will only go along within certain guidelines. I hope you understand that."

Sara stepped back, smiling. "I understand. Whatever you say, goes."

Lillian rolled her eyes. "I sincerely doubt that. Not once your mother gets into the act. She'll have the Shanghai Circus in my living room."

"I wouldn't want anything like that at my celebration. Maybe just a flock of doves released at midnight," Sara teased.

Lillian winced. "That's exactly what I'm afraid of!"

SARA MET EMILY THE NEXT DAY FOR LUNCH AT THE Clam Box and sprang the news. "Here's what we'd like to do for our celebration. We'd like to have a big party at Lillian's house. You know how we've been putting off planning it until we knew she could attend? Well, this solves the problem."

Emily nearly choked on her sandwich. "Your grandmother's house? Does she know about this?"

"She's given her okay. As long we work within certain *guidelines.*"

"How in heaven's name did you ever get her to agree to that? Does she know what you meant—a big party, a lot like a wedding?"

"It wasn't nearly as difficult as you might guess. I had asked her to think about it. Then we got to talking about the past. I read some pages from this diary she kept when she was first married. She wrote about this wonderful party that her in-laws gave when she first became a Warwick. I have a feeling that thinking about those memories softened her up a bit," Sara admitted.

"Sounds like you got into the mysterious box. Did you actually look inside without her permission?" Emily gave a low laugh. "That was very daring of you."

"A few things fell out on the bed. I almost couldn't help it." Sara still wasn't very proud of snooping, but Lillian hadn't made that much of a fuss about it.

"I would love to have a look in that box someday myself," Emily admitted.

"Maybe you should ask her sometime and she'll show it to you."

"Maybe I should." Emily smiled at Sara, looking pleased by the news. "How does Luke feel about this? Does he want to have a party there?"

"Well, he did say we could hold off until the fall and make it a Halloween wedding. He was just kidding," she added quickly. "He makes jokes about it but he likes that house. He's already done so much painting and fixing up, we wouldn't have to do much more."

"It could be a spectacular setting," Emily agreed. Her eyes narrowed. "And you said you weren't into this wedding planning stuff, that it totally terrifies you. What happened to that girl?"

Sara grinned and sipped her tea. "I guess I've been bitten by the bride-bug."

Emily laughed. "Better late than never. Sounds like we

have our work cut out for us. Let's call Molly Willoughby. She'll know what to do."

Molly was Sam Morgan's younger sister, Jessica's sister-in-law, who ran her own gourmet food shop and catering business, and planned all the best parties in town.

"And Sara," Emily added, "I think it's wonderful that you're so concerned about your grandmother. You've devoted so much time to her lately and made sure she was part of your celebration. Truthfully, after the way she's treated you and Luke at times, I'm not sure she deserves so much loyalty. I'm not sure she appreciates it, either . . . but *I* do."

Sara met Emily's glance and nodded. "Lillian doesn't say much, but I think she does appreciate it."

LUCY NOTICED EMILY AND SARA HAVING LUNCH BUT didn't walk over to their table. Instead, she waved from a distance, pretending to be too busy to stop and chat.

Ironically, just when they were no longer desperate for extra help, Charlie had found a good waitress willing to work part-time for the meager wages he offered. Even though Lucy wasn't continuing school, he thought it was best to start the woman and see if it worked out, saying they could always use reliable extra help.

So the new waitress, Karen, had waited on Emily and Sara. Soon enough, Lucy saw them go. She felt bad that she had avoided her friend, but Sara still didn't know she had quit school and for some reason, of all the people Lucy knew, it seemed hardest to tell Sara. Maybe because Sara was the one who helped her apply to colleges and encouraged her to start.

She knew Sara would be disappointed in her. She wouldn't understand, and Lucy couldn't bear to see that disappointed look in anyone else's eyes.

Karen left soon after the lunch rush was over. Charlie took the slack time for his daily trip to the bank. Lucy wandered around the diner, collecting all the salt and pepper shakers to be refilled. It was a boring chore that she normally didn't mind. But for some reason, today it annoyed her. It made her feel as if she was frittering her life away with trivial, meaningless tasks.

The bell above the door jangled, and Lucy looked up to see who was coming in. She felt a catch in her throat and stood up straight. Jack Zabriskie. She couldn't believe it.

He looked around the diner and took a seat at the counter. He hadn't seen her; Lucy had an impulse to run into the kitchen and hide.

Then he looked her way and waved. She hesitated a moment before grabbing a menu and starting toward him. She wished she had had a minute to fix her hair and put on a little lipstick. And her uniform was smeared with ketchup and burger grease. How attractive.

Lucy sighed, resigned. There was no help for it. He was going to see exactly what she was—an old, worn-out waitress. Someone who wasn't smart enough to be a nurse.

"Hello, Jack. What brings you all the way down here?"

"I've been wondering what happened to you, Lucy. Nobody seemed to know or would tell me."

"You know what happened. You were right there. I nearly killed a patient," she reminded him.

He smiled at her kindly. "Oh, right. Well, she pulled through just fine. Didn't anyone tell you that?"

"Sure, I knew. Listen, can I get you something? You want a menu?"

"Just coffee, please."

Lucy turned and collected a mug, then poured out the coffee and set a pitcher of milk beside it.

It was clear that he had come to talk to her because he thought he could help. But he wasn't helping her. He was just rubbing salt in the wound.

"That accident you had," Jack said, "those things happen to everyone sooner or later. Didn't your supervisor tell you that?"

"No. She didn't say anything like that to me."

"Well, it's true. Maybe Margaret doesn't want to admit it—ruins the image—but nurses and doctors make mistakes. We're only human. Hopefully, the mistakes don't end up being life-threatening. When you weigh the mistakes against all the good we do, it's like a few grains of sand on one side of the scale and a mountain on the other, don't you think?"

Lucy had to agree with the analogy. "The problem is, I got stuck on the wrong side of the scale too many times."

"You had a scare, Lucy. You're still learning, so it almost doesn't count," he said. "Didn't you almost have a car accident once or twice when you were learning how to drive?"

"I did have a car accident," she answered emphatically. "No one was hurt, thank goodness."

"Oh, well, then . . . bad example I guess." He was half-frowning, half-smiling at her, and she felt the chemistry of their special friendship kicking in.

"I know what you're trying to say, Jack. But this is different."

"No, it's not," he insisted. "This is the work we choose to do, the work we were born to do. You can't give up without giving yourself a chance."

"I *gave* myself a chance. That's as far as I go. I don't want to kill someone the next time."

"Well, there's certainly no danger of that if you stay behind that counter, working as a waitress. You're not going to save anybody's life back there either, unless they need the Heimlich maneuver."

His words were a bit harsh, she thought. He seemed frustrated with her. He probably thought he would come in here and talk her into going back. What he didn't understand was that even his kind, encouraging words couldn't change the fact of her failure. She wished he would give up and go.

As if understanding her silent request, he stood up and put some bills on the counter.

Lucy pushed them back at him. "Don't be silly, Jack. I can buy you a coffee."

He ignored her, leaving them. "One more thing. Do you remember Helen Carter?" Lucy nodded. Of course she remembered Helen.

"She's started chemo and her prognosis is good. She asked about you and said to tell you that you really helped her at a moment in her life when she needed it. She said to tell you that once she gets stronger, she's thinking about going back to school, like you said to do. She said you were the one she would remember, the one who gave her some hope to keep going."

Lucy looked down, avoiding his eyes. She didn't know what to say. It was nice of him to pass on the story about Helen. That made her feel a little bit better about everything, but it didn't change her decision.

She forced a small smile. "Thank you for coming to see me, Jack. It was very thoughtful of you."

He pulled on his jacket and hat. "Good luck, Lucy. I hope you change your mind someday."

"Good luck to you, Jack. Happy New Year," she added as he walked out the door. He didn't turn and she wondered if he had even heard her.

LUCY NEVER LIKED TO MAKE A BIG FUSS OVER NEW Year's Eve. She liked to spend a quiet night at home with Charlie and her boys. This year was no different. If anything, she felt more determined to ignore the holiday.

The evening was shaping up to be even quieter than she expected. C.J. was going on an overnight ski trip with a friend's family. Jamie was going bowling and then sleeping at a friend's house. Even the Tulleys were occupied this year. It would be just her and Charlie, sending out for pizza and sitting by the TV.

On New Year's Eve, they usually closed the diner early. There had been very few customers at lunchtime, and Lucy was nearly done with all the cleanup and prep work by half past three. She hoped that when the last two customers left, she and Charlie could close up and go home.

A woman sat at the counter, sipping tea and nibbling on a toasted corn muffin. And there was a man in a booth near the window, wolfing down a bacon cheeseburger while he worked on some sheets of accounting paper with a pencil and a calculator. She guessed from the case he had stowed under the table that he was a salesman, passing through town. She wondered if he was on his way home and where that might be. She wondered if he sold anything interesting, but for once, didn't feel like starting a conversation.

Charlie came out from the kitchen with a tray of clean glasses and started putting them away. "How late do you want to stay open?" she asked him.

He shrugged. "I don't know. I could use a nap before dinner. I'll never make it to midnight otherwise."

She wasn't sure she would either. She and Charlie were such party animals, it was laughable.

The man in the booth raised his hand and waved but didn't turn around. "Guess he needs something," she murmured to Charlie. Lucy started off toward the customer then saw his hand drop sharply. He knocked over his coffee cup, spilling it all over the papers, but he didn't seem to notice. He was clutching his chest with both his hands.

Something was horribly wrong. Lucy ran to him. Was he choking? Was he having a stroke? A heart attack?

She reached his booth and looked down at his face. His skin was deathly pale. He stared up at her, his eyes bulging. "My chest . . . the pain." Before she could react, he leaned over and fell out of the booth on to the floor.

"Call nine-one-one! Charlie, call nine-one-one! It's a cardiac arrest!"

Lucy turned the man over. With her hands under his armpits, she dragged him until he was lying flat on his back on the floor. He was a big man, overweight, and she barely had the strength to move him on her own.

She checked his vital signs and pulse. He had stopped breathing. She immediately pushed his head back, checked his mouth for any food or objects, and began to administer mouth-to-mouth resuscitation and CPR, just as she had learned in nursing school: first breathing into his mouth until his lungs expanded, then pressing on his heart with the fingertips of one hand flattened to his chest.

She didn't stop to worry if she was doing something wrong. She didn't stop to think of anything. She moved on automatic, totally focused on keeping him alive until help arrived.

She suddenly became aware of Charlie crouched down beside her. "What should I do? Is he going to be all right? Is he dying, Lucy?"

"He's hanging in there," she murmured quickly as she compressed the man's chest again. "How long does it take that darn ambulance to come? They're just up the street—"

She heard the sound of the siren screaming down Main Street and saw the red flashing lights through the diner's front window.

She didn't stop her first aid, however, knowing that every drop of oxygen was precious to this man now. *Dear God, let him live,* she prayed silently as she pumped the man's heart again. *I don't even know this man, but let him wake up and survive this heart attack.*

The EMS workers rushed in and crouched down beside her. One slipped an oxygen mask over the man's face, the other took over the CPR. "Good job," he said to Lucy.

She nodded and stood up, stepping back so they could do their work. A police officer had also shown up, and he spoke to Charlie, taking down information on a small pad.

A few moments later she saw the man's eyes slowly open. The EMS worker stopped the CPR. The man's heart was beating on its own again. Lucy sent up a quick, silent prayer of thanks.

The man was quickly loaded onto a stretcher and taken

out to the ambulance. Lucy knew that there was medical equipment in the ambulance that would keep his heartbeat stable until he reached the hospital.

During all the excitement the woman at the counter had left the diner. When the ambulance finally rushed off, Lucy and Charlie were alone. It was very quiet and neither of them spoke.

Lucy, feeling suddenly exhausted, dropped down onto a counter stool. She rested her chin in her hand.

Charlie let out a long breath. "Lucy . . . for heaven's sake. Where the heck did you learn how to do that?"

"In nursing school. Where else?"

"You saved that man's life. You really saved him."

She couldn't help grinning at him, despite their scare. "Yeah, I think I did."

"He was checking out. His face was turning blue. I wouldn't have known what to do. What would have happened if you hadn't been here? That guy is one lucky son of a gun, I'll tell you that."

Charlie couldn't stand still; he was practically hopping around the diner. He seemed exhilarated by the emergency while Lucy felt totally drained.

"You know I'm not that big on religion," he said in a quieter voice.

"Yes, I know that, Charlie. Did you just find some?"

"Don't you think that was a . . . a sign of something?"

"A sign? Like, God doesn't want us to serve bacon cheeseburgers anymore? Too much cholesterol?"

"Not me, Lucy. I'm talking about you."

"What about me?" She frowned at him, though she could guess what he was getting at.

"You saved a man's life. Doesn't that mean anything to you?"

"Of course it does."

"Admit it, Lucy. You loved doing that. You loved saving that guy's life."

Lucy laughed at him. It had been fun in a strangely dramatic way. "It was simple first aid. Everyone should know CPR."

"Maybe they should. But most people don't have the interest in those things, not like you do. You should have seen yourself. You were really something. I hardly recognized you." He shook his head, looking genuinely impressed. "So serious and determined. So professional. You were . . . like another person," he admitted quietly.

That was the way she felt when she was nursing, she wanted to say. Lucy couldn't deny that she had been happier feeling she had some higher goal, some greater purpose to her life.

"Well, it's over now," she said. "I hope that guy does all right."

"Yeah. That's a great way to start the new year, with a heart attack."

"It's a tough break," she agreed. "But sometimes when bad things happen, it's for the best. It's a warning of something that could have been even worse, right?"

Charlie was staring at her now. "I guess that's true."

She suddenly felt self-conscious. She could tell he was thinking about her training and what had happened at the hospital. She didn't want to get into all that again. "Ready to go?"

"Yeah, I'll shut the lights off and lock up." He didn't move from where he stood, though. "Lucy, I'm sorry. I never understood what it meant to you. I never really . . . got it. But watching you keep that guy alive just now. Wow. I guess I finally do."

Lucy felt grateful for his admission. And sorry it had been so long in coming. "Better late than never," she said quietly.

"Is it too late, do you think? Couldn't you call somebody at the school and see if they'll give you another shot?"

Was Charlie suggesting that she go back to school? Lucy thought she might fall right off the stool.

"Now you're saying you want me to go back to school?" She stared at him, but he didn't answer. "What about the house being a mess and managing the kids? If I'm working at a hospital, it's going to be even longer hours," she warned him.

"I know. But better that than watching you walk around looking so unhappy. If you're home and miserable, we're all miserable. Even if we have enough clean underwear. Besides, I hate to see you quit. You're not a quitter, Lucy. A quitter never could have stayed married to me this long."

She finally smiled. "You got that right, pal."

"Maybe I've always known you could do it, but I just didn't want you to," he confessed. "Maybe I thought that if you finished your college degree and got to be a real nurse, you'd be moving away from me."

He sighed and looked down at the floor. She could tell it was hard for him to admit this to her. It was hard for her to hear it.

He took a breath. "It was selfish, I admit it. I guess I felt I was losing you. Now I see, I've lost you anyway. And I want you back. I want you happy again. I know you could do this if you just try. Look what you did just now, just clear out of the blue."

He walked up to her and took her hand. Lucy looked into his eyes, wondering a bit at just how much his bold admission and unexpected vote of confidence meant to her. More than he would ever know. She had never told him about Jack Zabriskie's visit the other day. It was funny how Jack's words hadn't moved her, but Charlie, who had always been undermining her, was the one who was able to get through.

"So, what do you think?"

"I appreciate what you just said, Charlie. It means a lot to me."

"I meant every word. That's still not an answer."

"I'll think it over. Maybe I'll call my advisor on Monday and see what she has to say."

"That's a start, Lucy. That's a good start." Charlie nodded approvingly.

Lucy smiled at him. "Life is very fragile, Charlie. It wasn't me that saved that customer. It was the man upstairs."

"I know. But you have to take some credit. You sure helped Him out tonight. I'd give you an A-plus."

He leaned over and hugged her and Lucy hugged him back. Gosh, life was strange sometimes. Wasn't it?

LUCY KNEW THAT MOST PEOPLE WOULD BE SLEEPING IN on New Year's Day. Charlie, though, was unusually eager to get to church. Lucy wondered if witnessing the near-fatal heart attack of a man about his own age had scared him, but she didn't ask.

The church was nearly empty, as she had expected. Tucker, who was a deacon, showed them to a seat near the front.

"Happy New Year, everyone. I wish you all a blessed, peaceful, healthy year to come," Reverend Ben greeted the congregation.

His sermon was about New Year's resolutions. Lucy had made a few of those over the years and broken most of them. She wondered if Reverend Ben had some advice on how to actually keep them.

"What do you think God is thinking, watching us make all these lists for self-improvement? I've sometimes wondered that. God loves and accepts us with all our faults, no matter how much we stumble and fall. No matter how quickly we give up on our resolutions and self-improvement plans, or even give up on our hopes and dreams, God never thinks we're failures."

Those words hit home. Lucy felt the sting. She had given up on herself, marked herself as a total failure.

"No matter how often we give up on healing our addictions or trying to mend broken relationships or curb our tempers or have better values," he continued, "God doesn't give up on us. He's always ready to inspire us with the will and courage to try again, to do it better another time—if we only keep our hearts and spirits open to His inspiration."

Had she closed her heart and spirit to God? Had she left God out of her dilemma? Maybe that's why it all seemed so hopeless, with no solution.

"We can expect perfection in heaven. But not on earth. Not from our fellow men and certainly not from ourselves. Our job here is to extend the same spirit of love and forgiveness God shows us, to everyone we meet. And to ourselves.

"One of my favorite sayings is, 'The greatest wisdom is kindness.' I would have to add it's the greatest philosophy and the greatest medicine, too. You can go far making one resolution this year—resolving simply to be kinder. To be more forgiving, accepting. It's a step in a whole new path through life that can surely make the world a better, more loving place."

The choir began to sing, and Lucy turned to the hymn "Amazing Grace." She wasn't very mindful of the music though, her thoughts wandering. She thought about what Jack had said, about the scales with doing good on one side and screwing up on the other. Did saving that stranger's life last night balance it all out for her again? Was it a sign, as Charlie had said?

Lucy wasn't so sure about that, but Reverend Ben's words had struck a chord. She needed to start by forgiving herself. By knowing she may have made a mistake, but that didn't make her a failure. Maybe God had given her a talent for helping people, for nursing, and it was her duty to keep trying, until she was really good at it.

# CHAPTER FOURTEEN

~≈~

*Southport Hospital, Early January,*
*Present-day*

NORA MARTIN WAS A MUCH BETTER TEACHER THAN Margaret Sherman, Lucy could tell that from the start. She was calm and clear with her instructions. She never made Lucy feel dumb for admitting she was unsure of something, and she was usually encouraging. Nora, who had heard Lucy's story and agreed to be her new supervisor, made Lucy feel as if she were truly being given a fresh start.

Lucy was now assigned to a different wing but with the same kind of cases she had dealt with before, patients who had noncritical conditions or who were recovering from surgery. Most of the doctors on this wing were new to her, so she was surprised to run into Jack her very first day back.

Things had been good with Charlie lately—better than usual since he was trying hard to be supportive of her—but she still felt that little spark of attraction when Jack smiled at her.

"Hey, Lucy. I didn't know you were back." He walked over and gave her a quick hug, and her heart raced.

"It's my first day. So far, so good."

"I knew you'd come back sooner or later."

"I didn't. But thanks—I'm grateful to you for coming out to talk to me that day."

"That was nothing. I knew you had the guts to stick it out. You just had to find them again."

"Yeah, maybe." She nodded and smiled at him. "So how's it going? How's your new year?"

"Pretty good." His face lit with a slow smile. "My wife and I are back together. We spent some time together over the holidays and decided to try again."

"Wow, that's great." She looked at him carefully. "You seem happy."

"I am," he admitted. "Very."

Lucy forced a bright smile. She heard a whooshing sound and knew it was the hot air, rushing out of her silly fantasy. She almost wanted to laugh out loud at herself.

"I'm glad for you, Jack. I hope it all works out. Listen, I have to run. Maybe we can have coffee sometime."

"Sure, I'd like that. See you," he said. "And good luck."

"Thanks." Lucy had the urge to add, "I need it!" but squelched the impulse. She was trying to cultivate a more positive, confident attitude.

Lucy returned to her rounds. With Nora overseeing her, she cared for several patients throughout the morning. At one point Nora asked her to change an IV bag and Lucy nearly lost her nerve, but she forced herself to feign a professional, confident air and double-checked every step in the process.

She had missed the hospital, she realized. She missed the interaction with the patients, and she missed applying all that information from nursing school to the real world.

Nursing was not exactly what she had imagined. It had demands she never expected, and tedious, routine work, too. But in most everything she did, Lucy felt she was bringing

254 THOMAS KINKADE AND KATHERINE SPENCER

comfort and doing good. A mountain of good, that with God's help, would always outweigh any grains of sand on the other side.


LILLIAN OFTEN RETREATED TO HER ROOM DURING THE month of January. A month was not a long time to plan a party, according to Sara, and she and Luke seemed to spend every spare minute preparing for the big event. It all made Lillian very cross.

"You two aren't big on patience, as far as I can see," Lillian commented one evening as Sara brought dinner in to her. "It's the influence of technology. It's conditioned your generation to instant gratification."

There was nothing instantly gratifying about fixing up Lillian's old house, Sara wanted to say. But any mention of the work that was under way sent Lillian into an automatic tizzy, so Sara held her tongue.

Luckily, Sam volunteered to help Luke with more painting and repairs. Lillian's precious oriental carpets, which were too delicate for the light of day, were rolled up and carried off to be cleaned, and the hardwood floors underneath polished to a high gloss.

The large rooms were crowded with furniture and bric-a-brac. While Sara knew that rearranging upset her grandmother, she did find a way to move out a number of small pedestal tables, plant stands, curio cabinets, and chairs, one by one—sometimes late at night, when Lillian was sleeping.

The process reminded Sara of a game she had when she was a little girl called *What's Missing?* There was a very complicated felt picture with many details, and you would close your eyes and the other person would take away one item. Then you had to guess what was gone.

Every morning Lillian would roll into the dining room for her breakfast and look around. "Is something missing in here? Over there, near the window. Didn't I have that little mahogany cupboard with the glass doors?"

Sara would feign her innocent stare. "I think Jessica took it back to her house for safekeeping when we did the floors. I'll ask her about it."

"You can parcel out the goodies when I'm dead and buried," Lillian snapped. "I'm not ready to have the place ransacked quite yet."

Sara grinned. "Don't worry, Lillian. You'll get it back." After the party, she meant. Sara wasn't about to watch all her guests bumping their knees on end tables. The guest list had grown long—too long, she thought. Even though Dan had warned her, Sara couldn't manage to control Emily's penchant for large parties. After all, Emily was the mayor. She knew everyone in town. Plus, she had been denied planning a big wedding, so Sara had to cut her a little slack.

Sara's entire family—her adoptive parents and other relatives—were coming up from Maryland. Luke's family, who lived mainly in Boston, were coming as well.

At first Luke couldn't quite believe Sara's plan to have their party at Lillian's house. He called it the Haunted Mansion and insisted he was coming dressed as Count Dracula.

But soon enough, he got into the idea. One night, while Lillian was sleeping, Sara slipped the photo of the Warwick party out of her box and showed it to him.

"That's Lillian? Are you sure?" His shock was genuine.

"That's her all right. Wasn't she stunning?"

"A regular knockout. No wonder she bagged a millionaire. He's not so bad, either. I like the white tie and tails, very classy."

Sara smiled up at him. "You would look gorgeous in white tie and tails, darling."

"Oh no . . ." Luke handed the photo back to her and shook his head. "I was thinking more of my good sports jacket and some new jeans, Sara. You are not going to make me dress up in that penguin suit, are you?"

Sara tilted her head. "It would really blow everyone

away if we did go for the glamour look. And I know how you love to do the unexpected, unconventional thing."

"I hate to tell you, but you've got the wrong guy."

"No," Sara said, "I don't. I'm sure of that."

As he kissed her she thought that there was a chance she might persuade him in time.

Time was passing quickly and despite Sara's careful lists, there was still so much to do. The party preparations often kept her up late into the night.

One night she was working on her laptop at the kitchen table when Luke appeared in the doorway, his hair mussed and his eyes squinting at the light. "Are you still up? It's nearly two A.M. What in the world are you doing?"

Sara looked up from the screen and shrugged. She didn't want to tell him. This was something secret, something special, a surprise for the whole family. She wasn't even sure yet if it would all work out.

"I'm doing some research on the Net," she said simply. She closed the program so he couldn't see the screen.

"For work, you mean?"

"Not exactly."

Luke stood at the sink, drinking a glass of water. "Well, I think you ought to come to bed now. Dark circles under your eyes won't look very good at the big party."

"No, they won't," she admitted. She was tired these days but sometimes so excited, she could hardly sleep.

On the day of the party, the caterers and the florist's crew arrived at the same time, one at the front door, the other at the back. Lillian's old house was like a beehive that somebody had picked up and shaken. Lillian locked herself in her room and used her phone to make periodic calls to Sara's and Emily's cell phones. She only opened the door to accept her meals.

"Isn't it over yet?" she yelled into the phone. "What are they doing out there? I heard glass breaking."

Hours later, the setup was completed and only the servers and kitchen crew remained, managed by Molly. Emily had brought her dress, so she could change at Lillian's house and help her mother get dressed.

It had been an ordeal to find a new dress for Lillian. She was fussy to begin with and there were the two casts to consider. But finally Jessica and Emily found her a peacock-blue gown, chiffon on top with a long satin skirt. The top was altered to accommodate one cast and the skirt was long enough to cover the other.

Sara was relieved that Emily was occupied with Lillian downstairs. She didn't want anyone to see her before she was ready, not even Luke.

Slowly but surely she had brainwashed him into wearing white tie and tails. He had tried on just the jacket for her, and she could tell he was going to look devastating. She hoped he wouldn't chicken out at the last minute.

When Luke knocked on her door at a quarter to six, Sara was ready. She opened the door slowly and stepped back.

"Sara . . . wow," he said on a long breath. "That's not the dress you bought with Emily, is it?"

"Shhhh. No, it isn't. I found this one last week. What do you think—too much?"

He shook his head, his eyes fixed on her. "You look gorgeous. Red carpet, all the way. Very glamorous."

Sara was pleased. That's what she had been going for. The off-the-shoulder coppery gold dress was not a replica of Lillian's gown in the photograph, but it was similar in style, with a retro look that created the same effect. It was not her usual "look," and Sara felt a bit self-conscious, but it was also daring and fun to dress up this way.

"They're waiting for us in the living room," Luke said. "They asked me to come get you."

"Are my folks here yet?"

"They just called. They're on their way."

Her parents had come up from Maryland during the day and checked into a nearby bed-and-breakfast. Sara had spoken to them over the phone and was eager to see them. But she was glad they were running a little late. She knew her folks still felt a bit out of place in Cape Light. She didn't want to have them come into the house all alone, before she and Luke could greet them.

"You think your folks will be okay?" Luke asked.

Sara considered. "Well, it was hard for them when they found out we eloped, and it didn't help when I told them we decided to have this party so far from Winston. But lots of my close relatives, like my aunt Ellen and uncle Bob, will be here tonight. And I know my parents just want me to be happy. When they see us together, they'll be happy for us."

"I hope so," Luke murmured, "since they're throwing us another party at their house in February. Let's hope they approve of your groom."

Luke offered his arm and Sara slipped her arm through his. They left the bedroom and started down the hallway, toward the long, curving staircase.

As per Sara's instructions, the foyer was filled with flowers, the staircase banister was covered in bunches of laurel and rhododendron, studded with colorful blooms and white and gold toile bows.

Large potted topiary trees with fragrant gardenia blossoms flanked the staircase, and swoops of gossamer fabric hung across the ceiling and over doorways. More flowers and garlands of green decked the entrance to the living room with a cascading arrangement in cream-colored roses, miniature orchids, and phlox.

Sara and Luke wouldn't have been able to afford decorating the entire house so lavishly, but Molly managed to gather some arrangements from other parties she had worked on during the week. A country club luncheon and a friendly landscaper she often did business with helped. With Molly's contributions and Sara's own ideas, they had been able to do up the foyer in grand style—very much like the decorations at Lilac Hall for her grandparents' marriage celebration.

"Sara, you turned this place into a tropical paradise," Luke whispered to her.

"Not a haunted garden? That's good news," she said.

Sara walked into the living room and stood in the doorway. She watched Emily and Jessica turn to look at her and saw their mouths drop open.

Emily looked confused. "That's not the dress we bought at Lord and Taylor's . . ."

"Uh, no. I found this one last week. I guess I should have told you. What do you think?"

"I think it's absolutely gorgeous."

Jessica walked over to get a better look. "It's stunning, Sara. I love the beading." The dress had tiny beads all over the bodice and more beading on the skirt.

Emily smiled and came over to her. "Me, too. I would have never picked that out for you, but you look beautiful in it. Truly." She leaned over and gave Sara a hug. "Let's go inside and see if your grandmother's ready. She wanted to see you when you came down."

When the three of them entered Lillian's room, they found the family matriarch sitting in her wheelchair, completely dressed and looking quite lovely in her new gown and shawl, which artfully concealed her casts.

Lillian sat with a hand mirror, slowly applying lipstick. She looked up at them, and Emily and Jessica stood back, each to one side, so that Sara could step forward.

"My word! Look at you . . ."

Sara waited without saying anything. She couldn't tell if her grandmother approved of the dress or not. It shouldn't have been important to her, but it was.

"Did you pick out that dress with her?" she asked Emily.

Emily shook her head. "No, Mother. That isn't the one."

"I didn't think so. You don't have the eye for a dress like

that, Emily. No offense, but your taste is rather . . . blah."
Lillian narrowed her eyes at Sara. "Come here, let me see it
up close."

Sara stepped forward dutifully, and Lillian put on her
reading glasses and felt the fabric between her fingertips
and then checked the seams and construction.

"Not badly made for workmanship these days. I had a
dress something like that once," she added, glancing up at
Sara. "Silver lamé."

"Yes, I know. I saw the picture, remember?"

"Oh, that's right." Lillian nodded. "Well, you look stunning. This is your night and you are the beautiful center-
piece of this soirée."

"Thank you, Lillian." Sara blinked back tears, moved
by her grandmother's uncharacteristic words of praise.

Lillian turned and took a long blue velvet jewelry case
from her vanity table. She opened it, and Sara thought she
was about to ask for help putting on a necklace.

Instead she handed the case up to Sara. "Open it," she
said. Sara did and saw an exquisite string of pearls inside.
"You know what those are, don't you?"

Sara felt her throat tighten with emotion. "Yes, I've
heard a lot about these pearls, Lillian. I never thought I
would get to wear them, though." After all, Lillian rarely ac-
knowledged her as her granddaughter. And Sara had eloped
and wasn't having a "real" wedding. Lillian set many con-
tingencies to the privilege of wearing the pearls, and Sara
had assumed that she would never be found worthy.

The pearls were an heirloom in Lillian's family, passed
down from her great-grandmother. All the Merchant brides
had worn them—except Lillian, because she had eloped.
Years later, when her mother died, her brother, Lawrence,
had sent Lillian the pearls. It was the only kind gesture he
had ever made to her.

Sara took the pearls from the box and held them out in
front of her. "They're beautiful."

"Of course they are. Go ahead, put them on," Lillian said impatiently. "Somebody help her, please?"

Emily stepped up behind her. "Here, I'll do it for you." She slipped the pearls around Sara's neck and fastened the diamond-studded clasp. "There. You look perfect," she said, kissing Sara's cheek.

"Oh, yes. She really does," Jessica agreed.

Sara glanced at herself in the mirror behind Lillian. She touched the pearls lightly with her hand. They felt smooth and warm against her skin. They really were the perfect touch. "Thank you . . . Grandmother," Sara said. She leaned over and kissed Lillian's cheek.

"You're welcome. A bride isn't really dressed without pearls," she added.

"How true, Mother." Emily got behind Lillian's chair and took the brakes off. "We'd better get inside. The guests will be here soon."

"Let the games begin." Lillian made a sweeping gesture with her good hand.

Lillian had only caught glimpses of the flowers and decorations before Emily wheeled her into the foyer. Now she gasped with disbelief. "What in heaven's name did you do? Is this my house? I don't recognize my own home anymore! Oh . . . those flowers are beautiful. And look at the trees!"

"Do you like it?" Sara asked, hardly daring to hear the answer.

"Indeed," Lillian said. "You've done a fine job, Sara, a job worthy of this house." She pointed to the garlands that draped the foyer. "This spot particularly reminds me of the way Lilac Hall looked the night my husband's family gave a party for us to celebrate our wedding."

"Yes . . . I thought it might," Sara said quietly. She had worked hard and now had her reward.

Luke strolled up to them. "Good evening, ladies. Lillian, you look lovely."

Lillian leaned back and looked him over from head to

toe. "Is it really you?" she asked quietly. "I can't believe my eyes."

"See what the right clothes can do for a guy?" he teased.

"Amazing," she agreed.

The front door opened then and Sara's parents entered, along with her aunt Ellen and uncle Bob.

"Mom, Dad! I'm so happy to see you." Sara walked over to them quickly and gave them each a big hug. She wasn't sure why, but she suddenly felt like crying.

"Sara, honey. You look so beautiful!" Laura Franklin actually was crying as she stepped back and appraised her daughter. "Look at her, Mike. She's a married woman."

"Yes, I know." Her father hugged her again. "She's got that newlywed glow. I think it agrees with her."

Sara was laughing and crying, then suddenly realized that she had totally forgotten about Luke, who stood beside her like a stalwart tree, waiting patiently to greet his new in-laws.

She touched his arm and he stepped forward. "Laura, Mike . . . thank you for coming to celebrate with us. I'm sorry about the elopement. You can blame it all on me," he added, glancing at Sara. "I just love her so much, I couldn't wait for us to be married. I only want to make her happy and take care of her for the rest of our lives."

Sara's father glanced at his wife and sighed. "I have to admit, I was looking forward to walking my daughter down the aisle and giving her away the old-fashioned way. But, besides all that, I guess that was all I really wanted to hear from my new son-in-law. Welcome to the family, Luke."

"Yes, Luke. Welcome to our family," Sara's mother said, and kissed him on the cheek.

Sara smiled and rubbed off the lipstick imprint for him as her aunt Ellen and uncle Bob stepped forward to offer their congratulations. They all moved off into the living room, while Sara and Luke remained to greet the rest of their guests, who were starting to fill the foyer.

Between Luke and Emily, it seemed as if more than half

the town had been invited. Sara, who had initially envisioned a smaller party, suddenly found herself glad so many people were there. She and Luke were blessed, she realized, to have so many close ties and good friends in their "adoptive" home town.

After most of the guests had arrived, Sara and Luke began to mingle. Sara had been afraid that her grandmother would feel overwhelmed or even forgotten in some corner, but she soon saw that her worries were needless. Lillian's wheelchair didn't seem to inhibit her in the least, and Dr. Elliot had volunteered to be her escort and driver for the evening, steering her in a new direction every few minutes at her command.

Meeting up with her parents again, Sara was pleased to see that they were having a good time. Emily and Dan had been introducing them to the other guests, and her mother had lost the tense look she'd always had when she visited Cape Light.

"I'm glad that you and Luke decided to have this party, after all," her mother said. "It's wonderful for us to meet all of your friends and see the Warwicks again. Everyone is so happy for the both of you. You know how I wished you had a wedding down in Winston, but I don't think it could have been any nicer."

Sara hugged her mother, feeling surrounded by all the love and good wishes her heart could hold. Lillian had been right, a marriage should be celebrated.

They were well into the festivities and about to serve the cake when Sara noticed a guest who arrived late—a woman about Emily's age. Sara couldn't place her, though something about her seemed vaguely familiar.

"You must be Sara," the woman said as Sara came to greet her. "I'm sorry I'm late. I didn't realize the drive was going to take so long. I'm Amanda, Beth's daughter."

"Oh, you've come. I didn't know you were going to come for sure." Sara impulsively leaned over and hugged her. "Thank you so much. My grandmother will be so surprised."

After hearing the story of Lillian's estrangement from her family, Sara had asked Emily if there were any surviving members of the Merchant family. Neither Emily nor Jessica knew of anyone, but Sara couldn't let it go. She had spent hours on the Internet, using the research skills she had honed as a reporter. She finally traced Beth's only daughter, Amanda Young, who now lived in Vermont.

Sara brought Amanda over to Lillian, wondering too late if she should have given her grandmother any warning. "Lillian," Sara began hesitantly. "I want you to meet somebody."

Lillian turned in her chair and peered up at Amanda.

"This is Amanda Young. She's related to you," Sara added.

"Related? I have no relations. Not that I know of."

"We've never met, but I'm Beth's daughter," Amanda said.

Lillian leaned back in her chair, her jaw dropping in astonishment. "Your voice . . . it's just like hers. I thought for a moment she was standing right there. You look a bit like her, too," she added, peering at Amanda's face. "You have her eyes. Beth had beautiful eyes."

"I'm sorry I never got in touch with you. I knew about you. My mother told me. But I was very young when she died, and when I was older, I had no idea how to find you."

"Oh . . . of course. It wasn't your place to find me. I saw you once, when you were a baby." Lillian nodded, remembering.

"I know my mother loved you very much," Amanda said. "She hoped you were happy in your new life and in your marriage."

Lillian looked up at her, her eyes glassy. "My fairy tale didn't last forever, but we had a good run. Our parents were right. Oliver Warwick did end up disappointing and disgracing me, but not the way they expected." She sighed and reached out to touch Amanda's hand. "Thank you for coming here to bring that message."

"I'm sorry it's taken so long," Amanda said quietly.

"It's never too late to bring a message like that. It makes all the difference to an old woman like me. And you must call me Aunt Lillian. You're the only one who ever will, you know."

"I'd be honored to," Amanda replied.

Lillian glanced up at Sara. "You're a busy girl—planning this big party and playing amateur detective as well. This was all your doing, I suspect?"

Sara nodded happily. "You got me."

"What do you think of my granddaughter, Amanda?" Lillian asked her niece. "Isn't she something? Brains and beauty, too. Quite a package." She glanced at each of the women, smiling to herself. "Somebody said that to me once. You wouldn't believe it to see me now. . . . But it's true."

Sara believed it. She had a good idea who Lillian was thinking about right now, too.

Soon it was time for Sara and Luke to cut the cake. Though it wasn't a real wedding, Sara had persuaded Luke to stand up before their guests and say a few words.

"Sara and I want to thank you all for coming here tonight to celebrate our marriage. As you all know, we never wanted to have a big, old-fashioned wedding. As usual, I've managed to do things a little backwards—"

"His own way," Sara cut in.

"—But I have to admit, we've felt so much love and so many good wishes tonight to start us on our way, I don't know what we were trying to run away from. I'm even enjoying being dressed like the guy on top of the cake."

"He's going to have to wear that every day from now on. He just doesn't know it," Sara added, making everyone laugh again.

Reverend Ben stepped forward, "Before we devour that beautiful cake, I'd like to offer a blessing."

Luke smiled at him. "Please do, Reverend."

The room grew quiet and everyone bowed their heads, "Dear heavenly Father, please bless the love and union of Sara and Luke. Please watch over them and guide them through their life together. Let the love and happiness that abounds in this room tonight remain with them always. Let them be thankful for the many blessings they will share in their lives together, and let them face all challenges bravely, holding on to faith and trust in their love for each other, and in Your love for both of them."

"Thank you, Reverend Ben. That was beautiful," Luke said.

Sara nodded. She couldn't speak. She felt her eyes fill with tears and Luke's arm around her shoulder, hugging her close.

She knew that she couldn't possibly always be this happy. But she knew she would always love Luke and cherish the memory of this night, the start of their lives together, for as long as she lived.